I0681315

Tribal Spirits

FORGED REDEMPTION

KATHERINE MCINTYRE

Forged Redemption
ISBN # 978-1-83943-812-7
©Copyright Katherine McIntyre 2019
Cover Art by Erin Dameron-Hill ©Copyright October 2019
Interior text design by Claire Siemaszkiewicz
Totally Bound Publishing

Totally Bound Publishing books by Katherine McIntyre

Tribal Spirits
Forged Alliances
Forged Decisions
Forged Contracts
Forged Futures
Forged Redemption

The Whitfield Files
Of Tinkers and Technomancers

FORGED
REDEMPTION

Dedication

To those who have or still struggle with
infertility — you are not broken.

Chapter One

Thanks, sweetheart.

Ally paused in the middle of brushing her teeth as bile rose in her throat. Sweat pricked her temple and she gagged the peppermint toothpaste into the sink. Mere minutes in Mackey Kendricks' presence and he haunted her nightmares again and again. And now she was heading out to stalk the beast to his own den.

A knock sounded on her front door.

Ally sagged over her sink, digging her palms into the cool porcelain. She knew who waited on the other side. Her heart lurched in response, a reflex she couldn't help whenever he was in proximity. If she was going to be spending the next stretch of days up close and personal with Drew Williams, then Ally needed to strap on Kevlar, because he infected her like a computer virus, scrambling her mind and heart every time. The idea that she had gotten tangled up over her ex-boyfriend was cute—their mess traveled down to the roots.

They might've kept it a secret from their packs and families, but Drew Williams was her mate.

Ally tugged her freshly highlighted hair back into a ponytail and clapped a hand on her scarred thigh as a reminder. Drew had changed, and so had she. They weren't the same people they'd been two years ago before she'd dumped him. Before Drew had joined up with the enemy and split their pack apart.

The knock sounded on her door again.

Ally splashed icy water on her face and headed out of the bathroom. Her pulse pounded in double time when she approached. *Nerves over the mission, obviously.* She was two steps from the door when it creaked open on its own.

"We don't have the thousand years necessary for you to finish getting ready." Drew's droll voice echoed through the house as he strode inside. The familiar tone made her bare her teeth on instinct while her mountain lion lunged in her chest.

"Try an ounce of patience, Williams," she responded through gritted teeth. "Not even asking for an average amount. An ounce."

Drew shut the door behind him and turned to face her. A breath hitched in her throat at the full sight of him. Even though he was a bad decision in human form, Drew's looks placed him in Hollywood territory. He had a jawline sharp enough to slice, an arrogant nose that fit him all too well, and tan skin that glowed like he'd spent days basking in the summer sun even though early spring had just arrived. His hair, long enough to tug, gleamed like molten gold and the wicked arc of his eyebrows complemented his mocking smile.

"Well, we both know I'm not average in anything — even my lack of patience," Drew drawled, hooking his thumbs through his belt loops. He leaned against the wall.

"Excuse me while I eyeroll myself into a seizure," Ally shot back. She dipped down to snag her blue tote from beside the couch. Even after living here a couple of months, she thought of this place as Lana's, not hers. Probably because her bestie's name was still on the deed—Ally just acted as caretaker for the cheap rent. Besides, any day now, Lana and her fearsome Tribe mate would be returning for a temporary stay to make this house comfortably crowded.

Ally sucked in a breath and made her way to the door. She'd had to argue with Dax for days to take this recon assignment even though the prospect terrified her. But her alpha's mate, Sierra, was due in less than a month with the first cub or pup between the united Red Rock and Silver Springs packs. Dax needed to be there for the birth of his kid. Ally wouldn't budge on that one.

"Let's get this misery tour on the road," Ally said, flicking off the lights. She followed Drew out to the landing and locked up behind her.

By the time she'd spun around, Drew had slipped his aviators on and sauntered toward his Cadillac. "I'm driving," he called.

Cocky asshole.

Ally tugged the tote at her shoulder and followed him to the car, to hop into the passenger seat before he'd even stepped in. She hated the way the familiar scent of vanilla and smoke stroked at her nerves, evening her breaths. How she sank into these worn cushions like an old memory.

Drew turned the key, bringing the engine to life. Music blared through the speakers, the same acoustic rock he'd always listened to. He didn't say a word as he pushed on the gas to speed out of the development before she could even cast another glance to Lana's house. She could understand why he wouldn't want to linger.

Her fingertips traced the scar on her thigh on instinct. The silver had burned her flesh beyond repair when the pipe bombs had gone off through this neighborhood. The bombs Drew and his defection had been behind.

And she'd been good on hating him too. She'd gotten real good at that. Until the bastard had returned to town and told them of how Mackey Kendricks had used compulsion, forcing Drew to commit horror after horror. Ally might've pretended she didn't understand how fucked up his whole situation was, mostly because hating him was better than the alternative. But then she'd experienced Mackey's compulsion for a flicker-flash of a second, *and holy hell.*

Ally rolled the window down. This car was getting way too stuffy.

"So, what's the plan, Williams?" Ally asked. She placed her hands behind her head and leaned back in the seat. "I'm assuming your lengthy history with the Landsliders gives you some indications here."

Drew didn't need to tilt his aviators up for her to feel the intensity of the gaze flashing her way. "Williams is what folks called the old man." He tipped his glasses down on his nose, passing her a scorching look. "I prefer babe, darling, light of my life. Sir, if you're feeling kinky."

"You'll be called dipshit next if you keep at it," Ally shot back. Drew Williams had been the one person on the planet to keep up with her acerbic humor, to let her unleash when she sank into a mean mood, because they'd always worked the same way. He might've deceived most of the pack into believing he chewed up their hatred and spat it back out in droll one-liners, but she'd always known better.

"We're heading to World's End State Park to narrow down where the hell Mackey planted his secret lair. So, while we sleuth out the specific location, we'll be staying at a cabin in the interim—it'll be our home base."

"World's End? How fucking poetic," Ally responded, tapping her fingers along the ledge. Focusing on the breeze and sunlight proved better than thinking of spending nights in the same room as Drew Williams. Close proximity and a flat surface to fuck had always been her kryptonite when it came to him. "Does Mackey Kendricks choose all of his spots for maximum dramatic impact?"

Drew snorted. "You have no idea. The bastard's a full-blown prima donna."

The sun winked at her as they sped across the highway leading away from their territory. Soon they'd be heading into different pack territories, hence their stay in the public cabins used by human hikers. Even with the warmth radiating through the car and the gentle scent of lilac traveling with the breeze, a chill swept through Ally.

"Ava's spell on Mackey's device—that's all that's keeping him from using it to blow our packs into ash, right?" Their clever shamanic friend had placed a spell over the anti-shifter device they'd fought Joe Ganzorig for. They'd lost. However, Drew and Lucas had calculated that one, a minor loss for the greater victory of tracking her spell's signature to the general vicinity of Mackey's lair, a secret that had eluded them for far too long.

"That's the rumor," Drew responded.

She and Drew had been waiting for the call to hunt down this lair at last. If their packs stood any hope of stopping Mackey Kendricks or his Landsliders, they needed to catch him in his home base.

"Are you ready to confront him?" Ally asked, her sharp edges softening. "Ava fixed the bond between you and Kendricks through the Landsliders' mark, right?"

Drew's cocky grin faltered. She didn't need the mating bond to sense the terror gripping him tight. "Our friendly neighborhood shaman did me one better. She managed to reverse the bond—I can resist his compulsion. At the end of the day, either one of the East Coast Tribe takes him down, or me. Luc and Navi have too much to lose, so you can bet I'm going to be the one to end his life, even if I go with him."

His words stung, though she didn't have any right to the hurt. Drew wasn't wrong. They weren't dating, and most of his former pack and family barely tolerated him. Only Lana had welcomed him back in, but Ally's cinnamon roll bestie couldn't hold a grudge. Hell, Lana would forgive a bumblebee for stinging her, so why not Drew?

Ally tugged out the flask of Jack Daniel's she'd packed and took a swig.

"We're five minutes into the drive and you're drinking?" Drew arched an eyebrow.

Ally saluted with the flask. "The astounding new lengths you bring me to. Also, you're the one who wanted to drive so badly."

What she could never admit aloud was how much his self-sacrificing pissed her off. His actions made her flip the mirror back around and look a little too hard at all the desperate maneuvers she'd pulled as beta. How she'd thrown herself into fighting fang and claw against Landsliders, even mutated ones, without a blink.

Her mountain lion prowled inside, restless, needing to fight or run. Her mother had always told her she was a firework—all flash before the burnout, and she hated, hated to prove Rylie Coleman right.

"Oh, we're making a detour along the way," Drew mentioned offhandedly.

Ally gritted her teeth—she'd wear them to nubs by the end of this recon mission. "Didn't think of mentioning at all? You know I'm not the type of soldier to fumble along blind."

Drew placed a hand over his chest. "No, really?" The sarcasm reached eleven. Even though he drove, Ally considered the option of reaching across to strangle him. "Luc asked me to check on a pack out here," he continued. "He wanted to gauge if Mackey had them under his thumb or not."

"Like Mackey hasn't pulled together enough shifters to form a fucked-up little family? What's his damage?" Ally leaned along the window, her hair rippling out with the breeze.

"Mommy and Daddy issues puts it lightly," Drew drawled before flicking a quick glance her way. "And you thought we were bad."

"How dare he," Ally responded. "Didn't you tell him I don't share the spotlight?"

Her comment earned a genuine grin from Drew, one that made his eyes crinkle at the edges. One that made her heart thump hard. Once upon a time, she'd have set a forest on fire for one of those smiles. If she were even an ounce honest with herself, she still might. Ally's gaze drifted to the trees ahead of her. Her brow furrowed. She hadn't been serious.

Smoke trailed from the trees, the dark plumes billowing with increasing urgency.

"Hey, Drew?" she asked, sitting up in the seat.

A frown creased between his eyebrows. "Looks like there's a fire in the forest."

"That wouldn't happen to be in the direction we're heading..." Ally let her words taper, unable to dispel the tug in her gut. Mackey might be behind this too.

"One way to find out," Drew said, slamming hard on the pedal. His Caddy soared across the highway even as a cool competency settled over him. Like this, he seemed so different from the cocky upstart she'd fallen for. He exuded a maturity she wasn't used to seeing in him.

Her claws pricked out in anticipation for a fight. She needed somewhere to channel all this nervous energy beyond bickering with Drew.

In the distance, the fringes of buildings signaled an approaching town, and Ally half-expected to see the properties alight with crimson and gold flames. So many times, her mind transported to the night of the pipe bombs, and her thigh ached. Drew slowed when he neared the town, the slate smoke coming from the left past the main stretch of Mildred. The small bone-white church and red-bricked post office ahead lay untouched, even as folks pulled to the side of the street to gawk at the big plumes of what was building into a rager of a fire.

"We're getting close," Drew murmured, his tone darkening with the same seriousness that had settled over her. "The pack lives just beyond the town, nearer to the creek."

Ally's nose pricked with the charred scent of smoke beginning to pervade the car. Drew veered down a side street, farther away from the town.

"And you said a pack of shifters lives here?" she asked, even though she knew the answer. Mackey and his Landsliders had wreaked enough havoc on her own pack to dispel any delusions that he might show restraint. That he might not tear families apart in his quest to destabilize the region.

"He doesn't care." Drew's voice had distanced, the same as his eyes, as if he'd gotten trapped in memories of a different life from that of the man she'd known. "Mackey hates the packs. He hates his kind, maybe more than the Coalition does."

Her stomach flipped. This monster's hatred radiated like Hiroshima, the effects stamped all across their region, their homes and their packs.

Drew turned down another side street. Ranchers and two-story colonials sprawled out around here, short driveways and lengthy yards bursting to life with the careful blossoms and sprigs of spring's first breath. The acrid stench of smoke grew even stronger when they neared the column of black pouring into the sky.

Drew reached the end of a cul-de-sac facing thick brush and towering oaks. Flames glimmered in the distance, and the cries echoed through the air, faint from here. Ally's blood thrummed, her body prepared to move, to fight, to lash out at the first bit of trouble to step in her way. He parked at the edge.

"The pack must be deeper in," he said before stepping out of his car. Ally vaulted out of her seat, her nails shifting to claws. Drew met her eyes on the other side of his Cadillac. "Let's shift and check the area."

This was the sort of job for the East Coast Tribe — most packs stuck to their own kind and stayed out of each other's business. But the escalating threat Mackey Kendricks had brought to this region affected them all. This might not be her pack, but she couldn't let innocents suffer. They both started stripping their clothes off to prepare for the shift.

"Follow my lead." Drew gave the command. He'd been spending too much time around the Tribe. As much as Ally wanted to argue on reflex, the *thump-thump-thump* of her heart drowned out any response. She nodded and began to shift.

Her bones transitioned and fur pricked out along her arms. Her mountain lion took over, the form coming as naturally as breathing. The second she crouched on all four paws, the scent of the smoke grew overbearing and the screams reverberated through the forest, clearer than ever. Beneath the stench, she caught the other trails of the wolf pack who resided around here.

Before Drew gave the cue, Ally launched into the woods. Drew raced alongside her within seconds, keeping pace like he always did. Her mountain lion never needed the confirmation that he was her mate — he'd always been able to keep up with her in every aspect of their lives when no one else could.

Even though the fringes of trees had begun to spark, the fire focused on a different target, one that became clear the deeper in they ran. A pack cabin similar to their own lay in the middle of these woods, one accessible by a thin dirt road lined with cars. The pack must've been in the middle of a meet, all of them gathered together when the Landsliders had struck.

And now, those innocents burned.

Chapter Two

For Drew, devastation had become a familiar sight.

During his time in the Landsliders, he'd seen bombs lit, fields razed and packs ruined. He'd participated in all the destruction, even as the bile rose in his throat and his mind screamed. His hands were stained with so much blood he could do good works for the rest of his life and never scour the taint away.

He raced side by side with Ally, kicking up stray leaves and churning mud. In their mountain lion forms, they soared. The closer they got to the burning cabin, the louder the screams and the howls grew and the louder his memories marched in. Of the splattered blood. Of the broken stares. Of the whimpers he couldn't erase no matter how hard he tried.

Yet Mackey continued his reign of terror over their section of central Pennsylvania. More packs would be shattered under his hand and more families would be fragmented by the loss. The smoke caused his nostrils to burn the closer he got, and his breaths heaved, ragged around the edges.

The crimson fire leapt higher, a hungry blaze that would spread to consume the forest, from the fragile shrubs to the towering oaks. The crackle grew louder, the pop echoing through the trees. Drew tilted his head to the right and Ally caught his directive. They'd run together so often and for so long that in this form, their communication was effortless. She loped to the right, while he took the left. When he burst past the final fringe of spruce trees blocking the way, the sight almost stopped him still.

Timbers of the cabin started to collapse from a large hole blown through the entrance. Several bodies littered the ground out front. A woman had been groping forward in a clear attempt to escape, and another man curled around a smaller figure his brain refused to process. Bile rose in his throat. Several guys staggered out from the back. Voices echoed in the air, urgent. A couple of teenagers reached the cars, their resounding sobs containing all the hopelessness of this scene.

A little boy stumbled past the cabin, his legs streaked in soot and his wide eyes flaring silver. Surrounded by the blaze, the chaos and the looming trees, he was so small, all trembling limbs and the sort of lost Drew understood too well. His ragged dark hair glued to his forehead, and he reached forward, grabbing at the air. Drew's breath snagged in his throat. The kid couldn't have been more than five years old.

"Mommy? Daddy?" The creaks and groans from the burning timber grew deafening, but in the moment, the kid's quavering voice was all he could hear. The words were so fragile they shattered the moment they hit the ground.

The boy whipped around toward the cabin again. "Where are you?" Tears glistened in his eyes, a rising hysteria threatening to break free. He took the first steps in the direction of the cabin, and Drew bolted. *No, no, no.*

"Where did you go?" the boy asked, his voice almost drowned out by a larger groan coming from the cabin. The roof would collapse. The timbers were going to fall.

Yet the boy didn't see that when he headed toward the cabin, toward the blaze.

Drew's feet separated from the ground. He didn't just run — he flew.

A creak came from above as one of the nearby oaks caught flame, and several of the massive branches trembled. Drew's focus never left the kid who stumbled toward the cabin in flames as he tried to find his parents. *Feet away.* The little boy had almost reached the giant hole formed in what was once a cabin wall, the flash of fire inside. This close, smoke singed his nostrils and blurred his eyes. The heat blasted at him as if he'd stepped foot inside a furnace.

The roof was going to collapse.

The beams began to shift, and Drew lunged forward. He tackled the boy with enough force to send them tumbling feet away. Roof tiles clattered onto the ground, shards spraying in the wake. They landed right where the boy had been, the shattered pieces smacking against Drew's fur when he crouched over the kid. The boy's claws emerged and some fur prickled over his skin.

Drew stepped away to nudge the boy in the side. Even though the kid's eyes were wide with terror, he pushed off from the ground. Flames popped around him, and heat tingled as it singed his fur. None of that mattered. He had to get the kid to safety. Drew pawed the ground with claws and tilted his head, pushing the boy forward. The boy had already half-shifted from shock alone, and in several steps, he stumbled on all fours. Silver fur with black streaks covered the wolf pup.

Drew didn't hesitate. He clamped his jaws around the pup and carried the little guy by the scruff. He brought the boy farther away from the cabin within seconds, trotting ahead as fast as he could manage. Once he reached the tree line, Drew let go and met the boy's gaze. He tilted his head in the direction of his car, and the little guy dipped his muzzle to nod. Drew bolted for the cabin again. The familiar tug in his gut hinted at the worst, but he'd do whatever he could to find the kid's parents.

A crash echoed through the clearing. The rest of the roof caved in, the timbers dropping to the ground. On the opposite side, Ally led a few teenagers farther away from the wreckage of their pack cabin and in the direction of his Cadillac. Cars remained out front, but driving along the narrow path would be dangerous while the fire spread to the trees, licking the bigger branches to send them crashing down.

Drew gave the dancing flames a wide berth as he circled around the back. The older guys who had stumbled out before crouched on the leaf-covered ground. One of them collapsed to the earth, his breathing slow and ragged.

A couple of coughs escaped from Drew's throat. He veered in closer, dipping his head in their direction as they stared at him.

"Can't move," the older guy choked out between coughs. He glanced down at his leg. The guy knelt, bone splintered past the skin. Blood leaked out at an alarming rate, soaking into the loam beneath him. A younger man crouched in front of the guy on the ground. "Sam, you've got to go."

The younger guy jerked his head no. The flames trailed out past the cabin to sear the nearest tree. Drew met the older man's gaze and nodded before launching forward. He clamped his jaws around Sam's arm, light enough to not break skin but firm enough to give direction. Sam pulled back in resistance until the older guy pushed him ahead. Drew's heart thumped harder. He should've been desensitized to these scenes after all he'd witnessed. Yet their pain still tore him to shreds every time.

Sam stumbled forward, and Drew led him away from the burning cabin.

They padded through the forest until the looming birches lessened and cut a quick distance from the cabin to where he'd parked. Drew's mind whirred like a roulette. Mackey making strikes against packs wasn't anything new, but in the past he'd acted through others—his pack, the Coalition. If the Landsliders were making direct strikes, they must be close to undoing Ava's spell on the anti-shifter device.

And if the device did what rumor suggested, the Landsliders would possess the sort of bomb to destroy not just a pack cabin, but an entire territory.

The remnants of the pack who'd escaped the blaze took note of their lead and headed through the woods in the same direction Ally had brought the kids. Not like many shifters had survived. The Landsliders had stuck to their modus operandi of sweeping in, setting bombs and darting away. He was far too familiar with the approach.

Drew padded past the trees to where the meager group waited by his Caddy. No way could he fit everyone inside to transport them anywhere, but the trees began to creak and groan in the blaze. Going back for the remaining cars would endanger lives.

The little boy he'd found before lay curled onto the grass, still in wolf form. Ally paced beside him and three other teenagers. Two older guys had managed to make it out, as well as Sam who lagged, pausing every couple of steps to glance to the pack members he'd left behind.

Drew's ears pricked. The whirr of the fire alarm sounded in the distance — a town this small and smoke that big, they would've caught the alert.

He slunk behind his car to where they'd dropped their clothes. Drew let the shift overtake him. His tawny fur transitioned to skin and his bones mutated until he no longer stood on four feet but two. Even in this form, his nose and eyes stung from all the smoke and his breaths came out sharp and ragged like he'd run a marathon. A film covered his skin, one he was desperate to scrub off.

Too bad he couldn't scrub away the memories.

Drew tugged on his jeans and tossed on his T-shirt next. Ally prowled beside him, sinking into her own shift. Within seconds, the elegant mountain lion no longer crouched before him. She'd transformed back to the desert-tan, honey-blonde stunner he'd fallen for. Drew had seen every inch of Ally's body up close and personal so many times the allure should've worn off. But he couldn't ignore the throb of attraction or pull his gaze away.

The years had developed her strong frame, all sanguine curves and coiled muscle similar to her mountain lion. And the sharp arch of her eyebrows, her full, sensual mouth always had him smitten, even when she slung her barbs. Not like he minded — cozy warmth was Lana's terrain, never theirs. He and Ally had been born for walking barefoot over broken glass. He'd either develop calluses or bleed out.

Ally caught his gaze. "Eyes up here, Williams," she drawled as she pulled her navy tank top over her head. "Besides, my body's nothing you haven't seen every inch of already."

Like that mattered. The hunger for her had been a mere ache he could deal with, but this proximity, the low, sensual tone of her voice and the sight of her gorgeous body pushed it to a full roar.

He smirked. "It's something I don't mind seeing again."

Ally rolled her eyes and lifted her middle finger, even though he caught the quirk at her lips like she might grin. Spirits above, a genuine smile from her would run his heart through a wood chipper. Not like he deserved even a second of her time after all the heinous things he'd done.

Drew sucked in a breath to focus on what he'd return to once he stepped past his Caddy. The sobs echoing in the air were telltale enough. One of the teenage boys broke down, gravel dusting his knees as he stared out at their burning pack cabin. The older pack members wrapped their arms around the other two teenagers in a guarded, parental way. Sam paced back and forth, wearing a tread into the grass.

What broke him was the sight of the boy still in his wolf form.

The little wolf stood with his ears perked, his muzzle lifted. He looked expectantly into the woods, searching for the parents who would never return.

Drew headed over to the kid and placed his hand on the little guy's head, stroking the soft, fuzzy fur. Touch was fundamental among shifters, a comfort they survived on. The kid looked up at him. Those silver eyes with their searching socked him in the gut. He wished he had the answers, but he'd never managed to find them for himself.

"Sam," Drew announced, his voice echoing through the clearing. "Can you explain what happened?"

The shifter stopped pacing and glanced to him. Drew kept his hand resting on the little one's head, stroking his palm over the fur until the kid's muscles relaxed and he sat. Even still, the little one's focus didn't leave the woods.

Sam ran a hand through his hair, a barren look in his eyes. "We heard word of one of the local packs getting torched, but we thought maybe they had a land dispute, or a freak accident had happened. But when we congregated to discuss it, we barely caught a whiff of the foreign scents or saw the people running away from the cabin before the bombs went off."

Drew met Ally's gaze. No question, the Landsliders had caused the forest fire. This close to World's End State Park where their main headquarters were situated, the blaze wasn't a coincidence.

"How many other smaller packs are in this area?" he asked.

Sam's mouth formed a thin line. They might have been on task to find Mackey's lair, but he couldn't leave others to the same fate as this pack. Already, he'd created too many broken homes.

Ally caught his eyes and nodded. "We're going to alert them so this doesn't happen to anyone else. The names would be helpful."

The little guy nudged at his hand—he'd stopped stroking his fur—so Drew continued again. The motion caused his throat to tighten. Pure innocence was something he'd never known. He already had Mackey's number, but he'd kill him a dozen times over for causing this kid any pain.

Sam let out a shaky breath. "Yeah, I can do that. Do you have a pen and paper?" Ally nodded and bolted for the car.

Drew snagged the attention of one of the older members of this pack and gestured him over. "This area isn't safe right now. If you need refuge, head to the Red Rock and Silver Springs packs. Tell them Drew and Ally sent you. They'll be able to offer you help while you recover."

"Why would someone do this?" the man asked, clutching tight to his teenage daughter.

Drew's gaze simmered. "That's what we're here to find out."

Sam scribbled onto the scratch paper Ally had brought him, jotting down the pack cabins they'd be stopping by. With the sound of the sirens growing louder, they'd need to jet fast, otherwise they'd get caught in human trivialities. Unlike when he rolled with Lucas, he didn't have the Tribe card to extricate himself. Sometimes, not often, there were perks to working for one of the Tribes who governed their kind.

Drew crouched to look into the eyes of the little silver wolf. "Hey, kiddo," he murmured, lowering his voice so only he could hear. "It's going to get tough coming up. Spirits, I wish it wasn't. But I'm going to need you to go with these guys, okay? They're going to take you somewhere safe with friends of mine. And I'll be coming to join you soon. I'll do my best to answer any questions you have then. Can you do that?"

The little guy dipped his muzzle in a nod even though Drew could see the way he trembled.

A shadow fell over him as Sam approached. "I'll make sure Eli gets there. I don't think the Ravines made it out."

Drew nodded, ignoring the thickness in his throat and the heat behind his eyes. He ran a hand through his hair. "We've got to jet before the authorities arrive. We'll make sure to warn the other packs."

Ally had already sauntered toward the car, and she stood at the passenger's side, tapping her finger on the roof. Drew tossed a wave to Sam and gave one more nod to Eli who sat watching him, tail flicking back and forth. All he could see was the flames. All he could hear were the screams. Drew jogged to his Caddy and slid into the driver's seat, but even when his hands rested on the steering wheel, he didn't feel in control.

"I know this will delay us a bit," he started, forming his argument as he spoke.

"We've got to warn them," Ally interrupted, her eyes flashing. "And when we track Mackey to his goddamned lair, we'll set the thing on fire. Payback's a bitch."

Chapter Three

The motel smelled like rust and regret.

After the fire this morning, they'd spent the rest of the day traveling from one pack cabin to another in the region, offering warnings wherever they could. Ally hoped Dax had prepared for the volume of shifters about to head their way, because these people needed refuge and she couldn't help but extend the offer.

By the time they'd reached the Pavilion with its seafoam-green canopies and nabbed themselves a room, exhaustion smacked her in the face. Not like they could head to the cabin in World's End now and remain vigilant. Better they had an actual locked room to work with away from wherever the Landsliders holed up inside World's End State Park.

Of course, that meant she was stuck in this podunk motel room the size of a peanut with Drew Williams.

Drew sank back in the solo bed they'd managed to square away, sprawled out like he owned the thing. Ally ran a hand through her waves. She wished she had some way to avoid the sight of him there, some way to hide from the overwhelming desire sweeping through her. Hell, she wished she had some way to bury the self-loathing that had resurrected for countless reasons, beginning at the sight of the kids who'd lost their family members and ending with the hardbacked seat she sank into because she was too much of a coward to sit on the bed.

Ally pulled out her still-steaming container of veggie lo mein, as if the Chinese food could shield from the way her cells rioted around him, like she'd been denying herself a limb, or a fragment of her soul.

"We'll get started on the search first thing tomorrow," Drew spoke up, his voice cutting through the quiet between them. He rolled from the bed to swipe his container of sweet and sour chicken from the overly full bag of takeout, given their shifter appetites. "Today was a setback, so we'll have to make up for the lost time."

"Today was necessary," Ally responded, the words coming out sharper than intended.

Drew unsnapped the pair of chopsticks and began to wolf down his food, setting the container of sauce on the bed, like they weren't going to be sleeping there tonight. Ally bit back her irritation and picked at her lo mein, snatching up the carrots and peas first. Even though she needed the fuel and the salty scent made her stomach rumble, she couldn't dispel the way the teenagers had shaken or the glimpse of the blood painting the walls inside the cabin.

Drew swallowed and lifted his gaze to look at her. He leaned back on his elbows, the carton of white rice teetering on the mattress. "We did the right thing, but it wasn't necessary. Necessary is taking down Mackey Kendricks no matter the cost."

Ally's gut twisted. "Nice try with the heartless act. This is me you're talking to." Out of everyone in the pack, she was one of the few to know what Drew had sacrificed and who saw past the cocky mask he flashed the rest of the world. She couldn't shut out the sight of him crouching in front of the little guy, Eli, even if the memory was a bare blade between the ribs. The gentleness in his eyes, the calm way he'd responded to the kid—Drew was destined to be a dad.

Drew arched an eyebrow. "Didn't I tell you? On top of the swank tattoo, they gave us heart replacements on our initiation to the Landsliders. Pure ice, this one." He rapped his chest.

Ally snorted and leaned back in the uncomfortable seat, her plastic food container resting on her thighs. "Come on now, you never needed that to be an asshole, Train Wreck."

The old nickname, one she wished she could swallow back, slipped out before she could help herself. It dropped in like a bomb, flooding the room with tension.

Drew's eyes flashed the electric blue of his mountain lion, a honeyed, dangerous gleam rolling through them. He cracked a grin, one that didn't settle her nerves. "You're one to talk, Car Crash."

The simple nickname on those perfect lips and she was sixteen and smitten.

They'd only hit the first night of working together. They couldn't return to the past, not after everything had changed between them. Not after everything he'd done. Ally hated him anyway.

Liar. Liar. Liar.

The bag crinkled, drawing her attention. Drew placed the remnants of his carton inside, inches away from her. This close, his tan skin held more scars than she remembered, but it gleamed even in the sallow motel lighting like a slice of summer. Their gazes snared, and the oxygen vanished from the room.

Train Wreck and Car Crash hadn't just referred to the continual disappointments they were to friends and family. Their collisions were legendary — and inevitable.

Ally might've been fully clothed, but his gaze stripped her bare. Once upon a time, she'd marveled at how he'd managed to make her feel seen. She'd thrived under his attention and emerged like a new bud from the barren earth her mother had tried to bury her under. However, time, secrets and tempers had shattered things for them both. She sucked in a breath of the heady air and closed the lid on her lo mein to toss her leftovers back in the bag. Her skin ached for his touch and her mountain lion paced in her chest. She needed to tamp her libido something fierce.

Ally found herself leaning forward before she registered the movement. She stroked his arm and Drew froze, mid-crouch. The sight of him in front of her was so familiar, and yet he stood a stranger. His features had grown more defined over the years and his eyes more haunted than ever in the brief glimpses he allowed.

"What's wrong, darlin'?" he drawled. "There something you need?" His gaze danced, the heat there enough to consume her. His tone was locked and loaded, and Ally couldn't stave off the visuals of him pinning her to the wall, or of the way he'd fucked her senseless too many times to count. That thick length had buried deep inside her until she'd surrendered to sheer oblivion.

Ally tightened her grip on his arm, the silken feel of his skin against hers sparking her synapses to life. "Don't ruin this by talking, babe."

Drew's grin widened, and he stood from his crouch to close the distance between them. This close, the vanilla and smoke weighed heavy in the air — she could taste it. Her pussy throbbed on reflex. He leaned forward, settling his hands on either side of the chair around her. She'd never felt caged by him, only a deep sense of safe that snagged her even as she free-fell. That terrified her more than anything.

Ally looked at him, meeting his stare in a challenge even as her tongue traced her lips, too, too dry. She should be careful, should back away, should keep her distance. Except all the excuses shattered the moment she caught hesitation from him, the flicker-flash of hurt in his eyes. No matter how she'd tried to distance or paint over her hurt with hate, the look in his eyes brought her to her knees every time.

To hell with the shoulds. She was shit at following orders anyway.

Ally leaned up to press her lips to his.

Holy fuck.

His kiss was pure possession, the sort that made her hot and the kind that filled her with flames when she'd been ice. He met her like the squealed brakes of a car returning home after a lifetime on the road. Drew slipped his fingers through her hair, pressing his palm against her nape as he brought her closer. Ally rose from the seat until their bodies aligned and their mouths met over and over.

She wanted him like the sunrise after endless night and her heart ached like she'd taken a crowbar to it. Too long had passed since they'd come together like this. She settled her hands around his waist, then moved to his back, the strong muscles flexing under her touch. She couldn't stop touching him, like she needed the reassurance he was here and real.

So many nights, she'd woken up alone in her bed, searching for him as if he remained a part of her life. As if they were still together, even though she'd been the one to call it quits the final time.

Ally melted into him. He brought his hands around her waist, the heat searing right through her clothes. Her breaths came out soft and ragged and she dove in for more. The fevered kisses rose to her head, infecting her brain and body until she forgot every reason she'd broken up with him. His lips were rough, demanding, and her body belonged against his, a fact he made clear by the way he curled his fingers into her hips.

"Spirits above, I fucking missed you," he murmured against her mouth.

Ally grinned. "What did I say about talking?" Even as the teasing words slipped out, her stomach twisted with all she wanted to speak locked away. Drew had always been the one to talk while her truth remained voiceless, but whether she said the words or not didn't matter. He always knew what she meant.

"Right. I've got far better things to do with my mouth," he whispered against her neck, the caress of his lips making her delirious. Ally twined her arms around his neck, brushing her hips against him. He pressed his hardness right against her core, and she almost gasped with relief, lust overtaking her with the intensity of a fever. His teeth sank down on her earlobe, her neck, her shoulders, and Ally became putty under his precision.

He bit harder on her shoulder, and a moan escaped her, exploding through the sounds of ragged breaths cycling through the quiet room. Ally threaded her fingers through his hair and tugged. All he'd done was put his mouth on her body and she'd ignited. This — she had missed this. She'd always been trash at summoning words to communicate what she felt, but they'd never needed words to speak. Their bodies spoke the truths their voices never could.

The scent of him made her delirious, the smoke from his cigarettes, the vanilla from his aftershave. It made her want to rub against him and purr like some wanton thing. She slipped her hand beneath his shirt, tracing the hardened muscle there, finding it hot and silken. Her mouth watered to lick and suck every inch of his sunlit skin.

Those skillful fingers snapped her bra and the straps drifted around her shoulders. The anticipation caused her nipples to stiffen at full attention, and Drew didn't disappoint. He swiped a thumb over the tip, the sensation traveling straight to her core. Ally shivered as he continued to caress her nipples, light teases that had her panting. She arched her back, grinding her hips while he toyed with her. He pressed his hard length against her core, making her more delirious.

Bad decisions be damned, she needed him. They could sort the rest out in the morning.

Ally's hands moved to the zipper of his pants, and she brought it down. The audible *snick* echoed in the air like a starter's pistol. This was where they were perfection — away from the self-loathing, away from their damage, away from every unsaid word they'd restrained.

Drew returned his mouth to hers, and she gasped for him. Her lips were swollen from the kisses, yet she collided with Drew again and again. This was too long pent-up, the longest she'd been away from him since they'd started dating at sixteen. He'd been her first everything — kiss, fuck, love. Not like she hadn't played the field when they'd been split — they both had — but no matter what separated them, the inexorable force of the mating bond kept drawing them back together.

Ally dragged his jeans down, bringing his CKs with. Too many layers separated them. She needed his skin against hers more than she needed her next breath.

Drew brought her pants down in a single motion. He continued to kiss her so hard she couldn't focus on anything else but the demand of his mouth. He swept his thumb over the elastic of her panties and he glided his palm along her thigh, exploring, memorizing. His hand paused, and Drew froze.

Her scar.

The ropy, knotted mess she earned the night of the bombings. Ally's breath caught in her throat. He pulled away from her to look down and the urge to step back, to run away and hide swept over her.

Drew's mouth dropped open and his eyes grew interminably dark. "Did that happen the night…" He trailed off, not able to finish the sentence.

Ally couldn't force a breath in. She staggered back a pace, even though her body rioted. All the explosive heat between them vanished like a candle's flame snuffed. She glanced off to the side, unable to meet his gaze, not wanting to see what lay in his eyes — pity or, worse, disgust.

"The night of the bombs, the colloidal silver burned into my skin, so it never healed right." She forced the words out as she stepped away. The backs of her knees hit the chair.

Drew ran a hand through his hair, and he stared at the mottled paisley carpet. "Fuck…I… Spirits above, Ally." He stumbled a pace away, then another, the horror in his tone ringing clear. "I'll be back. I need to step out for a smoke."

He stepped away and the brief comfort didn't just dissipate — it shattered. Drew crossed the room in quick strides, making his way to the door. Ally stood stock still, hands balled into fists, until the door creaked shut and he exited.

She sank to her knees, her arms trembling and her legs shaking. Ever since she'd gotten the scar, Ally had worn it like a badge of honor, the way most shifters did. Yet she couldn't help the twist in her chest every time she looked at the mottled flesh, at the ruined skin that would never heal smooth. Out of anyone in her pack, in this state, on this planet, she'd thought her mate would be able to handle it.

Ally sucked in a sharp breath. *Get it together.* She forced herself from the chair and tugged up her pants. Ally snapped her bra back in place then ran a hand through her hair. Trying to hook up with her ex was a massive mistake, one she'd known from the beginning. When she kept her distance from him, she could at least pretend the hollow thump in her heart didn't exist. She could drown out the sound with endless distraction and responsibilities.

Being around him made their bond impossible to avoid. His presence affected her like the escapes she made to the ocean every summer. She might be able to live and thrive without them, but she felt the tug of yearning in her chest every time she went without.

Ally went through the motions mechanically, popping the rest of their Chinese food in the fridge and stepping into the bathroom to brush her teeth and splash more water on her face, as if the cold might breach the numbness. She slid into the bed, not bothering to strip out of her clothes. Maybe she could fall asleep before Drew came back in. Before she had to face whatever pity or judgment he might wield.

All she could hear was her mother's voice over and over. *Better keep your looks, sweetie. No one's going to want you otherwise.*

Rylie Coleman might've been the parent who had stuck around, but there were some nights Ally wished she hadn't.

The door creaked and Ally yanked the down comforter tight around her, facing the wall.

Drew's footsteps pounded through the room, but she couldn't look at him.

She closed her eyes, hoping he'd leave her alone if she pretended to sleep. Several shuffles and creaks sounded before the cushion moved, and Drew settled in behind her. Even if his heat wasn't indicator enough, she could pick his presence out of a stadium. He settled his hand on her shoulder, the touch surprising her so much she didn't restrain her held breath.

"No one needs to tell me I'm a monster—I live with what I did in my time during the Landsliders every day," he murmured, his voice so quiet it might break, a rasp that shivered across her skin. "I'm sorry doesn't even cut it, Ally-cat. You have every right to hate me for the rest of your life. I knew the damage the bombs did, that injuries happened, but the idea that I was behind something that hurt you—fuck, I don't deserve to even be in this room with you, let alone this bed."

He lightened his grip on her shoulder, as though he might pull away. Ally's heart lurched. She should've known—Drew hadn't been disgusted with her, but himself. The words wouldn't escape her lips, but she reached up to rest her hand over his to keep it in place. He hesitated and she tugged on his arm, hoping beyond hope he'd understand what she was trying to communicate.

The bed creaked again and his weight settled behind her. She could feel his heat and smell the scent of the cigarette he'd smoked. Ally wanted to sag with relief at the familiar presence by her side, one she'd longed for on so many nights. She wanted to tell him she didn't blame him for what he'd been forced to do. She wanted to tell him she didn't hate him — at least, not for what he'd done in the Landsliders. But the words refused to come and her mouth remained glued shut. Ally pulled his arm around her tighter as he sidled behind her.

Tomorrow, they could track down the Landsliders' lair and face the complicated web of emotions between them, but tonight, she'd bask in the comfort of Drew's presence for the short moments she could steal.

Chapter Four

Drew hunched over the meat locker in the back of the country store, sorting through their limited options of slabs of chicken breast and beef. Out here, they didn't have big aisles of groceries, and he hadn't stocked up for meals—who knew how long finding Mackey's lair would take.

"Do you really need this much?" Ally asked, her hands on her hips. She kept casting glances to the front where two cashiers sat chatting with each other. "We're not going to be staying at the cabin for the next century."

Drew cocked an eyebrow at her and pulled out another package of beef. "What are you talking about? This is all for you. I'm well aware of the immense amount of meat you need for sustenance, darling."

Was goading her the best idea after what had happened last night? Probably not. But they'd heated like steel at a forge only to be quenched a moment later. Drew's skin prickled around her like rugburn after the encounter scraped him raw.

Ally balled her hands into fists, a low growl coming from deep in her throat. She was fucking exquisite, eyes flashing bronze in irritation, her whole body reacting like a livewire. Even with her honeyed locks slung into a side ponytail and a pair of scuffed-up jeans on, Ally Coleman was the sexiest thing in his world. Those curves mesmerized, as did the tilt of her lush lips. Her annoyance was a familiar sight, and he couldn't help how she turned him on.

"Maybe if I could find some quality, I wouldn't need quantity," Ally responded through gritted teeth, shooting him a look.

Even as she locked and loaded the barbs, he couldn't help the warmth in his chest at getting to share anything with her, even the stupid fights they'd always had. Toss two hotheads into a relationship and they'd always be baking soda and vinegar.

"Grade A, right here," Drew said, lifting the package and pointing to the label. He didn't bother hiding his grin when Ally rolled her eyes. "Let's go pay and get out of here," he said, casting another glance. "All your complaining is holding us up."

Ally's perfect eyebrows drew together, and her mouth dropped. He sauntered past her toward the checkout, aware of the imminent explosion he'd left behind. The door creaked open and the bell tinkled, drawing his attention.

Two guys strolled in and Drew froze.

He didn't recognize the big hulker on the right, but the other one caused him to stop still. The narrow eyes, long chin and languid movements—he remembered those from his Landslider days. Harry was one of the mainstays, a bear shifter that had been with Mackey for years. Someone who would recognize him.

Drew took a few steps back and reached out to snag Ally's hand. The grocery trip didn't matter. If they didn't escape here unseen, they might as well just call the whole recon mission quits. To his relief, Ally didn't argue, reacting with the calm poise and assessment he'd expected from the beta of his former pack. They ducked behind one of the shelves which barely came up past his shoulders.

Drew met Ally's eyes and mouthed, "Landsliders."

She nodded, crouching by his side. Drew let his mountain lion take the reins, focusing on the scuff of their shoes as they strode past the registers up front. Harry's voice ghosted across his skin like spiderwebs, as if Drew had never left the Landsliders behind. As if he'd never broken free. Truth be told, if he hadn't been under Tribe protection, he wouldn't feel safe unless he evacuated the country.

Drew placed his groceries on the ground and crept forward, closer to the front of the country store. If Harry decided to stroll down this aisle to nab some pancake mix, they were fucked. The cashier murmured something, and Harry let out a bark of a laugh. The front door was the only exit, which left them no other options. With a start he realized he still held Ally's hand, but he didn't let go. If he needed to make any sudden movements, a quick tug worked better than trying to catch her gaze and whisper.

Besides, the simple touch of her hand quieted his beast like nothing else.

Drew reached the end of the aisle, crouched beside the display of dish soap and laundry detergent, but he didn't dare peer out. Not yet. The chatter from up front had died, and the footsteps scraped the hardwood again. *Closer.* Drew sucked in a sharp breath, half a second away from shifting.

He clutched the shelf, his nails turning to claws in preparation. He cast a glance at Ally who brimmed as much as he did.

The footsteps sounded louder, until they headed down the aisle beside them. This close, he could smell their scent clear in the air. Those steps paused.

They couldn't wait here any longer.

Drew slipped past the shelf to take the long way around to the registers, careful to keep his head down. The door lay feet away. Ally's grip tightened when they walked hand in hand toward it. He didn't dare look back, because Harry might catch a glimpse of his features, and they'd be caught before they ever uncovered Kendricks' lair. His back prickled at the vulnerability. The cashiers scanned them over, pausing at their empty hands.

Drew jerked his head no, not daring to speak. So close. He didn't dare quicken his pace, even though his calves tensed with the urge to bolt. Already, Ally's palm grew sweaty against his.

They stepped through the door, and Drew winced as the bell tinkled behind them. The moment he hit the sunlight, he bolted for his car. He slammed against the side of his Caddy before unlocking the door and diving in. He didn't take a breath until the passenger door clicked shut and Ally settled in beside him.

Drew leaned back in the seat, pumping the brake pedal on reflex. Even though he gripped his keys, he didn't put them in the ignition.

"Those were Landsliders I recognized," he muttered, hating to admit the words out loud. Every mention of his past with the group coated him in a new tar-thick coating of shame and self-loathing, until he might not ever be able to extricate himself.

Ally lifted an eyebrow. "So why aren't we peeling out of this place to leave them in the dust?" He opened his mouth to respond—his brain leapt to the next step—when Ally's blue eyes grew clear with understanding, and she continued, "Because you're waiting for them to come out so we can tail them."

Drew cracked a grin. His chest warmed at his mate's quick thinking. Ally was bright, tough and creative, all things her mother, Rylie, had tried to pound out of her at an early age. Not like he'd been much help. Every time they made steps forward, they'd tumble back three. And when his father had strong-armed him into joining the Landsliders, he'd detached more and more with every secret he shouldered.

Ally might've been the one who'd broken up with him, but he didn't question for a moment who was to blame.

"Bingo, beautiful," he responded. "We're lying low until they emerge."

Ally's features softened for a moment, the flash of vulnerability something he never could defend against. When it came to Ally, he'd always been unable to help the way he felt or how they careened together. Yet, he had no right to touch her, let alone be near her after all the terrible things he'd done. She deserved someone strong, someone good. Someone who hadn't been forever marred by their scars.

He winked, needing to dodge past the tension between them. "If you've got any ideas for how to pass the time, I'm listening."

Ally pursed her lips, leveling him with a look. "Let's not pretend you're capable of multitasking, Train Wreck."

Drew swallowed hard at the nickname. Yesterday, it had awakened part of him he'd thought had died, his hollowed husk of a heart. He'd needed to drown in the sensations of his hands on her hips and his mouth against hers to stave away the complicated weight of everything he'd buried away. That had worked swimmingly.

The door to the country store creaked open, saving him from responding. Drew placed his key in the ignition as Harry and his friend headed over to their car. He and Ally ducked under the view of the dash, peering past to keep watch. Within seconds, the Landsliders hopped into their car and the engine rumbled to life. The vehicle pulled out of the spot.

Drew didn't waste any time. He started his engine, waiting for the moment they hopped onto the road. Once the Landsliders turned to the left, his car crawled across the parking lot in pursuit.

"So, what happens when they lead us straight to World's End State Park in the main parking lot?" Ally commented as they trailed down the highway. He could still spot the red Chevy in the distance, but he kept enough space between them in hopes they wouldn't notice they had a tail.

"Then that tells us the lair is closer to the main parking lot," he responded, tightening his grip on the steering wheel. "There are multiple entrances, so whichever one they decide to take will narrow things down for us."

Ally let out a low whistle. "When did you become more than just a pretty face?"

"Let's be real. I'm not much without my looks," Drew drawled in response. "I blame Lucas and his band of Tribe for all this planning-ahead nonsense."

"Sure, all the bad Tribe influence," Ally shot back. "Just like the Boy Scouts are out to corrupt wayward kids into learning discipline."

Drew pumped on the gas, speeding to catch up with the car they tailed. All the dips in the road made it even harder to keep track of them. "Hey, we start teaching kids discipline and the next thing you'll have is upstanding citizens. No one wants that. Chaos and malarkey for all."

"Malarkey? What are you, eighty?" Ally cracked the window and leaned her arm out of the side. Her golden hair streamed in the breeze, silken strands he longed to run his fingers through. Spirits above, every inch of her body was pure temptation.

"Yep. Mackey better watch out, because I'm coming for him, walker and all." Even as Drew joked around, the bastard's name on his lips this close to his lair had his heart slamming. Ally snorted and Drew stole a glimpse in her direction right in time to see the flicker of a grin. He cherished each and every one of those, savored them like the first sip of whiskey after a long day.

In the distance, the sign for World's End State Park rose into view, the bold yellow lettering against red-brown wood. His stomach churned at the sight. They were so close to the man who had commanded his mind and body for far too long. Bile rose in his throat. All he could see was the speckled pattern of crimson. All he could smell was the rust.

His fingers numbed, and for a moment he stood back there in yet another cabin to deliver a punishment to innocents who didn't deserve the pain. His limbs didn't belong to him and his claws weren't his own, even as they sliced and sliced and sliced. Even as they grew stained beyond recognition.

"Drew?" Ally's voice sounded.

The road stretched out ahead of him, but he'd strayed to the other side.

Fuck. Drew swerved back into line, his heart thumping so hard the sound drowned out the radio. He glanced ahead — the red Chevy still drove ahead of them in the distance. He'd almost lost track of the Landsliders. Ally stared at him — he could feel the press of her gaze even as he kept his on the winding road. Shame flushed through him. He couldn't even do something simple like this without freezing up like a fucking coward.

And the worst thing about it?

He deserved every second of the pain and the repercussions.

Lucas and the others had repeated over and over how he had no control, how Mackey's compulsion forced him to do unthinkable things. Yet, he was the one who lived with the memories. His claws were the ones that had sliced, and his orders were the ones that had left his pack in shambles and had broken up families in their feud. He couldn't erase the horror in their eyes, that crystalline fear, no matter how much he tried.

Ally didn't say anything, but she reached for him to rest her hand on his thigh. The touch brought him to the present like nothing else. They both were trash at talking the talk, but he understood.

Ahead, the road branched into a side entrance of World's End State Park, and the Chevy they followed made the turn. *Bingo.*

The scent of berries lingered in the air. *Ally's scent.* One that reminded him of the younger, better times when his world wasn't composed of pain and regret. Her hand remained on his thigh, a steadiness he didn't deserve, but one he drew upon anyway. He forced his breaths to step into line.

They followed the Landsliders into the state park. His car crawled at this point—they'd gotten plenty of intel already, since this entrance led to the west side of the park, not the front. Yet he couldn't help but chase the lead further. The sooner they found Mackey's lair, the sooner they could rally an army to torch the fucker, then maybe, just maybe he'd stop appearing in Drew's nightmares every night.

"Let's see if we can get a head start and follow the scent trail," Drew said, his voice sounding foreign in the quiet of the car. Ally remaining silent was a rarity, but it happened every time a loaded situation descended. She'd rather get declawed than talk feelings. He couldn't blame her.

"Yeah, the sooner we find their lair, the better," Ally responded, drawing her hand away as though it flickered with flames. He already missed the touch, something he'd taken for granted in their time together. The past two years had been more painful than he could ever have imagined with no hope of reprieve in grasp. Truth be told, the sole thing keeping him going was the hollow revenge he planned for Mackey.

Beyond that, nothing else mattered. At least, not anymore.

By the time he pulled into the dirt parking lot, the Chevy sat parked alongside two other cars with no one still inside them. Drew breathed a sigh of relief and settled his Cadillac into Park.

He met Ally's eyes, ignoring how his heart skipped a beat. Golden sunlight threaded through her hair and gleamed on her lickable olive skin. She donned a self-possessed liar's smile he knew she didn't feel, and he wanted to slam his mouth to hers to claim his former mate until her moans filled this car.

"Get your head in the game, Train Wreck," Ally said, her ocean eyes dancing with amusement. "Unless you're planning on leveling all that lust at the Landsliders we're tracking, but I'm pretty sure we're here to fight them, not fuck them."

He snorted and set to motion, hopping out of his car. She wasn't wrong—he needed to focus. "All right," he said, kicking his sneakers underneath his car. "Let's shift and track these bastards."

Drew tugged off his T-shirt and brought his jeans down next, moving with the efficiency of years shifting. Ally stripped on the other side of the car, and he couldn't help the glimpse from searing into his mind. He'd never in a thousand years deserve a stunner like her. Fate was an unforgiveable asshole for mating Ally with someone like him.

He sank into the shift, and his nails transitioned to claws first, the fur prickling along his skin next. His mountain lion begged to come out, the pounding in his chest as constant as a heartbeat. That form, with the predator instincts keeping him focused on the present, offered the only peace he'd found as of late. Before Drew could intake another breath, he slipped onto all fours and padded past his car.

Ally trailed a couple of paces behind him, streaks of gold on her coat glinting under the sun, the same color as her hair. He stepped past the first few looming oaks and placed his muzzle to the bed of moss and crushed leaves that had become mulch. His nose twitched. He caught the strong scents of the Landsliders, particularly Harry's. Having a specific one to track helped him separate the other ones.

Drew loped through the forest, the birds whistling through the trees and the soft ground sinking underneath his paws. The loam of the moss and earth grew richer as the first electric green sprouts peeked through the muck. The breeze carried a breath of warmth, one he drank in as he raced along, as if he could pretend it was hope.

He scanned his surroundings for snapped twigs, pawprints or any sign of the other shifters who would be running around here. Not like they'd be kind enough to leave a 'Mackey's Lair Here' sign. Even as he tuned in to his surroundings, he couldn't hear much more than the gentle breezes, the distant thrum of water and the woodland creatures light enough to skitter through the bushes.

At least until the steady thump of pawprints filtered in.

Drew trotted behind a large oak and tried to gauge the source of the sound. Ally slipped beside him with ease, taking the cues even when he didn't give them.

The thump continued, a regular sound growing louder and louder. He crouched, trying to hide behind the trunk and fringe of surrounding bushes. A silver wolf emerged and Drew's blood turned Arctic. The last time he'd seen one of those creatures had been back in the caves.

The wolf was a mixture of silver fur and stone, crags of mottled rock protruding from spots and melding with open skin and pus, like wounds that wouldn't close. The eyes were vacant, gray, as if the creature had risen from six feet under, and the patches of stone traveling all the way down the legs caused its stride to falter and wobble.

One of Ganzorig's mutants had arrived.

Chapter Five

Ally had heard stories about the shifters-turned-mutant Lana and Drew had encountered in the face-off against Joe Ganzorig, but to be honest, she had trouble wrapping her mind around the idea. Now one of those mottled beasts approached in all its fucked-up glory, and the sight settled over her like frost.

The patches of shale coating the beast's skin looked painful, like a disease had wrecked the wolf or it had stepped halfway into Medusa's stare. Those pale, limpid eyes belonged on a corpse, not a living creature, yet it strode toward them on weighty, uneven steps.

Ally crouched, waiting for a signal from Drew to run. Taking on this hulking monster didn't seem to be in the best-plan agenda.

If one of Mackey's mutants roamed the forest around here on patrol, they were closing in on his lair.

Drew nudged her in the side. She stepped back a pace, then another, her pads settling with care on the soft mosses. The wolf roamed in the clearing ahead of them, but its gaze hadn't seized upon their tree yet.

They could still escape unnoticed. She trod lightly, careful not to crack any twigs as she backtracked with Drew, trying to stay behind the cover of the big oak and the flush of bushes around them.

The mutated wolf paced back and forth in the clearing, but then it snapped up, muzzle tilted in the air. It seemed to catch a scent.

Ally froze even as Drew took another step back.

The creature sniffed again.

Those milky eyes honed in on the tree they crouched behind. One step. Two steps forward.

Ally met Drew's gaze. *Run, or stay and fight?*

Drew didn't bother responding. The impetuous bastard's hind legs tensed, and he sailed forward. Drew flew over the bushes, the tips scraping against his fur, and he landed smack in the center of the clearing. Clouds of dust rose in his wake. Ally let out a growl and charged behind him. She kicked up grit and mulched leaves as she closed the distance to the mutant.

The moment Drew landed, the wolf launched into motion. The creature bolted with more speed than she would've imagined given the drag of its stone-covered paw. Ally pounded across the ground faster. If the mutant alerted other Landsliders to their presence, not only was their whole operation blasted to shards, but she doubted they'd make it out of World's End alive.

That is, if they even escaped this clearing.

Drew charged with his thick forehead down like a battering ram. He vaulted across the ground at a blurring speed. The wolf whipped around to face him. It bared its teeth, revealing a jagged maw crusted with more bits of stone. Drew didn't stop, a juggernaut on a singular mission, and Ally flew in behind him, closing the distance as fast as she could.

Drew rammed in with the blunt of his forehead. At the last moment, the wolf swerved. His head thudded against a patch of stone along the creature's flank, and Drew stumbled back, unsteady on his paws.

Ally loped around the side, teeth bared. She lashed out, but the wolf whipped away faster, even with the scraping drag to its foot. A nauseating rotten eggs smell surrounded the beast, making her nose sting. Her jaw snagged on fur right when it pivoted out of the way again. The beast loomed compared to the wolf shifters they sparred with, the massive size part of the mutation.

Drew launched around the other side, his claws extended. He raked out. The tips scraped against stone and fur alike, and the beast let out a low growl that vibrated in the air between them. Before Ally could lunge in, the wolf whipped toward her, leaping into the offensive.

She tried to dart away, too late. The beast crashed overtop her, and the force knocked the breath from her lungs. She thrashed beneath the crushing weight of the creature. Ally lashed out with her claws, scoring red streaks along the beast's legs. Not like the creature budged. She slashed her tips against the patches of stone, which caused a high-pitched screech that made her wince. The wolf snapped and snarled, a glob of drool dropping into her fur. The milky eyes looked like they'd been plucked off a dead fish.

A thud reverberated over her. Drew rammed headfirst into the beast's side.

Ally seized upon the slight shift in weight and threw her body into a roll. She tumbled past the wolf. It settled on four paws, the claws slamming to hit the earth instead of her.

She righted herself in a fluid motion, and the wolf whipped toward her again. Drew wouldn't give up. He plunged his fangs into the beast's flank right when it jerked forward to lunge for her. The moment the creature surged, Drew sank his teeth in deeper.

Ally charged from the opposite side, her forehead lowered.

It turned to try to shake Drew, but she slammed her thick skull against the wolf's flank.

Even as the creature staggered, Drew kept it pinned. Ally lunged in, ignoring the blast of heat from its gaping maw and the acrid stench that made her eyes water. The creature's teeth scraped against her flank when she slammed headfirst into it again. Pain prickled through her as blood welled to the surface, but she rammed harder. Stone scraped against her fur, her skin, the abrasion stinging.

A garbled growl came from the beast's throat, and its muzzle slammed against her side. The force of the blow sent her staggering back. Drew let go of the beast's backside, sailing overtop. He landed with a thud, piercing his claws past skin on both sides. The mutant wolf bucked, trying to shake Drew off, but he was a stubborn bastard.

Ally lunged forward, her teeth bared. She sank her fangs into the throat and they scraped against more stone. One of the paws knocked her square in the chest. She ignored the hitch in her breath and tried for another bite. This time the mutant dug its claws in past skin. Her shoulder screamed in response, but Ally refused to give up.

This beast needed to die, before it alerted the others.

She nipped out again, and her fangs found purchase in the skin. Ally clenched her jaw tight onto the bit and tugged. Copper filled her mouth when she tore a piece of flesh.

Drew sank his teeth into the wolf's ear and twisted his head to the side, dragging the ear clean off with an audible rip. A garbled mix between a whine and a growl rumbled from the mutant's chest, echoing through the clearing.

Ally reared back to ram into it again, but the beast slammed her with the stony foot. The force sent her stumbling. In a deft movement, the creature bucked, vaulting Drew overhead. He flew through the air but somehow landed on all fours. The wolf bled from multiple gashes and its breaths came out ragged. The mutant charged for her, a fury in its limbs fueled by desperation.

Ally crouched low to the ground. She hadn't missed the tilt of Drew's head or how he pawed the earth, ready to launch.

They'd worked as a team time and time again. Despite their countless clashes, when in their mountain lion forms, they'd always been united.

The milky eyes leveled on her, the muzzle dripping. The wolf neared, closer and closer.

Ally's haunches tensed as she prepared herself. The creature's muzzle opened, revealing sickly gray teeth stained by crimson and brown. The heat from its breath blasted her.

Yet she waited.

Feet away, the beast lunged.

Ally crouched so low she'd almost flattened herself to the ground.

It sailed toward her open flank, teeth bared. Right as the beast descended, she threw her entire weight forward. She collided with the wolf, the resounding smack echoing through the air and reverberating through her bones. Drew hadn't been sitting idle.

He'd crept around the side, and once they smashed together, he lunged in.

He sank his teeth around the creature's neck from the left. He tore the bit of exposed flesh amidst the stone coating the beast, and the wet slap echoed in the air. Blood sprayed from the spot, and the beast staggered away, thrashing back and forth. Ally shook herself off even though her muscles ached after the way she'd hurled her body against a rock wall. Drew crouched, his muzzle stained in crimson.

Together, they circled the wolf. The blood poured from the gashes at this point, puddles forming by the beast's feet. It took one shaky step forward, then another.

The beast swayed and a moment later crashed to the ground.

Ally's flank heaved, and the cuts and slices she'd earned began to sting in the wake of the immediate threat. Her eyes met Drew's, and he dipped his muzzle toward the creature. They would have to find somewhere to hide the body.

* * * *

Ally lounged on the bed they were somehow supposed to share without jumping each other's bones. Though, she couldn't fast forget how Drew had backed away last night or the anguish in his tone. He'd let her shower off the blood and dirt first, and the second she'd cleaned out her scratches, they'd begun to shrink. By the morning, most of them would be healed.

The cabin in World's End possessed a quaint charm similar to that of the cabins scattered around Ricketts Glen. Hickory panels surrounded her from the walls to the floors and ceiling. The rich scent of the wood mingled with the encroaching loam from the surrounding earth, the sap from the trees and the lemon polish that must've been used once in a while to gussy the place up. The cabin had the basics—a fridge, a kitchenette and a separate bathroom, but yet again they were left with a single bed.

The sound of the shower outside reminded her of rain, which brought on too many memories. Most people loved to live in the sunlight, but Ally preferred her rainy days—they were more real, more visceral than any trickery of the golden rays. She just needed to hold strong one more day, maybe two. Once she and Drew weren't in this close proximity any longer, her mountain lion wouldn't be ramming inside her chest like she was going insane. Maybe then, her heart wouldn't feel like it tore in two with every glance to him.

Her phone buzzed with more messages from Dax and the others back at Silver Springs, one of the only spots she'd gotten cell service since they'd driven up. Apparently, some of the refugees had reached Ricketts Glen and were settling in. Eli, the wolf pup Drew had dragged from the cabin, was asking for him. Ally's chest had squeezed tight at the message, and she forgot to breathe. Every time she witnessed how good he was with kids and every time she saw his tenderness, the sight threatened to unmake her a little bit more.

The shower shut off, and after a bit of rustling, the cabin door creaked open. Drew strolled out in nothing but a towel. Ally restrained her groan. *Not fucking fair.*

The fabric hung low on his hips, revealing those toned abs, the defined 'v' that traveled straight down into tempting territory, and all his delicious tan skin. Her tongue traced her lips on instinct. His blond hair was slicked back, still wet, and when he glanced up to meet her eyes, the brief flash of surprise was the biggest turn-on. Like he didn't realize how much he made her hot.

Seconds later, a smirk stole to his lips. "Eyes up here, Car Crash. I'm not a haunch of meat."

Parroting her own words at her. Cute. Ally rolled her eyes and swung her legs over the end of the bed. "Don't strain yourself too hard, coming up with all that original content."

"I'm a fan of the classics," he said, sliding the towel off his hips. He grabbed a pair of sweats from his pack. Like Ally could look away when he was bending low like that. His muscles moved in perfect symmetry, and she got an eyeful of his back flexing, and an ass so perfect it might as well be a Michelangelo. With the way he got her core pulsing, she might just steal into the outside shower and masturbate the tension away.

He turned around, sweatpants hanging low on his hips, and strode toward her. Ally opened her legs, leaning back with her elbows digging into the mattress. Drew stopped right in front of her, his blue eyes scorching as his stare traveled up and down. She had thrown on a pair of jogging shorts and a heather-gray tee to crash out in, but the way he looked at her made her more aware of every ounce of skin showing.

Drew crooked an eyebrow. "You aren't going to make space for me on the bed?" His tone teased, and Ally warred between the urge to punch him in the face or tug down those pants and wrap her lips around his cock. The thought alone had her tilting her head back, her breaths coming out a little more uneven. He nudged at her knee, even though his gaze never departed from hers.

She wanted his hands on her hips and his mouth on hers, but she couldn't bear a repeat of last night. Ally swung her legs over and crawled up the bed to the side she'd staked out. She slipped under the sheets and flipped onto her side. If she didn't get asleep and soon, she was liable to cause trouble.

Drew's heavy tread sounded as the floorboards creaked, and a moment later the main lamp shut off, casting the room into darkness.

"So, tomorrow we narrow down the entrance for Mackey's lair?" Ally said, needing to pull her thoughts to something other than the warm body settling into bed beside her. Drew leaned in, and like last night, he slid his hand to her shoulder, as if asking permission. Ally bit her lip and shifted his way in the bed, closing the space between them. He slid his arm around her waist, the heavy weight making her feel safe in a way she had forgotten existed.

"Yeah, we know the general radius, which will make tracking his lair a hell of a lot easier." His hot breath on the back of her neck made her shiver. Everything about the way they lay together made her hurt, like a bruise refusing to heal. Yet she couldn't pull away from him if she tried.

"The pack from yesterday made it to Ricketts Glen," she murmured. "Eli was asking for you." She didn't know why she said those words. Maybe because he needed to know he'd done some good, or maybe because she liked to bleed.

Drew's grip around her tightened, and their silence swam with the memories they both tried to bury. Every breath she took, Ally swallowed more and more glass, the pain in her chest growing.

"He was a sweet kid who didn't deserve that sort of hell," Drew murmured against her neck. His words made her want to sob, for him, for…

"Do you ever wonder?" he continued, his voice a hoarse scrape. "What ours would've been like?"

Even after two years had passed, Ally couldn't voice the answer out loud. The words stuck in her throat, and the chasm in her chest throbbed anew. Drew simply hugged her tight to him, because he understood.

Every damn day.

Chapter Six

Drew should've gotten up an hour ago. He tended to wake with the sun and this day wasn't any exception — he'd blinked awake once the first citrine rays streamed through the window. However, every second in bed with Ally offered an escape, like he'd traveled back in time. Like he'd never joined the Landsliders and lost her.

She'd curled toward him in the middle of the night and nestled against his chest. Drew had been powerless to resist. He'd tugged her close and pressed his lips to her tousled strands, the spun honey gold that always smelled as sweet. He'd memorized her features a thousand times, the thick fringe of lashes, those pouty lips twisted in a smirk and the slender slope of her neck. Except the other times, they'd been together — they'd shared something.

Now he could only grasp at these moments, knowing they would never be more, even if Ally was the only woman he could imagine forever with. Even if being apart felt like he'd lost an arm, a leg, the phantom ache ever present. Even if she was his mate.

Ally's lashes fluttered, and she began to stir, and Drew forced himself to let her go. Her harsh words never bothered him—she'd always been as blunt as a baseball bat—but if she recoiled, if she pulled away from him in fear or disgust, he'd break. He floated through this life as a ghost of the former man he used to be, haunted by all the things he'd sacrificed when his father had forced him to join the Landsliders.

He had no pack to call his own. His remaining family hated him, and even his mate didn't want him. Drew's focus had narrowed to one goal—take down Mackey Kendricks. Nothing existed beyond that, because this was one mission he didn't plan to come back from.

Drew slipped out of the bed. Ally stretched her arms over her head, thrusting her chest out in a way that had him paying attention. Her big blues rested on him, and her lips curled into a seductive smile. Throughout everything, the nuclear explosion of chemistry that detonated every time they were near each other never changed.

His heart slammed hard with an unrepentant longing that ignored every ounce of self-loathing he heaped upon himself daily. Out of everyone in his life, he'd missed Ally the most.

"Let me get some coffee started," Drew said, striding to the kitchenette before the tempest in his head consumed him.

"If I'm going to be dealing with your ass all day, I'd better be caffeinated," Ally grumbled as she slipped out of the bed. Drew grinned, warmth soaking through his chest without permission. He and Ally had been ragging on each other ever since they were kids — their affection always came with an extra helping of insults.

"Want some more sugar to temper all that bitterness?" he commented. He set to the ritual of getting the coffeemaker going. "Might have to dump the whole bag in." Within seconds the thing chugged to life, a series of growls and hisses emerging from it.

Ally lifted her middle finger and snagged the pack of bacon and eggs they'd picked up on their later run for groceries. She nudged him out of the way of the single burner and pulled out a sketchy-looking pan from the cabinet.

"So, we've got the location narrowed down," Ally said, placing bacon on the skillet. "Think we'll find Mackey's lair today?" She continued to bustle around the small space, cracking the eggs and bringing out plates with a clank. The whole rhythm of this domestic moment between them made his throat tighten. He'd wanted this with her for so long, to start every morning by her side and to share breakfast with their family. To have a little one of their own.

A couple of years ago, they might've had the chance.

Except, as with everything in life, his hopes had splattered like rotting fruit on the pavement. Ever since then, things between him and Ally had changed. She'd grown more distant and he'd gotten more involved in the Landslider mess and the secrets that came with it, until he'd lost sight of who he even was anymore.

Drew ran his fingers through his hair as he leaned against the counter. "We have to find the lair," he responded, staring at the wooden ceiling. "The longer we're here, the more we risk discovery. And the longer Mackey runs around unchecked, the more innocent packs are going to suffer."

He tugged out two mugs from the narrow cabinet and poured them each hefty cups of coffee. Drew spent the time to doctor them up, extra cream and no sugar in hers, while he drank his with sugar, no cream. Even after all this time, he retained every detail about Ally, from the cans of strawberry-kiwi seltzer she pounded down to the fact that she changed her hair length and color as a form of stress relief.

Ally had already placed the bacon on a plate and begun the eggs. "Steal a piece, and I'll cut your fingers off."

"What fun is life without a little risk?" Drew responded, setting the cup of coffee by her side. "Besides, it's an empty threat. You wouldn't deprive the world of these fingers."

Ally made a gagging noise over the skillet. "I think the world would survive." Even as she chased around the eggs she'd cracked on the skillet, a hint of a smile clung to Ally's lips. Somehow, the sharpness between him and Ally had softened a little, and they'd slipped into a normal back and forth. That sort of comfort was dangerous.

Drew had come to the conclusion a while back that he'd never get the normal life he craved. Nor did he deserve that sort of peace and quiet after all the agony and ruin he'd caused.

Ally took a sip from her coffee, and her gaze flickered over to him. She didn't have to say anything for the intended look to land. Of course, he'd remembered. Even amidst the scent of bacon permeating the cabin, he caught a whiff of her gardenia perfume. He had missed her like the first breath from underwater.

She shoveled eggs onto two plates and divided the bacon between them. "All right, Train Wreck. Eat up."

His heart twisted. Some things never changed, even if everything else had. Drew grabbed the plate. "Thanks, babe," he said, taking a seat at the scratch-and-dent round table.

The chair squeaked as she pulled it out to sit on the opposite side. Here, with their plates of breakfast and their waning cups of coffee, he stole a piece of himself back, one he hadn't realized he'd been missing.

Ally glanced to him while she sipped at her coffee. "Stop making those weird faces at me. It's creepy."

Sweet, sweet, domestic bliss.

Drew's mouth quirked with a grin. "You mean my actual face? Should I just tear it off and start over from scratch?"

Ally laughed, the sound short and surprised. Her blue eyes crinkled at the corners, and like this, with her tangled blonde strands and all her gorgeous tan skin on display, she looked radiant.

Drew dipped his head to dive into the eggs and bacon, the salty explosion of the meat and the creaminess of the eggs pure perfection. Ally had always been a fantastic cook. He'd savor this moment, a brief flash of what might've been if he hadn't scorched the earth of his past life. Of what might've been if he still had Ally by his side. The ice had melted between them, but this tentative spring was one snap away from killing those fragile buds.

* * * *

They'd headed out to World's End first thing and parked in the same section as before. Where yesterday they'd prowled through on all fours, today they needed more vocal communication to try to suss out where

Mackey's lair might be. The foreign shifter scents tracked all over the area, which didn't hone into any trackable trail. Not like it would in the Landsliders' terrain. The job was to find the lair, then get the fuck out—recon only.

Revenge would come later.

Drew's nose wrinkled. They hiked through another section that would've been easier in their shifted forms. Yet even in this form he could catch the stench of the Landsliders who stomped through here.

"You'd think Mackey would leave signs to make things easier for us," Ally grumbled behind him. She'd slipped into a slim pair of jeans he wanted to peel off her lithe legs with his teeth. Her lilac tee displayed the soft curves of her breasts and the defined slope of her waist.

"Yeah, *Secret Lair Right Here* is what we should be looking for," Drew murmured as he dragged his focus front and forward. Everything about her scrambled his senses. She always had. "We should be on the lookout for caves or random buildings. Any manmade structures might leave hints of where to go."

The heights of this park were staggering. They loped along trails showcasing deep valleys of endless emerald covered by blooming trees. The Nettle Ridge area they strode through featured a beautiful river, the sun sparkling off the winding surface. Oaks stood erect on either side. He breathed in the life exploding through this place, from the first tender sprouts trying to poke through the ground to the bright green and pale pink blossoms overtaking branches that had been spiny and brittle from winter mere months ago.

Ally's breaths beside him grew rhythmic, a gentle cycle melding with the steady thrum of the river below.

They tromped through the area with care, not wanting to alert any other sentries who might've been sent to patrol. He had the feeling the mutant wasn't the last one in Mackey's arsenal.

Along the path, several brightly colored markers attached to the trees, directing the normal hikers to whatever loop they followed. Drew scanned over the tree, his focus snagging at the base. A symbol had been carved into it.

"Hold on," Drew said, crouching by the base of the tree. His knees brushed against the matted leaves getting overtaken by green. He traced the carving with his fingertip, knowing it at once. Not like he needed a reminder when the same marking had been carved into his skin. Some nights, when the memories got bad, he struggled with the temptation to take a lighter to the Landsliders mark. To burn it from his skin, as if that might absolve him too.

Ally swung down beside him. "Is that..." She trailed off. He didn't miss how her gaze swept to his hip. Even covered up, he was always aware of his mark.

Drew nodded. "Yeah, we're in the right direction." He glanced to her, forcing a grin. "Looks like Mackey did leave a sign." Not like it'd be direct in the slightest. The man was far too clever for that. However, if anyone could figure out the pattern, one of his Landsliders, even an ex-Landslider, should. Chances were, these markings indicated to newer members the claim on the land rather than giving an actual direction. However, they'd be a clue.

"Follow me," he said, pushing himself from the ground. Drew jogged ahead, tracking the markers this time. Some of the signs on the trees were normal, while others held the Landslider mark at the base. He continued to weave through at a quick clip, glancing to the bases of the oaks and pines he passed. The trail brought them farther from the big vista overlooking the valley and deeper into the forest.

Even though he had his claws and fangs, Drew felt underprepared as they trekked through the woods. He bypassed the twigs that would crunch and sections of withered leaves sure to cause noise while they walked. Mackey might be lurking anywhere around here. Drew could have a flamethrower and an M61 grenade and he'd still feel underprepared to face the monster again. After all, Mackey needed only one command to seize control.

Ava had done her shamanic mojo and supposedly broke him from the influence of Mackey's compulsion, but he had a hard time believing. The ex-Tribe member had abused those abilities on so many shifters, for so long.

A shudder coursed down his spine, and he shook his hands out as he continued to trek deeper into these woods. Ally cast him a questioning look, but Drew just offered a half-assed grin.

"We'll stop him," Ally murmured, the words so quiet he almost didn't hear them.

Drew nodded. He couldn't voice how much it meant that she knew when he flashed fake smiles, and that she could figure out why he was fucked in the head. Yet he was too damaged to deal with, and even if she chipped away at the surface, she didn't deserve the burden of the twisted, charred grove his mind had become.

Ahead, stacks of granite and shale dominated the area, cutting through the thick grove of trees.

A massive oak in the center stretched to the sky, branches like grasping fingers while tender buds exposed green along the stark surface. Even from here, Drew caught the glimpse of the mark carved into the base, looking different from the others. He jogged ahead for a better view. When he got closer, he slowed to a careful walk. This wasn't one of the ordinary marks, a bit off-color from the taupe shade of the tree bark. He knelt to the ground in front of it and sniffed.

Drew knew the scent of dried blood anywhere.

"His lair has to be around here," Drew said, his words coming out thick and clumsy. Fear coated him like sap, and his fingers numbed. *Blood, blood and more blood.* That was the legacy of the Landsliders from the moment he'd entered the fold to the crimson they'd spilled out on the field.

He didn't question this was the site. Somewhere amidst these stone stacks they would find Mackey Kendricks' lair. His mouth dried even while he forced himself upright. Ally buzzed with nerves of her own. She paced back and forth through the clearing. Her gaze darted at the slightest sounds, like she was a violin string begging for the bow.

"Check the stones," Drew said while he toed the ground before him in case the earth might reveal the planks of a secret hatch beneath the leaves.

"I'll check what I want," Ally mouthed off even as she sauntered toward the rock faces and columns of stones. She tried to stay calm and collected, same as him.

His heart thundered louder than the falls of Ricketts Glen. He wandered to the stacks himself, checking the ground every couple of seconds to see if he bypassed hidden doors.

He passed one of the stacks that towered high enough for a climb, olive moss crawling over the surface and thick striations and cracks from the top to bottom.

Drew slipped his fingers into the cracks, hoping to find a button, a trigger to some secret entrance. Kendricks was the king of hidden entrances and turning the simple into something more complex. Only stood to reason his private hideout would be as tricky to find.

"Drew," Ally called, her voice quieter than normal. This close, who knew where the Landsliders might be lurking.

He jogged over to her side. She stood in front of one of the crags, tracing her fingertips across the surface. Even feet away, he could see the shape she traced, a large rectangle a shade lighter than the rest of the weathered stone, as if it hadn't been hit by the same storms of time. This must be the spot.

Even though his mission was to find the entrance to Mackey's lair, part of him hoped they'd never find it. Part of him wanted the man to fade out of existence or just vanish to another part of the globe. Not like that would ever happen. Mackey Kendricks had a blood vendetta involving this area, a plan he'd been unfolding for years. That sort of revenge didn't just dissipate—the same way the urge to murder the leader of the Landsliders had been Drew's driving force ever since he left.

"This has got to be it," he said, keeping his voice quiet. "Look for any type of lever or dip in the stone." His fingers trailed along the ledges, and he slipped them into the striations, looking for anything. He stepped past Ally who traced the outline of the rock, and he began checking the base. If Mackey left all his other hints there, stood to reason this one would be too.

He paused on the bit of metal his fingertip snagged on, the surface smoother than the grain of the stone.

Drew pushed the metal, and the piece flipped, like a lever.

A sharp gasp came from Ally, feet away.

Drew whipped around in time to see the stone veneer slide back, a mechanized door opening into a pit of darkness. She took the first step, peering in before she cast a glance to him. Drew nodded, slipping behind her. The scent inside was stale, musty, like a cave, but no lights decorated this entrance. Ally disappeared through the opening and he took the couple of steps in to follow.

His eyes adjusted to the darkness, black blobs solidifying and growing grayer. Nothing jumped out at him and no scratches or shuffles followed. He took another tentative step forward, even as Ally stilled.

A scrape sounded behind them, and the door slid shut.

Chapter Seven

They were trapped.

Ally whipped around in time to watch the door slide shut, leaving them in pitch darkness. They'd entered this place sans flashlight and sans weapon apart from their own claws and fangs, which meant no tools to work the thing open. Unless they found a lever on the interior cave wall, they weren't getting out. She sank to a crouch and began to feel around the door for a latch, a knob, anything to get it back open. As she trailed her fingertips along the bumpy edges, her stomach dropped.

This entrance traveled one-way. The door was sealed tight. Why post guards at the door when the biggest monsters lurked inside?

"Stick with me," Drew whispered, reaching out for her hand. She threaded her fingers through his. Even in the dark, in the lair of their worst enemy, his touch grounded her. Even here, she caught the whiff of vanilla and smoke.

Ally's heart pounded louder than a tolling church bell. They both dropped into silence before taking tentative steps ahead. No sentries lurked in this entrance and she switched to the eyes of her mountain lion to get a better view of the room before her. The bare circular area emptied into three narrow corridors sloping down and pale wooden beams laid out against the carved stone. Shelving jutted from the walls and crates were stacked on either side. This looked more like a storage spot than any grand entrance. For that, she was grateful.

Ally tugged at their joined hands. "Which one?" she asked, her voice scant above a whisper.

Drew tilted his head in the direction of the tunnel to the far left. "His scent is all over this place, but strongest that way."

"Joy," she responded, sarcasm her sole defense against the subzero cold imprinting her bones. She and Drew were stuck in the monster's lair and a veritable swarm of Landsliders could roam these halls. They needed to get out of here and fast—any confrontation would be suicide.

Every step deeper into this place made her throat tighten. A million things could go wrong, yet if they were discovered, no one from their packs would even find out what happened to them. They'd die alone in this mausoleum of a lair. Drew moved with a steadfast purpose she didn't envy. She recognized the glint of hopelessness in his eyes, the abandon of someone who'd lost everything they lived for. Ally hated that look on him.

Except, she didn't have any room to judge. She hadn't reached out with open arms when he'd returned.

The air grew more stifling when they approached the tunnels, and Drew took the first step. Her palm grew sweaty against his, but she didn't let go. The steep angle of the floor stretched out into oblivion, like taking steps into the forest on a new moon. She had never been afraid of the dark in the past, but there was a first time for everything. The stench of all the shifters that passed through this place pricked her nostrils, making her mountain lion pace inside her chest.

They headed down the narrow tunnel, stone scraping against her elbows on either side. The ground beneath her had worn down from tread, different from Ganzorig's caves in Ricketts Glen. Her entire focus zeroed in on one foot in front of the other and the warmth of Drew's palm against hers. His grip hadn't faltered once, a steadying force she needed right now.

The slope of the ground had her feeling like she tripped forward and a few times she almost stumbled into Drew. He remained steady, even though they headed deeper into the home of his mortal enemy. For as much as she ribbed at him and they bickered, Ally couldn't imagine how he remained standing after everything he'd suffered at the hands of that monster.

Spending this much time around him was dangerous. Proximity caused past clashes and hurts to melt away. Even though her heart had been beaten and battered, it pumped with intoxicating hope every time she was around him, making her feel young and stupid again.

The cool stone pressed in on all sides and for a moment, her vision swirled. She sucked in a shaky breath. *Focus.* Drew slowed as he stepped to the base of the tunnel where it spilled out into a different room. Ally didn't bother to stop herself and collided with his back. She craved the heat of his body right now, the one thing keeping her from spinning out. Give her a threat to sink her fangs into, not all this sneaking around.

A hallway opened beneath here, the walls painted the bleach white of sunbaked bones. Fluorescent lights flickered overhead, a stark difference from the dim room they'd arrived into. Not like any of the lights offered comfort when the biggest menace of the East Coast lurked through these halls. She strained to hear anything beyond the static quiet stretching through this place. *Footsteps, voices, shuffling—any of that would be normal.*

But no. Silence dominated this tomb.

Ally leaned in, so close to Drew her lips brushed against his ear. "We should look around while we're here." Really, the plan had been to find the lair and report to the Tribe, but if they were stuck here, they might as well make the most of it. As much as every fiber of her being screamed run, they'd never get this opportunity again.

He nodded and squeezed her hand in reassurance. The quiet through these halls disturbed her. This place was too calm.

They crept past the first of the rooms which had been set up with Ikea desks and more storage space that was dominated by packed boxes and sealed shipping crates. Given the Landsliders' meth trade, they were probably filled with something illegal. Even as she peered in, her skin prickled. Based on the scents of all the different shifters alone, these halls got a lot of traffic, but the offices were well-lived-in, from the array of pencils scattered across the desk to the stacks of papers, some peeking out of folders.

Drew tugged at her hand, directing her farther in. They continued, one slow pace at a time. Ally measured each breath, each step, not daring to make extra sound. Who knew what roamed these halls, mutant or shifter.

Each door they approached could spell discovery and her breath caught in her throat before she peered into another room. This one featured a long obsidian table stretched out across the center with plenty of chairs. Corduroy couches lined the walls, along with a big flat-screen TV, giving the room a lounge feel, far different from Ganzorig's cave hideouts. Drew's shoulders stiffened.

This time, Ally tugged his hand. He passed her a grateful look, those gorgeous blue eyes flashing electric. Her traitorous heart sped up. No matter how mad she'd been at Drew or how much she tried to hate him, he held the master key to the padlock and chains surrounding her core, and they clicked with an ease she'd never found in another soul. Ally stepped out of the room and continued through the corridor, which began to curve. Her mountain lion perked to attention at the distant scrape of what might be footsteps farther down.

Massive double doors to her left snared her gaze, and she slowed. Most of the other doorways had been wide open, but this lay closed. Glass windows displayed the room inside.

Ally stopped still.

Two skeletons were speared by their skulls into the far wall of the room, a button-down and khakis hanging loosely on one and a blue-and-pink floral print dress on the other. Ally pushed at the black-framed double doors to enter the room. The scent of old books mixed with the coppery stench of dried blood, but one glimpse of the spattered altar on the other side of the room and she figured out the cause.

Drew approached beside her, their hands still intertwined as they walked through this twisted shrine of a room. Hundreds of yellowed news articles were pinned and pasted to corkboards, featuring all different shades of recrimination against the Tribe, shifter attacks gone wrong and situations where shifters were punished for injuring humans. Mackey Kendricks had an issue with the governing system among their kind, that had always been clear. But this mess of papers and photos comprised what must've been years of searching into a Martha-Stewart-meets-conspiracy-theory collage.

The polished obsidian floor had been cleaned often, based on the pristine glow. With the sheer number of dried bloodstains spattering the concrete altar on the other side of the room, she didn't question why. As she soaked in more details from the articles along the walls, the dressed skeletons and the leather steamer trunks lining the way, the purpose of this room was clear — Mackey's inner workings splashed onto a canvas.

Her heart raced at the sight of all of this, like they'd uncovered a secret. In a way, they had. Throughout the bombings, the infected meth and the Coalition attacks, their packs had been searching for why this region had become the target. For a while, the Red Rock and Silver Springs packs had sworn they were cursed. However, as they got closer to the altar, a picture of a house snared her attention — the old Landsliders' hideout where they'd taken down the Coalition. Except in this picture, the building wasn't dilapidated.

"His parents' house." Drew's voice snapped her out of her thoughts. "That's what the first Landsliders' lair was — Mackey Kendricks' childhood home."

Ally's mouth dried as certain realizations clicked into place. She glanced to the skeletons speared to the wall. "So, dear old mom and dad?"

"They were the first on his hit list." Drew ran a hand through his hair, staring at the vacant-eyed, agape figures. "Back when we hunted for Ganzorig, Lucas found a list of names. They'd all been crossed off."

Ally's gaze traveled to the shadowbox displayed over the altar, featuring the very list he mentioned. The blood splatters on the altar grew chilling with clarity. "But why?" she whispered. Even with how much she hated her mom and Drew's father, she couldn't imagine crossing the line to kill them.

Drew cast her a sidelong glance. She couldn't look away from the despair in his eyes or the flicker of understanding. Her mom might've been shitty, but Drew's father had been worse. If Dax knew half of the shit Drew protected him from, their relationship might've been different.

"Lucas and I talked it over a while back," Drew said, tearing his gaze away. His voice grew monotone, as if he sank into the throes of his own memories. "Every person on the list was a friend of his parents, most of them successful or rich beyond ordinary. If you follow the rabbit hole down, their competition went missing, or they suddenly got promotions, all within the same five- to ten-year span."

Ally's stomach bottomed out. She couldn't look away from the skeletons pinned above them, as if the gaping hollows where the eyes once existed held answers. "When Mackey had become a Tribe member," she murmured, drawing the conclusion Drew hinted at. His mouth formed a thin line, and he didn't respond. Right now, he couldn't.

"So, all those years, they exploited his compulsion." Ally's mind buzzed like a hornet's nest. She'd been in the grips of those Tribe abilities at Mackey Kendricks' hand and understood the danger. She hadn't been able to move her own limbs, like she'd been wrapped in cellophane. Who knew how Drew suffered after the heinous acts he'd been forced to commit or witness, unable to fight back. She hadn't let herself go there, because the mere imagining howled in the back of her mind like a winter storm.

When she looked at Drew and the despair dulling his eyes, she couldn't avoid the raw throb of pain. Not while their palms pressed together and their fingers were intertwined. Her eyes heated. Fuck, she couldn't hate him if she tried.

She'd seen the bruises when he'd showed up at her house, limping.

She'd lain there with him in the woods when he'd been reduced to a shell, unresponsive and breathing shallow after one of his father's training sessions.

Yet, she'd never even known what he'd suffered during his time at the Landsliders. One thing grew clear—what had been done to him there had broken him beyond all his father's abuse.

Ally wanted to scream, wanted to cry, wanted to rage that the world was so ugly. At how innocent kids got hurt. Sometimes, the cycle continued—the Kendricks' abuse creating the monster Mackey Kendricks became. But other times…her throat tightened at how Drew had knelt before Eli just the other day. At how soft his voice had become, how gentle. And sometimes, even when rare ones broke the cycle, life continued to destroy them. Her eyes burned and her soul scorched.

"So, he killed them, and everyone else involved." Drew's voice cut through the quiet. "Thus, the Landsliders were born. Mackey preached far and wide about corruption in the Tribe, how shifters would never be free under their regime. And he had the data to back up his claims. Plenty have been dissatisfied with rulings the Tribe have made, so he found those folks. He went to the fringes, the outcasts and the criminals, gathering anyone without a home or pack and making stupid kids feel like they were a part of something."

"Or kids whose idiot fathers got them caught up in something they never wanted to be a part of," Ally murmured. He didn't look her way, but his jaw tightened, and he squeezed her hand. She wanted to tell him she understood, that she could forgive him for everything he'd done while under Mackey's hold, but the words gummed in her mouth. If she did, he'd latch on to the forgiveness and all the barriers she'd constructed to keep them apart would crumble away.

Drew deserved more than the shadow of a future she could offer him. He deserved the family he'd always longed for, one he'd never be able to have with her.

The hollowness threatened to consume her, the deep ache in her chest lurking even on her best days. That ache had emerged ever since the fateful trip to the hospital two years ago, ever since the blood had started to trickle between her legs. Even though they'd stopped it, her heart continued to bleed, even now.

"Let's get out of here," he responded, keeping his tone low. "We've found his lair, which is what we came here for."

Ally nodded, her voice not working. As a stylist, she might be able to babble meaningless nonsense with her clients for hours upon hours, but when it mattered, the words never reached her lips.

She let Drew lead her out into the hall, away from Mackey's shrine to his fucked-up childhood. Ally sucked in a deep breath, trying to summon her focus. They continued down the corridor, measuring their paces. Similar rooms to the earlier ones cropped up on either side, most of the wide-open doors and frames leaving them more exposed. If any random fucker could wander in here, they wouldn't keep plans of importance in this section, not without a guard.

After the grotesque display in the other room, Ally wanted to run out of this place more than ever. Her skin crawled at the long, long list of crossed-out names and the bloodstains marring the altar. She wouldn't be able to take a deep breath until she and Drew had settled back in his Caddy and were heading home.

A scuffing sound came from the end of the corridor, followed by the echo of voices.

Her eyes widened. They couldn't get caught here.

She headed for the nearest doorway, dragging Drew with her. Another office. Drew pulled his hand from hers at last. He ducked behind one of the broad ivory desks, gesturing for her to follow. She crouched with him.

The voices trailed through the hallway even clearer when whoever had arrived came closer. Sweat pricked her palms. The low murmur of discussion and the volume of footsteps increased, enough to pick out at least six or seven people. They'd be outnumbered.

Then she heard the voice, the one that repeated over and over in her nightmares.

Mackey Kendricks had arrived.

Chapter Eight

The moment Mackey Kendricks' voice sounded from down the hall, Drew's blood iced.

He crouched behind the desk, but he might as well have been buck naked in the middle of the hall with the way his chest raised hell. *Fuck, fuck, fuck.* The man wasn't omniscient, and he wasn't a god. Yet a single word from him and Drew would've sliced his own neck open. He'd witnessed other shifters fall victim, seen the crimson spill and their gaze flicker out before they collapsed after Kendricks had given the order. The helplessness inside him had expanded until he'd burst, all while words had come from his mouth that weren't his and his hands had made motions he didn't command.

Most times, he'd separated. His mind had buzzed, buzzed, buzzed while he'd watched from a distance as his body and mouth had moved without his permission. The footsteps grew louder. His palms pricked with a fresh coating of sweat — he needed to get out of here now.

Ally crouched next to him, her blue eyes wide and her hands balled into fists so tight her knuckles whitened. She'd had a taste of Mackey's abilities, and Drew thanked the Spirits one small command had been the extent she'd experienced. He would offer himself up every time if he could spare her from the nightmares that randomly seized his mind or the freeze-ups when the memories roared into focus.

"Once it's done, we'll be able to kick back and relax." Mackey's rich voice resonated through the halls. *Close.* They were so close. Drew hesitated to even breathe. Mackey Kendricks supposedly didn't have a claim over Drew anymore, but the monster would kill Ally in a second.

"Right, boss," another familiar voice sounded, one Drew couldn't place. "Because taking down entire packs is such a cakewalk."

"Hey, that's why Ganzorig's device was necessary," Kendricks responded. "We've got a crystal-clear advantage. It's about time we stepped up the pace."

They were close enough to catch the stench of them — Drew only prayed his and Ally's mixed with too many others to identify. He strained for any hint of what the device did, because their packs were still fumbling blind.

At this point, he could gauge about seven or eight pairs of footsteps. Drew's heart beat so loud the sound drowned out almost everything else. Ally nudged her knee against his. He latched onto the grounding point with all his might, otherwise he might float away, his mind retreating and his fingers numb.

Right there. The creak in the wood, the hiss of breaths and the timbre of their voices. They were right there, passing the room.

Drew didn't dare move. He didn't dare peek out the side and try to steal a glance. If Mackey Kendricks discovered them here, they'd both be dead, and their packs royally fucked.

'Have the crew set bombs on the houses in Silver Springs. We need you tearing the pack apart,' Mackey had drawled, the command in his voice.

No. No. No.

He couldn't. That was his family. His home. His people. He had hated his father with all his might, and when the man had died, for a flicker of a moment, he'd thought he might be free from all this. However, Mackey Kendricks had had plans, and they hadn't involved his brother becoming alpha.

'What are you going to do?' Mackey had asked, a glint in his dark eyes and the hint of a smile playing on his lips. The fucker was enjoying this. He enjoyed his inexorable control over others, reveled in it.

A voice that wasn't his had responded, *'I'm going to have the crew set bombs on the Silver Springs houses.'*

Oh Spirits, he'd wanted to die.

Drew shuddered and his whole body shivered, but it was a memory, a memory, not now, not the present. Their shoes scraped against the floor when they passed by.

"If the fuckers would retreat, this would be a lot easier," one of the Landsliders jumped in. "How many times are they going to interfere with our business?"

"The packs joining together made things more irritating," Kendricks said.

Drew and his mountain lion both perked to alert. They had to be talking about the Red Rock and Silver Springs packs.

"But that ends today," Kendricks continued in the casual drawl that had always drenched Drew with fear. "Once we launch the direct attack, there won't be enough survivors to band into anything worthwhile."

"Thank fuck," Harry responded. "If we could catch the East Coast Tribe and the traitor in the mix, it'd be A plus."

Traitor. They meant him.

The footsteps continued onward down the hall, past their room. He remained as still as the stone stacks above, until double doors creaked and the steady pound of the steps halted.

Drew met Ally's eyes and she nodded. Her forehead creased with the same concern swirling in his own mind. Mackey was going to attack their packs, maybe tonight, maybe in mere hours. And Kendricks would use the device that Drew had heard whispers about in his Landslider days, the one meant to destroy an entire region of shifters.

He tried to move, but his limbs locked. Drew sucked in a breath, focusing on his fingers, then his hands and his forearms to follow in the methodical way he'd learned to after he'd left the Landsliders. When the Tribe had first dragged him away, he'd thought they were going to execute him. However, Lucas, Jess, Navi and the others—they had been nothing but understanding. They'd given him purpose again, and Lucas had walked him through techniques to handle the freeze-ups with a patience he hadn't deserved.

How Mackey could have betrayed that loyal, wonderful family was beyond him.

Ally offered her hand, the simple act meaning the world to him right now. He slipped his through hers and together, they rose from the floor. With her palm pressed against his, he could feel the divots there from where her nails had turned to claws and pierced the skin. Drew forced his focus into placing one step in front of the other. Mackey walked around mere rooms away. At any moment the Landsliders could step out and he and Ally would be discovered.

They reached the doorframe and he peered out first.

Empty. His nails threatened to shift to claws as he clutched the frame. He should bolt, but he forced his breaths, one and two, waiting to see if movement emerged. The murmur of discussion could be heard from where he stood. If they didn't try now, they might never get the chance. He tilted his head in a nod, signaling to Ally before he took the first tentative steps forward.

Mackey and the crew had come from this direction, meaning an alternate exit lay somewhere there.

Drew kept his steps careful and slow, even though every cell in his body buzzed. He'd wanted to run from the moment they entered this place. The rec room they'd lounged in and the cozy quarters where they chilled after bombing innocent shifters and murdering families reminded him of the past. Dad had strong-armed him into joining, but only the twisted combination of terror and wanting to make his father proud had kept him there. Mackey's manifesto hadn't surprised him in the slightest, even though it had lodged in his gut. Given a few more wrong turns, that could've been him.

His dad had fucked him up, well and truly, but that made him more determined to be the furthest thing from the man. Even if everyone had looked at him like he was the worst sort of monster.

His neck prickled as they continued down the empty corridor sloping to the right. He hated having his back exposed to the group of Landsliders in the rooms behind him. Mackey Kendricks moved with the silent swiftness of a specter and Drew didn't trust his senses in this place.

As they headed around the bend, Ally stepped a few paces past him, though they still held hands. The corridor stretched out farther ahead, the end disappearing into inky darkness while another hallway intersected, this one leading to the right.

"Which way?" Drew whispered in Ally's ear.

A wrinkle formed on her forehead as she scrutinized the two areas. Drew sucked in another deep breath, this time trying to drag in any scents. He let his mountain lion take the reins, and he soaked in the wet dog from some of the Landsliders, the metallic edge of the surrounding stone and the rich loam of earth. Straight ahead, he caught the hint of ozone trailing with the breeze.

His eyes met Ally's, and they nodded. Together, they continued through the corridor. Drew cast a glance behind him. The hall remained empty, but he couldn't help how his skin crawled.

They passed the corridor to the right, and based on the increased sconces lighting the way, they'd be heading farther into the lair. Fuck that, he wanted to get out.

His claws threatened to protrude at a moment's notice, his mountain lion at the fore. They wandered deeper into the hallway even though fewer lights stretched this way. A crispness threaded the air here that hadn't existed deeper in and he grasped onto the hint with all his might. They couldn't afford to get caught. If they failed to escape, no one could alert the Red Rock and Silver Springs packs about the imminent attack.

"Up ahead," Ally mouthed, her eyes flashing bronze.

His eyes shifted to those of his mountain lion and the murky grays grew sharper and clearer. A steel door lay ahead, this one with a handle. Mackey and his crew must've entered here. Drew slowed upon approach, even though his gut tugged. Escape couldn't be this easy. The lack of guards stationed through the lair meant whoever got in wasn't meant to get out.

"Let me take a look at the door," Drew said, brushing past Ally. He hated to drop her hand. The connection between them was the one thing he'd been holding on to. Back when they'd been stuck in their shifted forms, her gentle headbutts, the brushes against his side and the way she'd curled up with him had been a balm. Their connection had never changed over the years, even as they had. He reached out, the metal of the door cool to the touch. When he tried the knob, it didn't budge. Locked, of course. He needed to find a mechanism.

"See if there's something on the bottom," he murmured to Ally. She dropped to a crouch, running her fingers along the seam of the door.

Drew trailed his fingertips along the base of the knob, and he probed for any buttons to press. A beep sounded, and he almost jumped back in surprise. He hadn't touched anything.

Before he could process, the door swung open.

Three guys stood in the doorway.

Oh, fuck.

Ally didn't even rise from her crouch, just lunged. Drew's instincts took the helm and he leapt behind her.

She dove through the opening between the guys, but Drew wasn't so lucky. He didn't pause, slamming into the nearest guy on his way out with enough force to hurt. Their shouts of surprise hit the air a second later, but Drew and Ally seized the seconds. As soon as he'd exited the door, he had begun to shift.

His nails mutated to claws, and beige fur sprouted across his arms, but Drew continued at a flat run after Ally who had also begun the transition. She crouched to the ground and within seconds, she'd shifted to all fours, her long honeyed mane replaced by a coat of fur the same color. His bones shifted, making his run uneven as he went from two feet then lowered to the ground in his mountain lion form. The scraps of his clothing fluttered behind him when he lunged forward.

Drew didn't dare glance back. The Landsliders would be following close behind. However, if they were going to dive into a confrontation, he sure as hell wanted to be farther away from the lair's entrance where Mackey Kendricks waited inside.

His pads pounded against the ground, and he lunged through a different part of this unfamiliar forest. In a race through their woods, the Landsliders would win. Dirt and pebbles flew under his feet as the scents of pine needles, of fresh air, of hesitant crocuses barraged him in this form, each one distinct and nuanced in a way his human nose could never have told. Ally loped ahead past dozens of trees, the tawny lion moving with the gracefulness she'd always possessed.

She slowed when she reached a clearing ahead. Drew didn't even need a look from her to understand. He slowed in tandem, listening to the *thump-thump-thump* of the Landsliders behind him racing to catch up.

Once Drew reached the open space, he whipped around. The three Landsliders transformed, a black wolf, a russet one and a coyote. He crouched low to the ground, waiting as they closed in at a speed fast enough that their feet blurred. Ally brimmed by his side, a firecracker waiting to explode.

He cast her a glance—she locked onto the middle wolf. He'd take the coyote first. Neither of them moved. They'd played the defensive game a thousand times before, and he'd take whatever precious seconds he could to gauge his opponent. The coyote led with his right foot, moved faster than the wolves and zeroed in on Ally.

Closer. Closer.

The distance vanished between them and the coyote leapt in first.

Ally ducked beneath him to slam headfirst into the russet wolf. Drew didn't waste any time. The coyote had barely landed on the ground when he charged in. He snapped at the coyote's throat, but before his fangs could sink deep, the guy whipped his head to the side. The coyote blocked with his longer muzzle, Drew's teeth catching air. The coyote backtracked a pace, but Drew slammed in again, this time, headfirst.

He smacked the flat of his skull against the coyote's chest, sending him staggering. Drew couldn't pause to evaluate, not while both wolves gunned after Ally. He pursued, slamming into him. The force reverberated through his entire body. The coyote couldn't shake him off let alone launch a counter under this fast, frenetic attack. Even as the beast pivoted to the side, Drew slammed into him again, this time hard enough the *whump* of a lost breath cracked through the air.

The coyote ducked low, attempting to roll away. Spry fucker would run for help.

Drew couldn't let him leave alive.

He launched on top of him, claws sinking in first before he pressed down. The coyote thrashed beneath him, latching his sharp fangs onto Drew's front leg. He didn't budge, flexing his claws so they pierced into flesh before he let his full weight drop onto the shifter. The beast sank the tips in deep, but he ignored the tendrils of pain that followed. The coyote bucked underneath, but he refused to move, each flail driving his claws in deeper. Drew dipped his head before lashing out with his fangs.

The tips scraped against the coyote's muzzle as he whipped back and forth. Time to end this. Drew lifted his front paws to slam them to the ground on either side. The coyote leapt for any purchase he could manage. Even if it was a trap.

When he tried to dart away, Drew still pinned his lower half down, so he fell short.

Drew struck, sinking his fangs deep into the coyote's throat. He whipped his head to the side, and the tear of flesh followed. Drops of blood flecked against his coat as he took a step back.

The coyote thudded to the ground and Drew's front leg pulsed from the pain. Not like he had time to indulge. A low growl came from Ally who backed away from the two hulking wolves striding toward her. Her muzzle already dripped with crimson and both of her attackers had received their fair share of scratches even if she'd gained a few in return. The Landsliders focused on her, their backs to him.

Their mistake.

Drew launched himself forward, crossing the short distance. Grass and mud churned beneath his paws when he settled his weight on his haunches. Drew leapt toward them, soaring through the air. The breezes rifled his fur and the thrill of the hunt pounded through his veins.

He landed claws first on the black wolf, slamming with the full force of his weight. The shifter let out a growl, and he whipped around to try to spot him. Drew caught Ally's eye. The Landsliders might work together in crews, but their casual alliances couldn't compete with a mated pair in tandem.

Ally didn't need to signal. He pre-empted her move. Drew dropped from the wolf's back and slipped around to the left. Ally leapt in from the right, her ivory fangs glinting in the sunlight. Before her attack landed, Drew had already weaved past the two of them toward the russet wolf.

When the Landslider in his sights lunged for Ally, Drew landed between them to intercept. He'd leave her to tackle the black wolf and he'd take this one. His gaze darted past the russet wolf, scanning his peripheral. No sign of others amid the trees or crouching behind the stone stacks. Even in this form, he couldn't shake the unraveling knot he'd become at hearing Mackey Kendricks' voice again. So close to the man who appeared in every nightmare and the time, distance and healing just disappeared.

Jaws snapped in front of him, hot breath puffing against his face. Drew swerved just in time. The claws raked out a moment later, scoring him in the side. He paused to regain his focus, and those claws descended again. This time he was ready. Drew let the wolf slash at his side, but the moment the tips snagged, he lunged forward. The russet pivoted his muzzle to the side, out of the way. Drew didn't stop. He slammed the flat of his head into the beast's throat.

The wolf let out a choking noise and wove two steps around to try and dodge his next blow. Drew followed the path, sticking his neck out with his teeth bared. The Landslider swerved to the side, escaping his fangs but landing right in front of Drew's claws speeding his way. He raked his claws deep, and they snagged in the beast's flank. Before the russet could dodge, Drew rammed his head closer to the neck. Another wheeze came from the wolf's throat.

The russet wolf took two steps back and ducked his head as if he might spring forward.

Except a tawny mountain lion stalked him from behind.

Before he could lunge, Ally leapt onto his back.

She sank her fangs into his back, and a rip sounded through the air as flesh rent. Crimson droplets flew, several landing on his coat. Drew swept in to ram the wolf in the side. Ally dropped her hold and the Landslider's body tumbled away from them. Those ragged breaths lifted the chest one, two, three, and stopped.

Ally's bronze eyes flashed, and her gaze settled on Drew. She didn't need telepathy — he understood the next step.

Run.

Chapter Nine

The window was down, but Ally couldn't feel a bit of the breezes whipping her hair around.

They had run through the woods of World's End State Park until they reached the car. From there, Ally and Drew peeled out of the parking lot and raced to the cabin, and after making quick work of hurling their belongings into Drew's Cadillac, they got on the road. She'd tried to fire off texts to Sierra and Dax, but reception was spotty as shit. She was half-tempted to hurl her phone out of the window.

Nothing moved fast enough.

Her heart hammered so hard it might leap out of her chest. Mackey Kendricks and the Landsliders had planned an all-out assault on her home. They could be heading out hours from now, or they could already be on the road, soaring across the asphalt to destroy her friends and family.

Drew white-knuckled the steering wheel, his gaze focused ahead. He sped across the highway faster than normal, but Ally fought the temptation to kick him over to the passenger's side and take the helm. She hated the lack of control, but out of the two of them, he needed to be in the driver's seat more right now.

"I, for one, am disappointed our woodland vacation got cut short," Ally said, needing to slice through the silence with something. She couldn't stay in her head any longer or she'd go crazy. "If they could all just stay in one spot, I'd happily set World's End ablaze, Smokey the Bear be damned."

Drew snorted. "Thought you couldn't take another night sharing a bed with me? All that complaining sounds a lot like you can't get enough of it."

Ally's breath rushed out in a huff. She sank into the irritation, preferable to the chasm she teetered on the edge of at the thought of their destination. "What do you mean by sharing? You ended up committing a full bed takeover. I was clutching the edge of the mattress every morning."

His lips tilted in one of those half-grins that never failed to make her heart skip a beat. Their time in the cabin, in the forest, in the lair—she couldn't forget it, even if she wanted to. A switch had flipped on between them, one she'd been fighting with all her might to keep off. When she didn't feel the desperate tug toward him, she could dull the pain to an ache, like an old injury. However, this freefall when she glanced at the softness in his blue eyes, a hint of self-loathing and concern there—she dropped onto jagged rocks every time.

"Well now, is that an admission of defeat, Ally-cat?" he drawled. "Color me shocked." When everyone else called her the nickname, it sounded endearing, sweet. On Drew's lips, the name was pure seduction.

Ally licked her lips, grasping at the distraction he offered. "You wish, boy wonder. You want to fight over the bed, I'll go to battle any time."

Drew crooked an eyebrow, his grin growing wider, the cocky shit. "I'll take you up on that. Name the time and place and I'll bring the champagne, babe."

"Unless you want the bottle cracked over your head, leave it at home," Ally shot back, pouring all of herself into this conversation. Her body hummed, livewire tense when they roared across the highway. The engine vibrated beneath her feet and the reverberations traveled from her toes to her fingers.

His gaze flickered her way, a seriousness there reflecting the spiraling depths she felt.

"We'll have to split up when we get there." Drew didn't need to say the rest of the statement—his worries buzzed in the air, the same as hers. After all the time they'd spent apart, this trip together, however harrowing, had been a solace. Somehow it began to heal the ragged edges between them though she hadn't even tried.

"I'll take the Silver Springs cabin," Ally said. "As the pack beta, they're my top priority."

"And I'll head to the Red Rock cabin," Drew responded. Neither mentioned the fact that either of them might rush headfirst into whatever Mackey planned. Duty had always come first, every time. Before their relationship, before their happiness, before their mental health, and they'd ended up here, broken beyond repair.

She tapped her fingers along the edge of the window, staring at the twisted oak trees flickering by. If she was someone else, maybe she could tell Drew she still cared. That she hadn't forgotten him even after all the shrapnel scarred them both. Unfortunately, she was defective.

Happy-ever-afters didn't exist for her.

"He's not going to stop until this region's in chaos, will he?" Ally murmured, her mouth switching the subject for her, tearing away from the yawning void in her mind.

Drew shook his head. "I won't let it come to that. We're going to stop his attack on our packs, then we're going to take the fight to him." He spoke those words with a conviction that didn't reach his eyes, one she couldn't summon for herself. Drew hid the freeze-ups well, but she'd seen them, ones he never used to have, like a 'Nam survivor dealing with memories of the war. His time with the Landsliders had left permanent scars.

Except Ally was the beta of the Silver Springs pack. She understood the importance of bravado, of the lies pronounced until they became hope.

"Now that we know the location of his lair, he has nowhere to run and hide," she growled. "Between our combined packs and the Tribe, we'll make sure he's finished."

"Your combined packs," Drew corrected, the bitterness corroding his voice. "You know as well as I do that I don't have a place there anymore."

Ally's throat tightened. She'd seen the ugly reactions any time Drew walked into the room. Hell, she'd even participated at first. "Anger can fade," she murmured, not knowing what else to say. She focused her gaze on the road ahead, unable to look at the alcohol-on-a-wound pain in those eyes.

"Not after the things I've done," Drew responded, resignation clear in his tone. "Some sins can't be forgiven."

"Where do you plan on going after all this is over then?" she asked, her heart thumping hard. Somehow, she'd gotten the idea in her head that he had returned for good. As though Drew was a part of their community again, a part of her life. The alternative rolled out like a bleak winter's morning, a gray day that stretched on forever.

Drew didn't respond.

The reality of his silence sank into her bones. He didn't plan on returning from this. The weight of the self-loathing in his eyes when he'd realized she'd gained her scar during the bombs sank in at last. This wasn't the garden-variety hatred they'd always levied at themselves. After everything he'd done in the Landsliders and after the way that left him with his former family, he didn't have anything to live for.

Ally swallowed bile. "You know what?" The words leapt to her lips before she could help herself. "Fuck you."

Drew's eyebrows lifted, confusion in his eyes even as he remained steady on the gas, the Cadillac coasting across the asphalt.

"You can't just crash back into our lives, deliver the news you'd been controlled by Mackey the entire time and check the fuck out." Her voice heated, but she couldn't stop. He'd been sacrificing his sanity and his soul since they were kids, dealing with his father's abuse so Dax didn't have to, then taking the Landslider-shaped bullet. And after his mind had been violated beyond anything she could imagine, he still hated himself.

Fuck, fuck, fuck. Every time.

Every time, Drew made it impossible to hide behind her own excuses. Because she'd always done the same damn thing.

"Sure, the pack might hate you now, but look, you've already begun to win some of them over. Lana's forgiven you, and out of everyone, she's the one with the biggest grudge to bear," Ally continued, fueled by anger and nerves.

"That's like saying Jesus forgave his enemies," Drew responded, his voice tight. "She's not the litmus test for forgiveness."

"Don't take the coward's way out, Drew." Pleading crept into her voice, a raw realness she hated. Because as much as she kept pushing him away, the time apart from him had been agony. She'd convinced herself she was living, but her world had been monochrome, more and more color sapping from the canvas with every passing day.

His gaze flickered her way, the sheer emotion in those heartbreaker blues slicing into her like a cracked whip.

"Tell me what I've got to live for, Ally-cat." His lowered voice held a razor's edge tension. She knew what he asked, but every time she opened her mouth to answer, the words pasted to her throat. She wanted to tell him how much she missed him, how she needed him every day he was gone. All the excuses she'd hidden behind to keep her distance disintegrated like ash in the breeze. Why save him from her own broken self if he didn't even believe he had a future?

Yet her mouth dried, her chest squeezed tight and she didn't respond.

Drew simply pumped harder on the gas.

The surrounding trees had already grown familiar, these roads ones she'd traveled a thousand times over.

They reached the Ricketts Glen area, which meant they were moments away from Lana's house. Moments away from each going their separate ways to alert the packs to the imminent danger. Her pulse rioted with everything unsaid stretching between them.

The silences threatened to smother her, the fears multiplying until she could barely feel the sun's rays on her arm. She leaned against the window ledge. The sky was the sort of blue that broke her heart, the same shade as Drew's eyes. She stared at it, wishing for some answer that made sense, wishing she could speak, wishing she felt the confidence she projected to the world, a mask to cover the hollowness within.

All too fast, the familiar streets cropped into view, the winding path toward the development where most of the Silver Springs pack lived. Drew's Cadillac slowed when he reached the circle of houses, Lana's in the middle of the ring. Ally's heart thundered, so deafening she couldn't hear anything else. Some of the houses had the construction wraps around them, even now in the midst of repair from back when Drew had been forced to bomb his own people.

Fuck, he deserved kindness, he deserved love and he deserved better than her.

Her nails shifted to claws as she gripped tight to the ledge. He pulled in front of the house where her car still sat in the driveway.

"Guess this is goodbye," he murmured, breaking the silence.

Ally turned to him. Drew clutched tight to the steering wheel, staring forward as if he couldn't bear to look her way. He was all sloping muscle and tan skin with a proud nose and carved chin that belonged on a statue. Yet his Hollywood looks weren't what had lured her in. It was the shadows in his eyes, the scars up and down his forearms and the hesitation in his lips, because he could never speak his truth either.

The sight of him there, so lonely and devastated, plunged shears through her chest. She leaned forward, crossing the distance between them. Drew looked at her right when she traced the firm lines of his chin. Right as she pressed her lips to his.

He tasted like coffee and destruction and Ally couldn't get enough. His mouth was hot on hers and the moment their lips connected, his fingers wove through her hair, his grip turning possessive. Ally kissed him with all her might, needing to communicate the truth that refused to leave her lips. That he had something to live for. That she hadn't forgotten him or left him—not truly.

Inside, she ached like she was dying at the thought of what they faced and everything they never got to explore. Her mouth surrendered to his, each kiss scorching, the caress of his lips a balm to her fears. This communication between them was real and true— these were the moments with Drew she lived for, when they bared themselves in the one way they knew how. He might not speak the words aloud, but she could feel them in the way his fingers tightened around her strands, in the hungry way his tongue explored her mouth, and in the crushing way his mouth met hers like this might be the last time.

Ally lost herself in the seconds that stretched on like every day they hadn't been together, a whole year and a half's worth of memories they'd lost. Yet, all too fast, Drew pulled away.

All too fast, they separated, the burden of duty summoning them both.

"Stay safe," she whispered before she exited the car. The hollow click of the door shutting echoed through the air. Ally watched as Drew's Cadillac tore across the pavement, heading toward the Red Rock cabin. Her heart heavy, she took one step, then another, until she bolted for her car.

Time to alert her pack.

Chapter Ten

Drew raced along the highway at top speed, heading for the Red Rock pack cabin.

His mind roared, and he fought to focus on the present, not the depth of sorrow in Ally's blues or how his lips tingled from the force of their kiss. In the brief exchange, they'd ripped open too many scabs, and right now, he bled. He hated that they'd separated to face this, and even more, he hated the idea that they might've left each other unresolved. One thing had become clear from their time together in the cabin — as much as they'd both tried to bury them, their feelings had resurfaced every time.

The oak and birch trees loomed along the highway, dashes of green unfurling along the branches. Ally's words jangled in his head, tangled there with the hyacinth in the breeze, the time-old scent of spring in this region. This had always been his home, but after everything that had happened here, he'd made no plans for a future. How could he? Every time he stepped into Beaver Tavern and pulled up to the Silver Springs houses, shrapnel sliced him open anew.

He hurtled closer to the dirt roads leading to the Red Rock cabin, fear pounding in the back of his head louder and louder with every passing minute. He wouldn't know until he arrived if he was too late or not. They'd moved as fast as they could from World's End State Park, and Ally's texts must've gone through by now, but Mackey and the others could've headed out mere moments after.

They might already be too late.

His insides thrummed. Sierra and Dax were staying in the Red Rock cabin more and more as of late rather than their own places. With Sierra so far along in the pregnancy, she didn't feel like running back and forth every time a crisis popped up, which had grown too frequent.

He screeched to slow down when he reached the long gravel drive leading to the picturesque cabin. A furl of smoke poured out from the chimney, which seemed intact, like the rest of the building. He hadn't arrived to a smoking ruin. Two cars sat in the driveway, a Jeep he recognized as Jer's, along with Sierra's junker. Drew pulled up behind them, the gravel crunching beneath his tires. The second he parked the car, he leapt out of the driver's side.

No foreign scents in the air. No screams. Everything appeared normal.

Drew approached one careful step at a time. The murmur of voices could be heard from the door, familiar ones. He knocked, then opened the door with a creak.

Sierra sat at the roundtable near the kitchenette, her bare feet propped up on the nearest chair and her stomach swollen with the little one. His niece or nephew. Her phone lay on the ledge out of reach—she must not have seen Ally's text yet. Jer leaned against the counter, his arms folded and his lips pressed tight as if in mid-argument. The Red Rock beta wore his usual leather jacket, his wavy hair swept back with a slickness fitting the smiles he flashed. Drew recognized them as hollow the moment he met Jer.

Sierra cast Drew a sideways glance. "Back so soon, Williams?" She dropped her feet to sit upright, concern gleaming in her eyes. The woman's levels of perception were staggering. "What's wrong?"

Drew exhaled a breath. He hadn't realized his shoulders heaved and his hands formed fists. "Mackey Kendricks and the Landsliders are on their way here, maybe even as we speak. They're about to launch an attack on the packs. I thought he might target this place."

"You and Ally found the lair?" Jer asked, pushing himself from his slouch.

Drew nodded, beginning to pace. Either they'd descend upon this place, or they'd already struck one of the other pack areas. "We snuck in," he said. "That's where we overheard Kendricks. We need to get out of here, now."

"We need to rally the packs," Sierra said, shooting up from her seat as if she wasn't eight months pregnant. She pocketed her phone and slipped on her shoes. The woman brimmed with nerves, her dark eyebrows tugging together like slashes. His brother had picked a formidable mate, but if anyone could keep his wise-cracking ass in place, it was the Red Rock alpha.

Jer headed for the front door. However, the Red Rock beta stopped in his tracks, feet from the entrance. His nose wrinkled, and he sniffed the air. Tires crunched over gravel outside the house.

Drew's veins flooded with ice.

"We're not expecting anyone," Sierra murmured, answering his question before he asked it. Drew moved on the honed instinct of a predator, striding toward the back of the cabin. He didn't question for a moment who had arrived. Sierra slunk behind him and Jer followed close after, moving with the quietness of a wolf.

The thump of footsteps didn't ensue, a fact Drew hadn't missed. The Landsliders could be quiet when they wanted to, but he found it hard to believe he wouldn't catch a scant sound from an army marching to descend upon this place.

They snuck past the side bedroom, heading toward the veranda out back. At least from this vantage point, the Landsliders needed to climb a couple of feet to attack them. He stepped out onto the painted planks, the spring breezes coasting across his bare arms. His skin prickled. Something was wrong. The forest was far too quiet.

Déjà vu kicked him in the teeth. He'd been here before on the opposite side, too many times.

"Run." Drew gave the command. He couldn't explain the impulse, but they needed to get as far away from this place as possible.

Jer leapt to the wooden rail and began climbing, right as Sierra went to push herself up and over. Drew crouched and placed his hands out to offer her a boost, even though his mind screamed *Run, run, run.* Her gaze met his, pure seriousness, and she nodded. Sierra heaved herself over the side, Jer helping her down from his spot. Drew didn't hesitate. He grabbed ahold of the rail and vaulted over.

The moment his boots slammed to the leaf-covered ground, the force of the jump reverberated up his shins. Even now, they might be too late. If Mackey had brought enough Landsliders, how fast they ran didn't matter.

He had to try. Drew's eyes locked with Sierra's and all three of them bolted for the thick forest that lay behind the cabin.

His mountain lion bucked in his chest, desperate to take the reins. The need to shift pounded through his veins, his claws close to pricking out, and the predator side of him roared to the front lines. His boots beat against the hardened ground. He raced toward the deep woods that stretched far behind the Red Rock cabin.

He dared a glance back, even as he scrambled forward. No movement. He'd expected Landsliders to be loping around the house. This should've been a merciless attack, yet not even a squirrel stirred around them.

Caution clanged like church bells on a Sunday.

Jer vaulted a pace ahead, and Sierra took the lead. They reached the fringes of the cragged trees guarding the entrance of the woods. He hadn't gotten two steps past the looming oaks when his fangs threatened to poke out. Something was wrong. His mountain lion thrashed around in his chest like he'd been lit on fire. Drew sucked in a breath, trying to focus. Silence, silence, silence—except—a shrill, faint sound came from the house.

The sound grew louder by the second.

"What is that?" Sierra asked, whipping around.

Jer began to shift in response, his jacket shucked to the ground as the patchy fur sprouted across his skin.

The shrill noise grew loud, so achingly loud, like it burrowed beneath his skin and rattled around in his mind. Drew's nails shifted into claws, and the beginnings of a shift overtook him even as he tried to force the urge back. The impulse to run rode him as steady as his heartbeat. He needed to go, needed to move, needed to do something.

When he tried to take those next steps forward, his limbs refused to listen. Bile rose in his throat. All he could see was the grin on Mackey's lips from his Landslider days, and all he could hear was the slick voice delivering the command. Just like then, he couldn't move and couldn't do a damned thing apart from what the bastard ordered.

The sound grew loud, so fucking loud he couldn't stand it. The buzzing rang and rang and rang until he wanted to tear his own ears off, and a scream froze in his throat. Drew stared ahead at the pack cabin, at the fringe of trees and the surrounding land, waiting for the Landsliders to crest over the horizon, waiting for them to lunge in on the attack.

Nobody arrived.

Nothing in this forest moved, and a familiar thickness settled in the air, one he'd encountered before.

Drew's mouth dried, and the realization hit him. He tried turning to shout to Sierra and Jer, but he was frozen. Paralyzed.

So. Damn. Loud.

He blinked, the world spinning around him, the grays, greens and browns all bleeding together. Drew couldn't keep his eyes open. He wanted to rip out his own mind, his ears, anything to make the shrill sound stop. His eyes slipped shut again — lights out.

* * * *

The splitting headache hit first. The thumping rattled around in his skull so hard he didn't even want to open his eyes. He began to move his arms and his legs. His skin brushed against leaves while sharp twigs jabbed at him. Outside. He was outside.

Drew forced his eyes open. He seemed to be in the same spot he had been when he'd passed out, in the sprawl of woods behind the pack cabin. His muscles ached, and his mind throbbed, but he pushed himself from the ground. Jer and Sierra still lay collapsed there with their eyes closed, but he caught the steady rise and fall of their chests. Whatever had conked them all out hadn't killed them.

The device.

They'd been waiting for Mackey to use it. He had suspected the thing was a bomb, and everyone whispered about the device affecting shifters, but he should've guessed. Mackey Kendricks had always been about control. Why develop something as simple as a bomb when he could create a device to paralyze mass groups of shifters? Bile rose in his throat. The drive-by knockout nagged at him. He dusted some of the dirt and dried grass from his pants and faced the pack cabin.

Oh, shit.

Oily tendrils of black smoke poured skyward from what remained of the Red Rock cabin. That fast, the pieces clicked into place. The Landsliders were never short on strategy. His hands balled into fists. Paralyze everyone inside then bomb the place, the perfect recipe for no survivors.

Guaranteed, they'd be heading to Silver Springs cabin to pull the same maneuver.

Drew's heart jackhammered, and he wrinkled his nose at the acrid taste on his tongue. He needed to get to Ally. Jer began to stir, a groan coming from the Red Rock beta while he stretched his arms over his head.

"What happened?" The words came out groggy and thick as Jer sat up.

"Kendricks used the device then nuked the cabin," Drew said, making the strides over to Sierra. The very pregnant alpha remained passed out, and his stomach tightened with fear that the fall might've hurt the baby.

"Shit," Jer said, his voice trailing off. "We've got to get to Beaver Tavern." He ran a hand through his curls, a dazed look on his face as he stared at the flicker of flames coming from their former home.

"We need to get out of here," Drew said. The flames would draw the authorities at any moment and they didn't have the time to sit around and explain. Drew crouched to the ground and slipped his hands under Sierra's shoulders. He glanced to Jer. "Help me carry her to your Jeep?"

Jer nodded, the order snapping him to focus. He jogged over and crouched by Sierra's legs to boost her from the other end.

Jer might have been heading for Beaver Tavern, but Drew would have to leave the Red Rock beta to the task. He needed to get to the Silver Springs cabin five minutes ago. His mountain lion thrashed in his chest, but nothing like the berserk way from before. Hell, he didn't know how much time had passed. If he was already too late. His heartbeat thundered in his ears.

"All right, heave-ho," Drew said, lifting Sierra with his arms looped through hers. Jer brought her legs up at the same time and together they began the march toward their cars—if they even remained. The closer they trekked, the more the noxious stench of smoke infiltrated his senses, scorching his mind clear of any other thought than reaching the car. Sierra blinked while they headed up the slope of the hill. Heat gusted out, the creaks and groans of timber reminding him of the other pack cabin they'd found on fire.

He kept his feet steady and, together with Jer, he made quick work of carrying Sierra past the cabin. His heart stumbled when he caught the crash of a timber when it dropped into the center. While he didn't have the breadth of memories Jer or Sierra might of the place, this spot had been his first reintroduction to the packs after he'd begun working with the Tribe. The mission they tasked onto him was the one thing that got him to wake up every morning, the one thing that kept him from getting in his Cadillac and driving off a cliff.

Ahead, he could see past the front of the house to the curving drive. By some miracle, his Caddy and Jer's Jeep were still intact. Drew swallowed a deep breath, regretting it at once as the smoke tickled his throat. In the distance, sirens wailed. Any moment either the cops or the firefighters would be on the scene, and they needed to be out of here.

"Let's get her into the Jeep," Drew said. "I'll head to Silver Springs and you guys can check on Beaver Tavern."

"I can get into the Jeep myself," Sierra croaked as she shifted back and forth in his arms. Drew caught Jer's eyes, and the Red Rock beta lowered his alpha's legs to the ground. Drew kept his grip on her longer, helping her get upright. Sierra met his eyes.

"Thanks," she said with a nod. She righted herself, and he let go. Her gaze lingered, and the further meaning clicked like a key in place.

"If he's at the cabin, I'll make sure he gets out," Drew murmured, needing to say something. His chest tightened. His feelings toward Dax had become a tangled thornbush—pride, love, resentment and jealousy all warring day and night—but he would always look out for his brother. He always had.

"Call and check in when you get there," Sierra said, heading for Jer's Jeep. He knew her agony far too well, the tear in two of having to go one direction while her mate was in another. Jer hopped in and turned on the ignition. His engine rumbled to life, kickstarting Drew into motion. He grabbed his keys and settled into the driver's seat of his Cadillac. He didn't realize he trembled until he'd started the car and set his hands to the wheel.

The Jeep rumbled up the drive and, with a screech, headed right along the highway. Drew followed close behind, the *tick-tick-tick* of the turn signal louder than ever as he wheeled left.

He turned his music on blast, yet the smooth rock that normally soothed his nerves now grated against them. His mind roared with panic, a suffocating chasm he tried to avoid at all costs. Ally would get them out. Ally would escape in time. She had to.

He couldn't face the alternative.

He soared across the asphalt at top speed, following roads he'd grown up racing along, whether with Greg and Dax or by himself at three in the morning. In the distance, the tall peaks of pines stretched out, the familiar ear marks of the pack cabin. He hadn't been there since the fight against Dax, and even now, shame coated his skin.

So many fights in the clearing, all under Mackey's orders. All for a position he never wanted. Bones had crunched. Blood had spattered on the dusty ground. And Drew's heart had shattered when his former friends and family had lined the crowd, cheering for his brother. Sure, his father's friends had backed him, other Silver Springs members who had been part of the Landsliders, and old, bitter folks like Ally's mom Rylie. Yet the ones who mattered despised him.

He approached the turn for the Silver Springs cabin, and his heart stopped in his chest.

Too late. He was too late.

Charred smoke rose higher than the tops of the trees. The Silver Springs cabin was on fire.

Chapter Eleven

Ally groaned. Her entire body felt like it had been run over by a tank.

She pushed herself from the ground, dust coating her skin from the fall. Heat blossomed in patches along her skin. Her throat tightened. *Oh, fuck.* Her nails turned to claws and she dug into the ground in front of her, hysteria rising. Her leg throbbed like the molten silver poured onto her skin all over again.

Hands descended around her shoulders, the grip rough. Even though she started in surprise, her body cooperated — she knew the presence like her own. *Safe.* He was safe. She sucked in a breath, but it caught in her throat. Coughs erupted from her chest, the smoke like sandpaper to her insides. She tried to blink, but her eyes crusted shut.

Ally staggered ahead, one step at a time, guided the entire way. Those hands remained on her shoulders and every time she sagged or stumbled, he helped her back up. He kept her moving, away from the heat and away from the smoke.

"Come on, Car Crash," he murmured in her ear. "Keep going."

Her chest squeezed tight, but she forced herself forward. After a few more paces, she drew in a blissful breath of fresh air. It tickled her throat, and she spluttered again. The heat dissipated and Ally blinked her eyes open. She faced the broad lake she'd spent a childhood swimming in, one she'd explored from top to bottom, unlike Lana who hung in the shallows. His hands still gripped her by the shoulders, rough, competent and achingly familiar.

"Thought you headed to the Red Rock cabin," she murmured, glancing at Drew. He closed in behind her, wrapping his arms around to pull her tight to his body. She sank against his firm chest, almost sagging from the relief coursing through her. All she remembered was staggering out of the back door of the cabin while that piercing noise had grown louder and louder, then heat had blasted before she'd passed out.

"Already did," he said. "Sierra, Jer and I were heading for the woods when they unleashed the device." He squeezed her close, the sort of solid she needed right now. Ally reached up to rest her hands on the corded forearms wrapped around her.

"Fuck." The word flew from her as she stood straight, almost barreling out of his grip. "Where are Dax and Lucas?"

"Here." Dax's voice came from feet away. The scrape of his approaching footsteps followed. "We all managed to make it out of the blast. Where's Sierra?"

Drew let go of her, though with reluctance. "She's safe. They're heading for Beaver Tavern right now."

Ally turned around to face Dax and Lucas who both appeared lightly toasted, smears of ash on their skin and fried strands. The motion brought the cabin into view.

Mackey might as well have torn the heart from her chest and stomped it on the ground. The Silver Springs cabin burned, fire ripping through the paint job they'd done a couple of years back and smoke pouring from the center like a volcano. Her throat tightened. This had been her home away from home. She and Drew had snuck here when they'd first started seeing each other, when she hadn't been able to stand her mom's barbs and his dad had decided to beat him up too much in 'training'.

This had been their safe space where they'd healed, where they'd fallen in love and where their pack had rallied after so many difficult blows. Hell, she'd seen a lot of the guest room when she'd been lying low after the bombing.

Yet, like their other homes, the Landsliders had taken this one too.

"We need to rally at Beaver Tavern," Dax said, taking the lead. Lucas had already begun walking toward the cars.

Ally's pocket buzzed at the same time multiple ringtones broke through the quiet. She pulled out her cell to check the message. From Sierra.

EMERGENCY MEET AT BEAVER TAVERN.

Her heart plummeted. Ally's eyebrows drew together, and she met Drew's gaze.

His mouth formed a tight line and he clutched his phone so hard he might break it.

"Let's head out," Lucas called to the rest of them, jogging ahead past the burning cabin. Soon, the fire engines would come to put out the blazes, unlike the one in her heart that was sparking into a wildfire.

* * * *

When she pulled into the gravel lot at Beaver Tavern, she'd half-expected the scene she'd stumbled onto before, of the flames burning through the place like they had the day Drew had led the Landsliders to attack before his fight with Dax. She stepped out of her car right when Drew slid his Caddy in beside her, the crunch of gravel the only sound that echoed. The stillness in the lot filled her with a silent terror.

Any normal day, Beaver Tavern burbled with idle conversation and the hum of activity from inside and out. However, a bleak quiet stained the spot, the doors barred shut. More cars lined the highway, blinkers on to turn into the lot. Sierra's message had spread fast and already the members of both packs arrived on the scene.

Drew stepped out of his car, slipping his aviators off and into his jeans pocket. He brimmed with thunderstorms of his own, his gaze wary as he looked at the place that had become a haven for not just the Red Rock pack, but the Silver Springs as well. Even in the late afternoon, cozy beams normally emanated through the windows, but the blinds and curtains had been pulled shut.

Ally reached out and slipped her hand into his. "Let's head in," she said, knowing he'd frozen on the spot. The shame and loathing must be suffocating right now faced with the bombs, the Landsliders and the place he'd torched.

He let out a shaky breath and his blue eyes cleared, a focus descending that hadn't been there moments before. Like this, she remembered the boy she'd fallen in love with far too well.

While other cars raced through the drive, screeching to park all around them, Ally and Drew took their first hesitant steps toward Beaver Tavern. Dax and Lucas had arrived moments before, but they must've already entered. The shut front door emanated a forbidding presence, like they'd stumbled upon a mausoleum. Ally ran a hand through her hair, unable to dispel the nerves traveling all the way to her fingertips.

The crunch of gravel sounded even louder, and sweat pricked her palm while she kept her hand pressed tight against Drew's. Her breathing hadn't returned to normal, ragged around the edges and her throat raw. Too many times, the Landsliders had violated their home, their territory.

Drew reached for the front door first and he yanked it open.

They both stopped in the doorway.

On any normal day, Beaver Tavern smelled like porter and hickory. The chatter drifted out from the often open windows, creating the warm and welcoming vibe she'd always adored from the day she, Dax and Kyle had first entered this place. That fateful day Dax had met Sierra, and they'd first joined forces. Always, always, always people crowded the roundtables, hanging around playing pool or sitting at the bar to chat. Every time she drove past, the mellow amber lights through the window soaked her with warmth, a comfort she had rarely found.

Today, Beaver Tavern smelled like blood.

Voices sounded, but not casual chatter. This was the harsh murmur of heartbreak and strangled sobs.

The lights had been snuffed out, only a few lamps illuminating the place, as if the darkness could hide the horror.

As if they could erase the stench of death or the dozens of corpses collapsed to the ground, sprawled over the tables and hunched over each other in protection.

Sierra crouched in the center of it all, Dax alongside her as she ran her fingertips over another body. Ally's jaw dropped, and her feet carried her inside, even though she couldn't feel her body. These weren't random shifters and this wasn't a random massacre. She knew every single face. Jared and his entire family sprawled around one table, their throats slit from silver, even their ten-year-old daughter, Molly. Fuck, just last week they'd taken her out for good grades on her report card.

Betty and Frank piled on top of the pool table, his body over hers as if he might shield her from a blow. His hand curled around her shoulder. Their blood drip, drip, dripped, crimson pooling on the ground next to the shattered pool cues.

A scream sounded from behind her, the sort of agony that would haunt her for years to come. Raven rushed past her to where Jer hunched over a body. Tears streamed unchecked down his face. Gene had been in his normal spot at the bar, his half-finished porter still on the counter. Now he lay lifeless on the floor.

No. No, no, no, the bar.

Ally walked, then she ran.

As Raven's screams, her sobs, filled the air, Ally's throat tightened. She wove around her, careening to the back of the bar.

Her feet stopped working.

Her knees hit the ground, and the air evacuated her lungs.

Kyle lay on the ground, slumped to the side. Crimson pooled around him, a neat slice across the throat. Her packmate, the one she'd gotten into thousands of stupid debates with, the one who she'd run recon alongside, and who she'd loped around the woods with when they'd been kids playing in their mountain lion forms. They had gotten Kyle.

Ally's entire body began to shake. So often, he'd flash her a quick grin or join in when they started teasing Dax. So often, he'd been there fighting alongside her, someone she trusted when her list was fragmented and short to begin with. Few knew about his dream to head to Philly and study law — to become a pack lawyer for the Silver Springs like Jer was for the Red Rocks. He'd been saving his money from the bar, stowing it away.

He had planned on enrolling in the fall.

Footsteps sounded behind her and a hand rested on her back. *Drew.*

"Oh, hell." The words slipped from him.

Her hands balled into fists, the nails shifting to claws. Silent sobs welled in her throat, refusing to come out. The hardwood dug into her knees, but she couldn't move. The sight eviscerated her.

"Kyle," she murmured, as if he might answer. As if those brown eyes hadn't dulled for good. Ally reached forward, but he lay feet away, out of reach. She couldn't bring herself to close the distance. Her heart thundered so loud the sound drowned out the sobs, the clatter of footsteps and the screams as more members of the packs arrived. More and more of her friends and family discovered who had been taken away from them.

For one brief moment, she'd believed they'd pulled this off. That they'd been clever and infiltrated Mackey's lair. That they could thwart Mackey Kendricks and the Landsliders. Even if they hadn't managed to save their pack cabins, she'd believed they'd kept their people safe.

Except in all their haste, they'd missed one integral spot.

Heat stung her eyes and hopelessness clawed in her chest. They'd gotten cocky, thinking they could take on the Landsliders and win.

Spirits above, they couldn't. Mackey Kendricks would destroy them like he had so many others, whether it was with bombs, flames or his Landsliders. Drew crouched beside her and rested his palms on her shoulders.

"Come on," he said, his voice firm, and his eyes as somber as a cemetery. "Time to get up, Silver Springs beta."

Her heart ached so hard it might burst. She snarled at him, the animal sound coming from her lips. Ally wanted to hate Drew for tugging her away. This was Kyle lying here on the floor, not some random shifter. This was her packmate, her comrade, her friend.

Drew didn't budge, the heat from his palms soaking into her shoulders. His mouth formed a firm line, strain around the corners. Even though his eyes had darkened and even though she caught the way he clenched his jaw like he held on by the motion alone, he remained steady. Drew was unshakeable, even in the face of devastation, like a leader should be.

He was right.

The pack needed their leaders and she'd signed on to this responsibility. Ally sucked in a shaky breath, focusing on the weight of Drew's hands on her shoulders. She stared hard at the wood grain by her feet, anywhere but the broken body lying mere feet from her. Bile rose in her throat again, but Ally kept forcing the breaths. *One, two, three. One, two, three.*

Even though her fingers trembled and her legs shook, Ally pushed herself from the ground. Drew rose with her, leaving one hand on her shoulder as if he knew she needed the lifeline he offered right now. As if he knew she needed her mate.

When she straightened, Ally rested her hand over his and met his gaze. The figure in her peripheral had her mind buzzing, a rising white noise threatening to crest at any moment. She focused on Drew, on the arched nose and carved eyebrows she thought arrogant. In the dim light of Beaver Tavern, she understood more than ever that all the definition had been honed by tragedy.

"I've got this," she murmured, trying to convince herself.

Drew nodded and at last he dropped his hand from her shoulder. "Go, rally your pack."

She slipped her hand in his to tug him forward. Drew's forehead furrowed, but he followed her as they stepped from behind the bar. Ally winced. Minefields existed everywhere her gaze landed. Raven knelt over Gene's body, her ink hair spilling over her shoulders like a shroud. Not a single tear trickled down her cheeks, because the woman had become broken-doll numb in the wake of this loss.

Where before a couple of the shifters from their packs had arrived, now Beaver Tavern was filled to the brim.

From Rick and Marcy to Lana, Silver Springs and Red Rocks alike filtered into the broken landscape that had once been their safe haven. Ally cast a glance to the bar again, half-expecting to see Kyle standing behind it. She sucked in a sharp breath, heat stinging her eyes.

Dax and Sierra strode toward her and they met in front of the bar, the back and center stage of this place. Drew's hand tugged as if he'd drift away, but Ally held on tight. After everything he'd sacrificed for their packs, he deserved to be up here as much as she did. Jer wiped at his eyes before he squeezed Raven tight and rose on shaky legs to join them.

Together, Dax and Sierra were a storm on the horizon—sharpened ozone and scorched clouds. Their expressions held all the rage and sorrow they both contained. Dax's gaze drifted to Drew and he tightened his grip on hers. For a moment, an argument leapt to Ally's lips. She prepared to lash out at the first person to give her trouble. Except Dax nodded, his mouth a firm line mirroring his brother's. Despite the past pain Drew had caused, he had earned his place here.

Ally lifted her chin and stared out at the familiar faces clustered in here, so many people she would lay down her life for. This was the pack she loved. This was the pride of her life.

Sierra stepped up, the woman's presence direct like a lightning rod. Her eyes blazed with a dark fury they all shared at the bodies littering the floor and the blood staining the planks. Sierra circled her hand around her stomach, a reminder of the future each and every one of them fought for.

"Mackey Kendricks has set bombs to our homes." Her voice rang out, clear and incisive. "He has infested the region with mutants and berserkers. He's tried to steal our land, and he's sent the Coalition to our doorstep. The man has taken far too many lives."

Dax nodded, resting his hand on his mate's shoulder. Gone was the calm, smiling alpha she knew. Only on rare occasion had she seen him like this, the terrifying rage that mutated to cool resolve.

"Now, we go to war."

Chapter Twelve

Drew could take a bath in turpentine and the stench of blood still wouldn't have left.

He rubbed the towel over his skin, not sure if he'd gotten the stains out, because it sure as hell felt like the scum clung on. Not like he could set a match to the new set of memories that imprinted after today, yet another scene of broken bodies—these ones former friends. He slung on a pair of sweats and strode through his old house, which had remained untouched for quite a few months now.

Unlike the others who lived in the communities, he'd picked a small rancher that lay tucked away, not too far from the Silver Springs cabin. After what happened earlier, he remained vigilant to every creak and groan from outside. The sound of a snapped twig from a rabbit earlier might as well have been a gunshot.

This house was familiar and strange all at the same time, like everything in his life. The worn slate couches, the wood shavings he never managed to clean completely from his countless projects and the small figures of their packmates he'd carved over the years. His guitar sat in the corner, begging to be plucked. Those all belonged to a guy who had a future, one who hadn't screwed over his own pack beyond redemption.

Drew plucked out the handle of Jameson from his tote and crashed into his couch. He tilted back the neck to steal a sip. The liquid coursed down his throat with a burn he needed badly right now. All he could see was the carousel of dead bodies and broken faces round and round on repeat. All he could see was the horror in Ally's eyes and how she'd trembled. His self-loathing roared even louder in the wake of another tragedy.

He should've known Mackey would pull something like this. He'd returned to do some good for the pack he ruined, and yet he failed. If that didn't sum up his life, he didn't know what did.

Failure of a son. Failure of a brother. Failure of a mate.

Drew stared at the ceiling, the worn beams he'd once looked at while sketching out a future with the love of his life nestled in his arms. But this — bruised and alone with a bottle late at night — this was what he deserved. To say he ached was the understatement of the century. Drew cracked into a wide-open chasm of pain, the sort of fucked-up no attempts at restitution could stitch together again.

He could earn the forgiveness of every damn person in this pack, but none of it would matter. None of their platitudes would change the charred hull where his heart had once existed, a void consuming him a little more every day.

Fuck, he should've taken the knife and sliced it across his throat back when his dad first brought him into the Landsliders, the first time Mackey used compulsion on him, something subtle. Drew should've spared everyone the misery. One quick cut.

The thought haunted him every damn day.

The crunch of tires had him rolling to his feet.

His claws pricked out and, as he whirled toward the door, the headlights of a car grew visible through the blinds. If Mackey backtracked to kill him, Drew would fight him fang and claw for all the damage the monster had done.

He strode over to the door, and the headlights clicked off. The soft pad of footsteps echoed as someone approached. Drew rested his hand on the knob when the scent of gardenia traveled his way, one he caught even in here. He sucked in a shaky breath, and his claws reverted to nails.

The knock sounded on the door and for a moment, he debated walking away. He was low tonight, the shit sort of company no one deserved, especially not her. Before he could make a decision, the door swung open.

Ally marched her way in, like she hadn't shown up at random. Like they'd reverted to years ago when she dropped by on a whim, when her toothbrush had perched on his bathroom sink, when they'd been inseparable. Her blonde hair had been swept back into a ponytail, a few wavy strands curling around her neck.

"Please tell me you've got something to drink," she announced, her gaze meeting his.

Drew's tongue traced his lips. He strode over to his couch and grabbed the handle of Jameson. "Hope you still drink whiskey, babe."

Ally lifted a carved eyebrow, and she sauntered past him like she hadn't a care in the world. Except Drew always knew her better than that. She might be casual looks and comments, but pain radiated off her like desperate beams from a lighthouse. Today had devastated her, no matter how she tried to hide her feelings.

"Please," she responded, slumping into his couch. "I got a taste for whiskey way before you ever took a shine to it."

"How dare I drink rum when there's oak-scented paint thinner to drown in," he drawled, pausing in front of her on the couch.

She sprawled over his loveseat, dominating it in a way she always had. The sight of her kickstarted his libido, a pulse of desire he could never ignore. Ally's long, tan legs were on full display in the blue running shorts she wore, and her white tank top might as well have been painted on. Ally was perfection, all slender shoulders, her tits straining the fabric of her shirt, and hips with a generous curve.

Her sultry gaze locked in on him, those blue eyes darkening with intent. He didn't question for a moment what she had in mind. When they'd been leaving Beaver Tavern, the claws had dug in hard at the sight of all the couples taking solace in each other. Dax had kept his arm around Sierra's shoulders, Lana had leaned against Lucas, and Jer and Raven had kept their hands clasped together.

Ally had twined her fingers through his back there, and the stupid fraction of him that dared to hope had leapt onto the comfort. However, in the dim light of his old house, reality set in. Comfort belonged to someone who hadn't ordered the bombs that scarred her.

"Going to just stand there gaping at me, or are we going to drink?" Ally asked, tapping the seat beside her. Her tone dripped sex, making what she'd come here for clear. He should feel used, but hell, he wanted her so badly the need drowned out reason.

Drew ran his hands through his hair and sank into his weathered couch, even though sex was a terrible idea. He leaned over to pass the handle of Jameson over, and she tilted the bottle. As Ally passed it back, he caught the gleam of the liquid on her lush lips curved into a smirk as fake as his own.

"Why aren't you at Lana's tonight?" he asked, spreading his arms along the back of the couch. He didn't miss how her gaze scorched when she lingered on his chest. "You know out of everyone she's the best with this sort of shit."

Ally stretched her arms over her head and stared at the ceiling. "Lana and Luc were doing their thing upstairs. I didn't want to bother them."

Drew lifted an eyebrow. "So, you chose to bother me instead?"

Ally pursed her lips. "What am I interrupting? Your romantic date with the bottle, or your hand?"

He snorted and lifted the bottle of whiskey to his lips again. The fiery liquid served as a reminder when it washed down his throat. As much as he wanted to sink between those luscious thighs, the damage he'd caused was still visible there. And if they continued the way they were, the casual drinks, back and forth taunts, he knew where they'd be heading.

"Ally, this isn't going to happen," he said, hating the words even as he said them out loud. Because truth be told, his soul ached with a weariness he couldn't fight anymore, and she'd been the first breath of relief he'd found. She flinched. Before she could say anything else, he forced himself to continue. "I don't blame you for hating me. Hell, join the damn club. But I can't help the way my body reacts around you, and we end up colliding every time. You deserve better than a hate fuck with the asshole who screwed up your leg."

Drew tilted the Jameson back again, unable to witness her reaction. If he were more selfish, maybe he'd just indulge. But when he'd started working with the Tribe, he had promised to make amends. Out of everyone, she deserved them the most.

He heard a rustle and his heart clenched. She was going to leave, in typical Ally fashion. This had been their holding pattern from the beginning—when shit got real, one of them would ditch. All their bickering, yet they never found the words to say.

He lowered the bottle to find her sitting inches from him. The scent of her, gardenia and fresh berries, surrounded him, enhancing the desire he fought to contain.

Ally's brow furrowed and she let out a shaky breath. Her gaze glided over the couch. "Look, I'm only going to say this once, so pay attention."

Like she needed to ask. She'd had his rapt attention from the moment she stepped into his house.

"I never hated you, Train Wreck," she said, her voice skating a whisper. Hearing the words out loud punched him in the chest, and Drew sucked in a sharp breath. She couldn't look at him, but he understood. Everything about opening up was more painful than the worst knock-down brawl he'd been in.

Ally reached out and placed her hand over his, the touch a connection that had never faded between them. Finally, she looked into his eyes. The lost hopelessness there drove shards into his chest.

"You never told me. We might've always been back and forth, and we might've fought a lot, but we shared everything. And when you joined the Landsliders — that's why I'm still pissed. You. Never. Told. Me." Her voice grew hoarse, a pleading there that slid right under his skin. The air grew tense between them, loaded with the truth she'd spoken, one she'd been silent on for so long.

Drew's throat squeezed. And what if he had? Maybe together they could've found a way to extricate him from the mess. Maybe he wouldn't have been so alone. But he'd boxed her out, distancing even when he hadn't tried to. And after the miscarriage, the tenuous bonds between them had fallen apart. He'd never blamed her for leaving.

Excuses bubbled to his lips, ones that had dwelled there for far too long. The ones he had made years ago to justify keeping her in the dark — her protection, to keep her safe, to keep her away from evil like Mackey Kendricks.

Yet she sat here baring herself before him in a way she rarely had before. All the excuses crumbled to dust.

Drew slipped his hands around hers and gripped tight. His heart hurt — right-hook hurt — at her admission. "I'm sorry, Car Crash," he murmured, the old name loaded with the timeworn affection that had never quite vanished, even as they'd both tried. "I should've told you."

As much as he wanted to say more, the simple truth stood on its own. They had shared everything. She had been a part of all his shitty history, from the fights he got into as a kid to the cracks in the head and hands around his throat his dad called 'training.' No matter how much they'd fought, they'd always shared everything, until he'd joined the Landsliders and they'd fallen apart for real.

Ally's lips tilted with a half-smile. "Was that so hard?" Even as she tried to return to her normal register, the vulnerability she'd exposed lingered in her words and the tender way she glanced to him. Those slips of soft were his kryptonite from the iron-edge woman who slung acid for a pastime.

He grinned. "Full-out evisceration."

In the wake of the horror they'd witnessed today, smiles and jokes felt sacrilege, like he was spitting on their corpses. However, life was too short, too glass-vase-fragile to waste. Relief radiated through him in a way he forgot was possible, like a hard shell cracked wide open. The heat inside spilled out, real feelings that existed beyond the numbness he'd sentenced himself to.

All the time he'd spent pushing Ally away had been a waste, because this gorgeous, resilient woman had never wanted any ideal. They'd collided together over and over throughout the years because they were both headfucks too stubborn and broken for anyone else to deal with. Somehow along the way, he'd forgotten that.

"Spirits above, Ally-cat," he murmured, the words thick in his throat. "I missed you so damn much."

The admission tore at the numbness, a mixture of pain and warmth he'd been avoiding for far too long. He might not recover from this riptide threatening to drag him away, but she'd taken the first step toward him. He'd rather soak in the hurt than cause her hesitant smile to falter.

She stared at him, eyes full of wonder, full of the hope he thought had been destroyed a long time ago. Spirits, those lush lips, the slender slope of her face, and the wicked curves of her features made for sin—all of it held him spellbound. She'd always been a beautiful destruction he'd embraced every time.

"Then enough about what I deserve," Ally growled, a grin spreading. Her gaze flashed the bronze of her mountain lion. "I want you, Drew Williams."

Like this, she was the hellcat he remembered, but she'd grown. The Ally from years ago would've never been able to voice the words out loud. Her bravery socked him in the gut, the push he needed to bypass the self-loathing in his brain.

Drew reached out to trace the slope of her jaw. He brushed his thumb across her lips, and she shivered in response, her gaze laser-focused on him. Everything about her screamed sex, from the way she tilted forward, revealing the shadowed slope of her cleavage, to the heat in her eyes, a lioness on the prowl.

"And how badly do you want me, babe?" he murmured, a grin rising to his lips. He continued to run his fingers across her skin, down the elegant column of her neck, and across those exposed collarbones.

"Keep your ego out of this, Williams," she shot back, the exact response he expected from her. "You're insufferable enough as is."

She was the only one who'd ever keep him in check. Others might not get their collisions, but they both understood when the other needed to hurt and when barbs at each other soothed pain that would otherwise consume. When he'd returned with the Tribe, Ally's barbs had been cool, none of the familiar heat in them. Those had hurt.

Yet with these, the glint returned to her eyes and a smile ghosted her lips.

Maybe he didn't deserve forgiveness, but she'd given it anyway. Maybe he could shove the shadows away and let the light in — at least for tonight. Drew's heart thundered.

"Take your swings now, babe," he drawled. He prowled closer on the couch, closing the space between them. "Because they'll all be gone when you're screaming my name."

"In your dreams," she responded. Ally licked her lips, the eagerness in her eyes stoking his libido. The mere scent of her got him hard, and her arousal was heavy in the air. Fuck, he wanted to drive into her again and again, to slip her golden hair through his fingers and tug. Drew needed Ally splayed beneath him, unfettered and raw. The slip of vulnerability from her before had stoked his coals in a way nothing else would.

All thoughts of stepping away vanished once she spoke up. Ever since the Tribe had dragged him out of the Landsliders, Drew had been running, running, running from those memories. He'd grown icebox numb, only the blackened tendrils of his self-loathing protruding through. Yet, if she could summon the bravery to voice her truth out loud, then maybe he could face a few of his demons.

Drew placed his palm on her cheek and drew her forward. The space vanished between them, and their lips met. They'd kissed before, a thousand times over, but he had never needed her this badly.

He sank into the kiss, his fingers threading through her hair. He gripped tight. Drew drank in the taste of her, of desire, of heartbreak, of salvation. This wasn't a chance encounter fueled on regret and old memories. This thing between them, this crazy collision they'd always fallen into — this was the way they healed.

Chapter Thirteen

The moment Drew's lips met hers, everything else vanished.

The pain, the excruciating pain from the losses earlier that made her forget how to breathe, how to function.

The raw scrape of nerves that buzzed after the words burst from her mouth, unbidden, the only way she'd ever manage to speak them.

The overwhelming fear of what would come next, of the retribution they'd promised the packs they would deliver.

When she had been sitting at home and flicking through the TV channels, the emotions had roared so loud she thought she would go insane. She'd only met one person who could shut away the noise, the one whose arms she'd fallen into time and time again. Ally couldn't place when she'd forgiven him, whether it had been the moment he returned, or the small connections along the way of fighting together again, of reconnecting back in the cabin, but she had.

Ally wrapped her arms around his neck and sank into the explosive heat of his kiss. That clever mouth coaxed moans from her. The way he switched from the gentle brush of his lips to the harsh bite of his teeth was pure poetry, and she couldn't help but surrender. His vanilla scent wrapped around her, the warmth traveling straight between her legs. He leaned over her and she fell onto the couch cushion with a thud, a grin rising to her lips.

Drew dipped to claim her mouth again, pure possession. This was the passion she'd craved that no amount of Tinder dates could compare to. Not like she'd ever admit it, but when she masturbated in the shower, she envisioned him, every fucking time. Her nipples tightened when he pressed her into the couch, his weight pinning her in a way she craved right now. Whenever her problems expanded to the point where her very cells threatened full breakdown, he brought her to the ground and pieced her back together.

Somehow, she'd forgotten that. Somehow, the years of secrets had poisoned their well, until each of them withered more and more.

"Spread for me, sweetheart," Drew commanded, showing the bossiness she only ever took from him in the bedroom. Ally opened her legs wider, desperate to feel his hardness between her thighs. He brushed another kiss to her lips even as his fingers skimmed the waistband of her running shorts. He tugged down, bringing her panties along too as they both hit her ankles. Ally toed her sneakers to the floor and kicked the fabric off the rest of the way.

Vulnerability crashed over her like the tide as she lay here, pussy bared to him. His gaze grew hot and hungry when he rested his big hands on her thighs. Her scar throbbed like it always did, and she tried to pull her legs together on reflex. Drew didn't budge, even though he cast a glance to the mottled skin, the disfigurement her thigh had become.

He met her stare, the desire there mind-melting. "You've never looked more beautiful."

Heat stung at her eyes, all the hateful words that rose in her mind banished. After the agony that had scored her today and the failure threatening to crush her, Ally just needed the reminder that something good existed out here. That she had a future to fight for too.

She and Drew had always been complicated—they would always be complicated. But she'd never wanted to chase after her dreams with anyone else but him.

He crawled down to sink between her thighs and her core clenched in anticipation. Drew lowered, brushing his lips against her thighs as he nipped and sucked at the skin. A breath escaped her. She was so drenched for him and had been the moment their lips met. The bristle along his jaw rubbed against her skin and the fevered kisses he pressed against her thighs had her spreading open on instinct. She tensed when his lips brushed across her scar, but he didn't hesitate, biting the knotted skin. He teased her to the point where she grew delirious, until her pussy pulsed with need. Ally slid her calf along his side.

"Something you want?" he teased, his eyes gleaming with amusement. "You know the currency, sweetheart."

Ally opened her mouth and shut it. The man was infuriating, obnoxious and, holy hell, he made her insane. With a smirk, he descended between her thighs. Once he slipped his tongue against her clit, Ally forgot everything. Drew lapped at her with a languid laziness, those slow strokes agonizing. They sent her careening toward oblivion. A moan slipped past her lips when he increased the pace.

"That's right," he murmured. "Show me how badly you need me."

He tightened his grip and descended again. The glimpse of him between her thighs was the hottest thing she'd ever seen, chin-length strands framing his gorgeous face. His eyes glowed the electric blue of his mountain lion. The breath escaped her at the scorching way he bit and sucked, and the tip of his tongue moved with exquisite precision. Everything she'd been holding back exploded outward, her moans growing louder and louder.

Ally bucked at the intense spike of pleasure rolling through her, and she thrust her hips toward his clever mouth. Drew gripped her so tight his nails dug into her skin, the delicious bite enhancing her pleasure. The way he devoured left her breathless as he wrung moan after moan from her. Each stroke brought her closer, closer, until everything vanished except the scent of vanilla, sweat and the feel of his mouth on her.

Drew increased his tempo, moving with a fury she was helpless to resist. The pressure built, built, built, until it twisted so tight she couldn't think, couldn't function and couldn't breathe.

Ally careened over the edge. White-hot pleasure flooded through her and the breath caught in her throat. Her core spasmed, the aftershocks radiating through her as she came. Every other thought bleached away in the wake of the mind-blowing bliss holding her captive. Drew relaxed his grip on her legs, and she lowered her hips to the couch again. His lips glistened from tasting her, and the wickedness simmering in his eyes promised they'd just begun.

Spirits above, she'd forgotten what being with a partner who knew every button to push, every switch to flip felt like. Drew understood her body and the way she ticked like her pack knew the forests of this region.

"On your knees, sweetheart," he commanded, a cocky grin on his lips.

Her core clenched tight at the desire hot in his tone. His erection strained the fabric of his sweats, and he slid off the couch to stand. Her mouth salivated at the sight of him, all sun-kissed skin and ridged muscles she wanted to sink her teeth into. He was the sort of gorgeous that made her heart ache. No matter how much they pissed each other off, or how they might argue and bicker, she'd forever fall for the concern shining in his eyes and the steadiness he offered every time she came apart at the seams.

Ally rose to her feet, a little unsteady in the wake of the orgasm he'd wrung from her. She stepped to him, slipping her fingers past the elastic of his sweats. She skimmed her fingertips across his silken length, enjoying how he closed his eyes at the touch. His breath hitched in his throat.

He wasn't the only one who knew every step of this dance.

"Time for a little payback, stud," she purred, bringing those pants down his powerful thighs, his defined calves. She sank to a crouch, and Drew kicked off his sweats. The sight of him standing above her, all cut muscle and lickable, smooth skin dosed her with lust that traveled right between her thighs. Spirits, she was soaked. As she switched to her knees, the hesitant tenderness in his eyes squeezed her chest tight. He looked at her like he wondered if he was allowed to have this sort of connection.

Like someone as fucked up as him could have a mate.

Ally licked her lips, unable to deny the emotion gripping her by the chest, because she'd always seen her own fears reflected in his eyes. Tonight, she wanted to prove to him the opposite. Maybe if she could convince him he deserved a future, she might begin to believe it too.

She ran her fingers along the length of his cock, near-salivating at how good he'd feel inside her. Ally lowered her mouth to his erection and slipped her tongue over the tip, tracing the lines to watch his thighs tense. She could tease too. He slipped his fingers through her strands and gripped her hair tight, the slight sting making her wetter.

Ally wrapped her lips around his cock and began to suck. A guttural groan escaped him, one she savored. She moved up and down along his length, running the tip of her tongue with the motion. The hardwood bit into her knees and her pussy pulsed to the point of pain. Spirits above, she wanted him to plunge straight inside her to the point she could think of little else.

She reached up to scrape her nails against his thighs, enjoying how he shuddered at the touch. Drew tilted his hips forward and thrust into her mouth, increasing the speed. The earthy musk of him shot straight to her core, the ache in her thighs demanding satiation. Ally worked his firm length, unable to dispel the memories of the way he rammed between her thighs.

He tightened his grip in her hair and his thighs stiffened. His cock spurted as he came in her mouth. She swallowed the salty liquid and slid her mouth off his length. Ally wiped the corners of her lips and rose from the ground. Drew slipped his hands around her waist, pulling her tight to him. Even though he'd just come, when she ground her ass against him, his cock began to respond.

"You're so damn sexy," he growled, slipping his hand beneath her tank top. Within seconds, her bra unsnapped, and he'd tossed her shirt to the ground with the other clothes. "Spirits, I want to fuck you so hard you're screaming my name."

"Like I'd add to your ego trip," she murmured, even as she slid her ass along the length of his cock. "Maybe I'll scream someone else's name."

"You wouldn't dare," he responded. He continued to bite and suck, his breath hot against her neck. Her core ached for him, so wet she was dripping. He slipped his hands around her breasts to grip them hard. As he swiped his thumbs across her nipples which formed into stiff peaks, a gasp flew from her. The desire pooling between her legs was whiskey warm, an inferno continuing to grow.

"Come on, babe," he said, sneaking a bite to her earlobe. "Admit it, no one else makes you feel like this."

Ally's lips pursed and she thrust her hips against him. He'd grown hard again, his steel length firm against her ass. "No one makes me as crazy as you do, Drew Williams."

"I'll take it," he responded. She could feel his grin against the skin of her back even though she couldn't see it. "Now, bend over."

Oh fuck, yes.

Ally leaned down, spreading her hands out on the couch in front of her. Drew settled his palms onto her hips. He brushed his cock against her drenched core and she almost shot forward at the sparks coursing through her. The need for him had grown violent, a yearning that pulsed through her whole body to the same steady thump as her heart. Drew slid the tip of his cock against her opening, but he stilled there. Ally groaned, almost stamping her foot.

"I don't know, all the sass has me wondering if you want this," he murmured, his tone low and wicked. Ally restrained a scream as she nudged her ass back again. Drew slipped his erection away. She panted for him like a cat in heat — how much more did he need? "Beg for me, babe."

She swallowed hard, unable to deny how the velvet command stroked right through her. Every time he pushed for her to surrender, even as she tried to keep parts of herself back, and he'd been the one man she'd trusted enough to.

Drew ran his fingers through her hair and gave a gentle tug. He teased her, brushing the tip of his cock against her drenched core.

"Spirits, I need you inside me," Ally gasped out, unable to resist anymore. "I want you slamming into me until my toes are numb, until I forget my own name." He nudged the head of his cock against her entrance, but she couldn't stop. "I want you to fuck me until I forget we were *ever* apart."

The words lay stark in the air, an admission she never meant to make out loud. However, before the embarrassment could crash down, he guided his cock into her, the smooth glide banishing away any other thought. Her core squeezed tight around him, and as he slid his full length in, her fingers curled into the sofa cushion. Drew began to rock inside her and Ally's throat tightened at the familiarity, at the relief coursing from her fingers to her toes.

Around him, she was home. No matter how much she'd tried to convince herself otherwise, the man had stamped an indelible mark on her heart, something hurt and time hadn't erased. She thrust her hips back, and Drew leaned over her, reaching forward to grip her breasts tight. She panted at the sensation, the tightness inside reaching a piercing crescendo.

Drew rammed into her, his strokes coming on fast and furious with a desperate need she felt deep inside. Ally's moans lit the air. The sting of their skin smacking together brought her closer and closer. He slid his palms all over her body, along the slope of her hips, around her waist. The motions scorched her skin like a brand, a possession in his hold she sorely missed.

He gripped tight to her hair and slammed into her, hard enough she could feel the reverberations through her legs, down to her toes. Every time he hit home, she blinked white, a gasp flying from her at the way her sensitized clit smacked against him. Drew moved like the churning waters of the falls, a powerful force she couldn't deny. Ally's heart thundered as she dug her nails into the cushions in front of her.

Sweat pricked on her forehead, drops sliding down her back. Their fevered breaths exploded through the air, a ragged cycle as he continued to slam into her. Drew was unrelenting with a stamina she'd missed. Hell, she had missed every damn thing about her mate. Even with the pain that dropped between them like nuclear bombs, and even though the fallout of their choices left them broken and battered, when she was with him, the hurt and sadness faded away.

Ally panted, the slap of skin to skin singing around the room. He filled her to the brim, and each time he hit home she came closer to the edge. Drew tightened his grip on her hair, the hard pull giving enough of a sting to ground her here in the present. Her core ached for him with a tension that grew by the second, tighter, tighter, tighter.

Drew rammed in hard enough that her clit throbbed in response and a gasp flew from her throat. Her pussy spasmed around him, the bliss radiating through her entire body. Ally was frozen in the moment as the orgasm crested over her. She was helpless in the waves of pleasure. A breath flew out while he continued to rock inside her. Ally almost collapsed forward.

A couple of thrusts later, and his cock pulsed. Heat flooded through her in spurts and Drew's nails left crescents on her hips. Ally's hold on the cushions in front of her threatened to slide, and her arms wobbled. Drew stilled behind her and he let go of her hair, the strands falling around her shoulders. He pulled out of her, but Ally didn't move, wishing they could stay like this for a few moments longer. Wishing they didn't have to return to a reality filled with problems she didn't know how to face.

Ally sagged onto the couch, and Drew crashed next to her. He slipped his arm around her shoulder, and she leaned in against him, drawing in his scent, vanilla, sweat and sex. Her heart hurt at how good this felt, at the sheer relief of curling into his arms instead of having to stay strong by her lonesome. Their ragged breaths were the only sounds in the air as their sweat-slicked skin pressed together. Several pieces of hair glued to her cheeks in the wake of the long overdue release.

Drew leaned in to brush his lips against her neck and her throat tightened. Spirits, why had she run away from this? However, the answer crashed in like always, the wrecking ball threatening her happiness at every turn.

Because now she couldn't run any longer. She would have to tell Drew about her infertility. This time, he would get to make the choice if he could still be with her, even if he'd never get the family he dreamed of.

The fear flooded her with ice and she shivered, even as he tugged her in closer. Because if Drew chose to walk away, she didn't know how she'd pull her broken pieces together again.

Chapter Fourteen

Yesterday had been whiplash.

The day had begun with the drag race away from Mackey's lair to stumble onto the ruin the Landsliders had caused. The pack cabins had been torched, and members of Silver Springs and Red Rocks lay dead on the floor of Beaver Tavern — people he'd grown up alongside. Yet, Drew's night had ended with the girl of his dreams in his arms and hope he hadn't expected or thought he deserved.

Today began with a burial. Nothing to douse the afterglow like a funeral.

Sierra and Dax had alerted the East Coast Tribe members yesterday, most of whom were already on their way when Lucas arrived in town. With how many times Mackey Kendricks had targeted the region, their packs had the big, bad, magic-wielding enforcers on speed dial. The Red Rock and Silver Springs packs had rallied last night and far too many of them had people to grieve.

The bathroom door clicked and steam rolled out as it opened. Ally strode out with a towel wrapped around her, her honeyed waves slick and pasted across her tan skin. Even now, he could smell the berry of her shampoo. The sight of her long legs and the sloping curves he'd traced with his palms last night had him wanting to mount her all over again. For once, both man and mountain lion were in agreement.

"Don't suppose you have any LBDs in my size tucked away?" she asked, sauntering up to him. Her gaze dripped sex, those blue eyes wicked in a way that got him hard.

Drew lifted an eyebrow. "LBD?"

Ally rolled her eyes. "Little black dress. I'm not showing up to the funeral buck-naked."

"I can think of plenty of other things I'd prefer to do with you buck-naked," Drew drawled. He fought to ignore the complicated mess of emotions at the sight of her in his house, like they'd transported back in time. Like they might stand a chance at a future. After everything he'd done and all the pain and suffering he'd been a part of with the Landsliders, he didn't deserve this. He didn't deserve hope, yet it twisted in his chest like a snowdrop begging to unfurl.

Ally snorted. "Down, boy. I'll have to head home to get changed then. We're honoring the fallen today and I've got responsibilities as pack beta."

"The responsibility looks good on you," he murmured, the words slipping out. Ally had always been fierce enough, but with all the time she'd spent rebelling against her mom, no one would've believed her capable of strapping on the seatbelt to become the second in command for the pack. For the right cause, Ally had become the most dedicated and loyal person he'd ever met — even if she wasted her time on hopeless cases like him.

Ally turned away, like he wouldn't catch the blush staining her cheeks. "It's just chasing after a bunch of overgrown toddlers. You wouldn't believe the petty shit most of the pack gets us involved in."

"You've always had way more patience for kids than adults, though," Drew commented, the memories warm in his chest. He'd seen Ally's gentleness around kids, how her twisted-metal edges softened.

Her lips pursed, and she twisted around to grab her clothes. "I've got to get on the road. Can't be late for this."

The temperature in the room plummeted, and Drew regretted the mention at once. Ever since the miscarriage, ever since their beautiful light had blinked out of the world, Ally had grown glacial at the mention of kids and families. Even now, the pain sank claws deep into his chest at what they'd lost. He couldn't imagine how she carried the weight every day.

Ally had already thrown her clothes on and run the towel through her hair a second time, leaving it curling into ringlets. She folded the towel and placed it on the couch beside him. Drew reached out to grab her hand before she darted off. He didn't want her leaving like this.

She looked into his eyes, a heartbreaking fragility flashing through hers. Drew swallowed hard, trying to tamp the futile rage bubbling within him. He would tear down the world to take that look away.

"I'll see you there," he said, his voice steady, even as his heart thumped harder. Of course, he'd let hope in too early. They couldn't just pick up where they'd left off, not after the broken glass splintering the path between them. They'd shred each other to pieces in the process. Yet, he couldn't help how his stomach twisted when she offered a hesitant grin, how he didn't just fall for her, he plummeted.

Ally brushed her lips against his. The soft give of her mouth was electric, and Drew wove his fingers through her hair, drawing her in to crush his lips to hers. He drank in her sweet taste, a brief respite from all the ugly thoughts threatening to drag him under.

She pulled away, but everything about her felt gentler, softer in the wake of their kiss. "I'll see you there."

Drew couldn't help but watch the swing of her hips when she walked to the door. Even after the click of it closing echoed through his place, his gaze remained glued. After everything that had shifted between them last night, she still held back. He'd been an idiot to think one spin in the sack might change their status quo or heal the rift that had grown Grand Canyon deep. Drew sucked in a sharp breath. He shouldn't be wasting his time on dreams that would never come true.

He'd been brought back for one task alone—Kill Mackey Kendricks.

* * * *

Twelve deaths to mourn today.

Drew rolled up to the site where a day ago his pack cabin had cast a long shadow. Now, all that remained was a husk, the charred planks reaching skyward, splintered and ruined, like the Landsliders had left everything. Individual families would bury their dead at the cemetery later, but there were too many to grieve. Dax and Sierra sent out the location of the Silver

Springs grounds, the clearing expansive enough to hold the packs as they honored everyone they'd lost yesterday. A couple of familiar cars were already parked in place, Jer's Jeep and Sierra's junker — most of the leaders had arrived.

He pulled into the gravel lot, but his legs refused to move. This place held too many memories he didn't want to face. This was the root of the greatest shames of his life. Of his dad bringing him to 'train'. He'd staggered out from here too many times clutching shattered limbs that seared like fire, swollen eyes that ached. No one had noticed, and if they did, they hadn't interfered — his dad was the alpha. Even Dax hadn't been aware.

As much as Drew had wanted to protect his brother, some small part of him had screamed out for someone, anyone to notice. For someone to stop his father.

No one had stopped that man.

Only Ally had been there to help him on the roughest nights. Only Lana and Ally had shouldered the secret. But they had all been kids back then, too scared to say anything against the formidable man who'd led their pack. Besides, half of the time he'd fought tooth and nail to earn the respect of the father he'd loathed. The real reason he'd entered the Landsliders wasn't just fear of failure. Part of him had hoped for the approval he'd been chasing after since he was a kid.

An unfamiliar Dodge Neon pulled beside him. Sam, the younger guy from the pack that had gotten torched, stepped out. The back door clicked open and shut and Eli hopped out, his dark hair in messy waves. The black pants he wore covered his shoes and the button-down shirt was three sizes too big.

Drew summoned his courage and stepped out of the car. At once, recognition gleamed in Eli's eyes and the kid raced over to him.

"How's it going, kiddo?" Drew asked, crouching to eye level.

Eli glanced to Sam and chewed on his lip. "He said a bunch of people are gone, like my mom and dad. That we're going to talk about them today."

Sam shrugged, a helpless look in his eyes. He kept glancing over to the campground, his hands in his pockets, obviously wanting to be anywhere but here.

Drew met Sam's eyes. "You can go on ahead." The 'I've got this' was understood. Sam nodded, flashing him a grateful grin before he bolted off toward the growing crowd at the clearing. Somehow, no one had claimed the kid yet, and Sam clearly wasn't eager to take on the burden. Drew switched his focus to Eli. "Want to come with me? We can go together."

Eli stared at the ground, kicking at one of the pieces of gravel. "I don't know anyone." He looked to Drew, the big, lost eyes twisting his insides to knots. Fuck, this poor kid. "I don't have anywhere. I don't fit in."

The kid's worry, one he felt deep inside, echoed in the lonely air. Drew ignored the heat rising to his eyes and the way his heart lurched at the simple words. He slipped his hand on Eli's shoulder and rose from his crouch. "Me too." He forced the words out, his throat thick.

Eli stared up at him. "But isn't this your home?" Spirits, the kid was pure innocence, those wide blinking eyes and the genuineness in his tone. He didn't understand how twisted and damaged Drew's terrain had become.

"It was, once," Drew murmured, trying to ignore the gravel in his voice. "But homes can change. We can make new ones."

If only he believed those words. However, as his hand dropped, a small one slipped into his. Eli looked at him with hope he wouldn't dare dash, with this pure light, like things might work out.

"We'll go together, okay?" Drew said, tightening his grip around the kid's. Eli's lips pressed tight, and his eyes grew glossy. Drew took the first steps toward the clearing. "We're here to honor your mom and dad too, don't forget."

A couple of tears slipped down Eli's cheeks and he nodded hard. Drew squeezed his hand when they approached the clearing his blood had splattered across a year ago. The guilt, the horror and the loathing should be gripping him fierce, but he focused on the little guy who trembled beside him. This kid was beyond amazing. He didn't deserve the hell the Landsliders had delivered. None of them did.

Dax and Sierra stood in the center of the clearing alongside Lucas and Lana. Jer and Raven lingered beside them, but once the rites began, the betas and significant others would be taking seats with everyone else. This ceremony would belong to the alphas of Red Rock and Silver Springs as well as to the Tribe. Already, members of the joined packs sat in the folding chairs they'd dragged out, and he caught sight of Sam sitting among them. Dax caught his gaze, which trailed to Eli by his side. His brother offered a nod, which Drew returned.

Lana's reminder clanged around in his head—at some point, he needed to dive into the past with his brother. Yet he didn't even know how to open the tome without unleashing all the ugliness that came along for the ride, the resentment, the jealousy and the fear — always, the fear.

"Come on, let's find ourselves a seat," Drew said, leading the way as he directed Eli toward the chairs. Every time he glanced back, the hope in the kid's eyes near broke him. He was the first person to look at him like he could achieve something in far too long, someone who hadn't been around for the thousands of times he'd fucked things up beyond repair. The way Eli looked at him made him want to try.

The slam of car doors echoed and a moment later, Sierra's jaw dropped. The Red Rock alpha almost broke into a run, which slowed when the heavy weight in front of her caught up. This far along into her pregnancy, the woman was encumbered, whether she wanted to admit it or not.

Navi sauntered forward, the tank top she wore revealing the Tribe tattoos along her arms, and her dark eyes soaked in her surroundings. The short woman emanated lethal. Out of the Tribe members, Akio and Navi were all fangs and growls while Jess and Lucas took care of the welcoming in and kumbayas. Still, he and Navi had shared a begrudging respect once his past with Kendricks had aired out in the open. The Tribe understood the weight of their abilities more than any other shifter. Out of everyone he'd encountered, they were the few who didn't fault him for what had happened.

Sierra's focus wasn't on the Tribe member, but on the muscular guy with a buzzcut and a broad grin who strode behind her. The former Red Rock beta hadn't been in town since he'd mated to Navi and hit the road with the Tribe. Finn Kelly loped up to Sierra and threw his arms around her, wrapping his former alpha in a fierce hug.

"Takes a funeral to see you, fucker," she muttered.

Finn offered a half-smile. "Or a kid. You know I'm not going to miss the birth of whatever nightmare spawn you and Williams created."

Dax snorted and Navi clapped a hand against his as they embraced. Drew watched the pack camaraderie from a distance. He'd been a part of that sort of kinship not so long ago, and he missed those connections with every beat of his heart.

A creak sounded, drawing his attention away from the scene. Lana had found the seat next to him. She'd been one of the first Silver Springs to offer forgiveness instead of baring her fangs, and for that, he'd always be grateful.

"Well now, who's your friend, Drew?" she asked. The brunette radiated the same gentleness she always did, like being around a sunbeam.

"I'm Eli," the kid said, sticking his hand out between them. Drew beamed at his manners—the little guy's parents had raised him right.

Lana's smile reached her green eyes, pure delight, and she reached to clasp his hand. "Pleased to meet you, Eli. My name's Lana." Her gaze flickered to Drew's. "Happen to know where Ally is?" He didn't miss the loaded question—Lana had always seen through their bullshit.

"On her way," he responded, fighting the tug at his lips threatening a smile.

As if on cue, another car door slammed, and within seconds, he caught the scent of her gardenia perfume. His entire body hummed at the arrival of his mate. His senses grew more aware when she was around, the slight breeze curling around the small hairs along his neck. The heat from the cool spring beams sank into the starch white of his button-down, and the earth beneath his feet grew that much more solid.

Ally strode into view and the breath caught in his throat. She walked with her chin lifted, her blue eyes focused and her hair streaming back in the beachy waves she'd perfected. The little black dress that came up to mid-calf enhanced the look, managing to be appropriate and devastatingly sexy all in one sweep. Her gaze snagged on his, and she bit her lip. The hint of softness she allowed while they were together reeled him in every time.

"Hey there, Eli." Ally walked over to them and took the seat beside the little guy. "I see you made it here safe?"

"Sam brought me," Eli said, straightening a little under her attention. He didn't blame the kid. He was smitten too.

"I'm glad you're here," she said, her voice gentling in a way he remembered. "You'll fit into the packs in no time."

Ally's approach with kids had always destined her for motherhood, strong and stern when she needed to be, but warm and coaxing most of the time. The sharp barbs she doled to adults vanished whenever she spoke to littles. If he ever needed a sign that life wasn't fair, the universe had delivered that when their chance at parenthood had been snatched from them in a single night.

Eli tilted his head to the side. "Even if I'm a wolf?"

Drew grinned and reached over to muss the kid's hair. "Didn't you see? The packs are combined, a mix of mountain lions and wolves. I bet there are some kids here who'd love to be your friend."

Ally's gaze snagged his overtop Eli's head, the longing there driving straight past his defenses and into his heart. On the rare nights he allowed himself to hope, that was the one he clung to. That someday he might be able to have the family he dreamed of with his mate.

The other Tribe members filtered into the clearing, Jess and Akio striding to greet Sierra and Dax. His brother shone up there, beaming with the calm confidence he'd always possessed, more like their mom than he'd ever been. Drew feared on his worst days his father's DNA would be a life sentence, one he knew he and Dax didn't share, even though they'd never talked about that revelation.

All around him, the lawn chairs filled in with members of their packs. Marcy and Rick arrived with their kids in tow and several families from the Red Rock pack found their seats. The little ones chattered and giggled, not understanding the somber occasion they'd arrived for. Drew kept looking around the crowd to spot Kyle's familiar face or Greg's wan smile, but the ghosts had tripled over the last year and loss struck hard blows.

Drew reached over Eli to tuck a couple of errant strands behind Ally's ear. The same heaviness weighted her eyes too. The Landsliders had threatened them time and time again. They had broken the packs until they shouldn't be able to stand up again. Yet here the fragments rallied, and as he stared across the clearing, despite the missing members, they stood unified, trying their damnedest.

Maybe if the packs could collect their shattered pieces and still fight, he could too.

"Members of the Red Rock pack," Sierra called out to the crowd.

"Members of the Silver Springs pack," Dax followed, his voice resonating through the air.

Lucas stepped beside them. "We gather here today to honor our fallen."

Chapter Fifteen

Ally's gut clenched like she'd been punched for the thousandth time today. Ever since she'd left the cozy embrace of Drew's house, reality had descended with jagged teeth.

The darkened lights of Beaver Tavern when she'd passed by. Because Kyle would never be standing behind the bar again, half-slouched and grinning at something stupid.

When she'd pulled up to the gravel lot, the hull of a cabin where their bastion, the Silver Springs' refuge, had once stood.

And Drew smiling and mussing the hair of the kid they'd saved from the first torched cabins they'd stumbled upon. The sights slammed into her like a high-speed train.

Ally sat beside the two of them, unable to help how her heart skipped a beat at the hope in Eli's big brown eyes, or the spasm in her chest when the ever-present reminder descended that she'd never get a kid of her own. Lana passed her a knowing glance. Ally pursed her lips and delivered a pointed look. Of course, her sunshine bestie would want to talk.

The Tribe had begun their ceremonial rites, the scent of incense heavy in the air. Navi and Lucas stood there alongside the Tribe members she didn't know as well, Akio and Jess. They ran through the steps of blessing the departed souls to the Great Spirits, since there had been too many deaths for individual services. Everyone brimmed in silence around them after the tragedy yesterday. That sort of violence left aftershocks, the tremors rocking through their community.

Sierra and Dax stood hand in hand, apart from the Tribe. Even though their faces were composed, solemn masks, Sierra's eyes radiated the anguish and rage brewing inside. Dax tapped his foot, a nervous tic he always busted out when he got upset. Ally had known him since they were kids and worked alongside him for too long to not catch the signs.

Sweat broke out on Ally's palms when the Tribe completed their ritual, the heaviness in the air signifying the shamanic magic present. All the ceremony was meant for comfort, because she could focus on the words, on the actions, and try to ignore the static roar in the back of her mind at everyone they'd lost. Hell, she still smelled the copper of the blood and still saw the splatters of crimson on the floorboards.

They would haunt her for a long time to come.

Dax and Sierra stepped in front of the members of the Tribe and began to speak about the departed. The buzz in Ally's mind reached a deafening roar. She swallowed hard, trying to drown out the words they spoke about Jared and his entire family who'd been slaughtered during their dinner at the tavern. Their little girl's life had been snuffed out before she could live it. Ally's hand pressed to her stomach on instinct, pain thundering in her bones.

Then Sierra spoke of Old Man Gene, one of the elders in Red Rock, and her tone rang out like a tolling bell, the crack of struck metal. Sobs filtered through the air, resounding through this clearing. The spring breezes coiled around their packs, carrying their grief out to the water and up to the sky.

Ally glanced over to Drew who watched, his face as composed as the alphas. Lana wept, tears rolling down her cheeks like streaks of silver. She'd always been able to express herself, something Ally sorely envied. Eli's lip trembled — he might not know the people they were talking about, but he'd lost his own parents to that monster.

"And we'll remember Kyle," Dax called out, "not just as the kid who used to follow me around all the time making wisecracks and goofy faces, but as the fighter who stood against the Coalition. The packmate who fought alongside us when we took down Joe Ganzorig, the Landsliders' right-hand shaman."

Ally's eyes burned. She should've spent more time with Kyle. She should've grabbed a pint with him last time he'd shot the text, not postponed it because her responsibilities as beta had chewed up too much of her time. Now she'd never get the chance.

She pressed her lips tight and looked at her hands, unable to listen anymore. She couldn't break down, not here. The pack expected her to remain strong, like Dax and Sierra. Ally was the Silver Springs beta, and she would make them proud. Their alphas continued to list the deceased, the calm register of their voices melding with the whimpers and sobs from the rest of the pack.

Ally gritted her teeth so hard they might break, trying to ignore the way sorrow prickled across her skin.

Ally cast a glance to Drew. Desperation flicker-flashed in his eyes, the same she'd seen when he'd talked about destroying Mackey no matter the cost.

They'd already lost so much. If she lost him too, there wouldn't be fragments to piece back together. She'd be obliterated.

* * * *

Ally pulled into Lana's driveway. With her best friend home for the time being, she couldn't make the adjustment to consider the place hers. Lana's car sat parked in the driveway, though Lucas' Explorer wasn't. He'd lingered with the other members of the Tribe who had more business to discuss. Dax had requested she attend a meeting at Sierra's place later, but for the time being, she'd seize the seconds away from the grief and the nightmare of a task mounting before them.

She sucked in a deep breath and cracked her car door open. If her best friend happened to be home, emotions-talks were probably in order. Even if Ally drove roundabouts around her feelings, Lana had a way of directing her straight down the path no matter how often she tried to find a detour. Ally wove her way to the front door, her chest scooped hollow after the send-off this morning.

It creaked open before she touched the handle.

Lana waited inside, the stiff black dress from before ditched in favor of sweats and a hoodie. Ally fired a lazy salute and kicked her heels off, watching them slide across the hardwood.

Forged Redemption

"Did you drive two miles an hour?" Lana teased, a low amusement in her voice.

"Stopped in the street to stare at some birds," Ally said, tugging her dress up and over her head. "All that time around the Red Rock wolves and I'm picking up their bad behavior." She stalked to the laundry basket she'd left by the couch and pulled on a clean pair of plaid pajama pants and gray tank top. No way would she maintain any level of civilized until she had to step up later.

"Did you want some coffee?" Lana asked, walking to the kitchen.

"Tea for me," Ally said, running a hand through her waves as she strode in after her. Her feet on the floor barely grounded her, not like Drew's presence did. Deep down, they both understood why, no matter how much they fought the bond. She let out a long breath. Her entire body felt bruised, the exhaustion increasing at a slow and steady pulse.

Already, Lana bustled around the kitchen, her coffeemaker gurgling and the electric kettle clicked on. Ally wandered over to the hickory cupboard, cracking it open to snag a bag of Earl Grey. Out of all the teas Lana cycled through, she always kept that one stocked. Lana's stare burrowed into her.

"Is this your version of subtle? Stare any harder and you'll be shooting laser beams out of those things," Ally cracked, tugging down two mugs from the cabinets.

Lana crossed her arms over her chest, not bothering with the glimpses anymore. "You and Drew."

"Are mortal enemies," Ally responded, refusing to look at her bestie. "Every time he opens his mouth I'm tempted to grab the hair-cutting shears from my station and let loose with the pointy end."

The electric kettle boiled, and Ally snagged it to pour the piping hot water into her cup. Lana nabbed the mug and began fixing herself a cup of coffee, drowning it in sugar.

Lana gave her the side-eye, eyebrow tilted in disbelief. "You can keep spouting that if you want, but you're not fooling anyone. I'm just surprised I didn't figure it out sooner. Like ages ago."

Ally paused to face her, the scorch of the hot tea against her palms something she needed right now. "Figure out what?"

Lana leaned against her countertop, the look in her eyes one Ally had dubbed 'the therapist stare' years ago. "I didn't have a frame of reference then to understand why you and Drew kept getting back together every damn time. At least, until I found my own mate."

Ally froze. She and Drew had kept the bond secret for so long, and no one believed for a second they were mated with the way they bickered. Mates were supposed to look like Lucas and Lana, all gooey and in love, not the lit match to an oil slick she and Drew had always been. Their fire had never been anything as tame as a hearth in a home. They'd been the blaze of a wildfire, colliding with strength enough to take a whole forest down.

"Why didn't you tell me?" Lana asked, tapping the side of her mug. "That's big stuff, Ally-cat."

Ally sagged against the counter, wanting to fall over. She loved her best friend, but she wanted to strangle her right now. Her heart ached, her body ached, her soul ached, and she wanted to power off for the next couple of hours until she strapped on her responsibilities like armor. However, Lana looked at her like a golden lab with her teeth on a toy. She wouldn't give up easily.

"We were young when we figured it out," Ally said, "so young we dove into the mating bond headfirst without thinking about what that actually meant. And you know how we were, hell, how we are. One moment we were all aces, running at ninety miles an hour over nothing but endless roads and sunsets. The next we'd either freeze each other out or get in another stupid fight."

Lana nodded, her pointer finger tap, tap, tapping on the side of her mug. "You know at any time you can call quits to my inquisition," she reassured. "Yesterday was a nightmare and today wasn't a Sunday picnic either."

Ally's heart squeezed tight. Every time she wanted to get pissed at Lana for taking a crowbar and prying open the rusted basement doors she'd stuffed her emotions into, she couldn't. Because truth be told, she'd been dying to speak for far too long. Yet every time she tried to open her mouth, all she could see was the kid she used to be at the dinner table growing up. When she'd start babbling about her day—about what Susie had said in school, the butterfly she'd drawn and how she'd outrun Dax.

Every time, her mom would let out the sigh, disappointment no amount of soap could scrub off. Then would come the comments—that mindless words were better off left in her head, that nobody liked obnoxious kids like her and the timeworn favorite, her eternal trump card—no wonder Dad had left.

Ally clutched her mug tighter. Lana was the exact opposite. She always encouraged her random babble and fought for the deeper stuff too.

"No, let's do this," she murmured. "I should've told you, Lan."

Lana shrugged, offering a small smile. "I know it's hard." Understanding slammed into her, the sort she'd spent all her younger years searching for. "But, fill in the blanks for me then," Lana continued, taking a sip from her steaming coffee. "The mating bond explains why you guys kept crashing together, but why did you break up with him for good? He's returned, and you're both smitten, so why are you holding back?"

The excuses leapt to Ally's lips, that they weren't good for each other, that his time in the Landsliders had screwed up their chances for good, that all they did was fight. But in the wake of the losses that had rocked their packs, those lies felt pathetic.

Ally stared hard at the tea bag floating in her mug. She couldn't look at Lana or she'd break.

"Lan, you saw him today with Eli. Drew would be such a good father." Her voice cracked and she stopped. She couldn't go there.

A clink sounded on the counter. Lana placed her mug down and closed the space between them. Ally sank against her best friend, the one who'd waited at the doctor's office the day she got the news. The miscarriage had fucked her up for good, and not just mentally. Because of some complications, she couldn't have kids, period.

Lana's arms crushed around her. "You're not broken," her best friend murmured. Every damn time, the woman saw right through her defenses.

A breath escaped her throat, one she hadn't realized she'd been holding. Her eyes stung and the first tears trailed down her cheeks. The dam she'd been holding back by her lonesome for far too long broke open. Her heart cracked in two, the pain worse than the scorch of silver when her fingers curled around Lana, holding on to her tighter than intended.

Broken. The word had cycled through her mind on repeat since the day at the doctor's. It was the only one to fit the void in her chest and the hollow thump in her womb where she'd once felt warmth, and light and joy. Nausea swirled through her again, the sweep of sickness that always descended when she confronted a future without the hope of a family, something she'd wanted since she was a kid.

Every time her mother had tried to douse her flickering candle of some beautiful future, Ally had clung to her dreams. Early on, she'd fallen headfirst for Drew, and when they'd discovered they were mates, it was a done deal. She'd known, *known*, she hurtled for that destiny a hundred miles a minute, for the family she could form of her own. One that wasn't the acid bitterness she'd grown up with. One that reflected the Silver Springs pack she loved.

Except her mother hadn't doused the candle—the light had shut out the moment those words descended. She couldn't tie Drew to her sentence.

Ally wasn't sure how long they stood there, minutes, an hour—the time didn't matter. She sank into her best friend's embrace in a way she never allowed herself to. She heaved a shaky breath as the tears slowed.

"Does he know?" Lana murmured.

She swallowed hard and pulled away. Ally allowed herself a second to scrub her cheeks, as if she could erase the evidence that she'd ever shed a tear. Even though she felt like she'd set down a hiking pack she'd carried for far too long, the rawness of what had erupted from her prickled across her skin. Admitting those things out loud came at a price.

"I can't," she said, hating the pleading in her voice. "Because you know Drew. He'd sacrifice everything for me, even if it cost him the thing he's dreamed of all this time."

Lana shook her head, her green eyes watery. "Shouldn't that be his choice?"

The words would barely come out, so she forced them at a whisper. "What if he resents me?"

Drew always looked at her like he stared at a sky full of stars. Ally couldn't bear the idea of his look souring with time, of one day waking up and him seeing her the same way she saw herself.

Lana offered a shrug, and a tear snuck down her cheek. "I'm not going to lie to you, Ally-cat. Maybe he will. But maybe you two will be able to move forward at last, to heal. A wise woman once told me you're so much bigger than that. You're allowed to heal."

Ally couldn't help the ghost of a smile at hearing her own words repeated at her. She bumped her best friend in the side, who gave her a watery grin in return. Seeing Lana's own tears somehow settled the rapids inside her. The miasma of grief, anger and loathing churning inside her slowed.

"Sounds like the lady was full of horseshit," she said back, her voice surprisingly steady.

Lana gave her the side-eye and tipped back her mug of coffee. "If I hadn't listened, I might still be sitting in this lonely house wasting away with grief. Taking the leap is terrifying. Trust me, I know."

Ally sucked in a breath and stared at the ceiling, wishing it would give her answers. The white surface glared at her.

"I'll do it. I'll tell him."

Chapter Sixteen

"We've got a problem."

Drew leaned up from his slouch against the bar to look at Lucas. The massive Tribe member stood beside him with his arms crossed and a grim expression on his face.

"Tell me something new," Drew responded. "Isn't that our state of always?"

The overwhelming scent of bleach torched his senses. Yesterday, they'd scrubbed this place top to bottom to get out the bloodstains. Yet even after they'd spit-polished Beaver Tavern, when he searched around the empty room, all he saw were the bodies that had piled up.

"Bigger than this region," Lucas said, creaking into the seat beside Drew with two pints he'd pulled from the taps. When Lucas called him in early, Drew had leapt on the chance — the longer he roamed around his house, the more the pressure of the past couple of days threatened to crush him.

"Well, fuck." Drew heaved out a sigh and lifted the pint to his lips. The foamy porter slid down his throat, not making enough of a dent to smooth out the chaos in his mind. Mackey Kendricks had done a lifetime's worth of damage to this region in this past several years, and he wasn't finished.

"He's not aiming to destabilize this area," Lucas said, his dark eyes burning with a weariness Drew felt. "Or at least, that was just the beginning of the plan. I hoped maybe once he got his revenge on us, he'd back the hell down."

"You know, unicorns exist and Bigfoot's waiting for you to find him in the forest too," Drew drawled, acid on his tongue. The bastard wouldn't give up. He'd seen the crazed light in the ex-Tribe member's eyes and felt the sheer power of the commands slam into him. Mackey was addicted to the control, a junkie returning for another fix.

Lucas lifted an eyebrow, delivering him an arch look. "Obviously. Don't go stomping all over my dreams." He took a sip from his porter, letting out a sigh of his own before he continued. "We started getting calls in from other Tribes. The South Atlantic, the Midwest ones. The Landsliders aren't just spreading, they're infecting the shifter populace. This is why we were trying to keep his presence and defection quiet."

"Our kind already possessed a healthy fear of the Tribe," Drew murmured, the realization crystallizing. "But one of you going rogue—well, I'm proof positive of the wrecked state that'll leave you in." He paused to look at Lucas. "Though some folks prove the Tribe are still worth trusting."

Lucas offered him a grateful grin, his eyes crinkling at the edges. Drew knew how much the guy struggled with the burden of his abilities. As much as Mackey Kendricks had locked and loaded the Landslider vendetta against his parents and the region who ruined him as a kid at first, he'd been privy to dozens of rants about the Tribe. Kendricks blamed the whole institution, so go figure he wanted to bring it toppling down.

The door creaked open, and Navi poked her head in first, followed by Finn then Jess. Drew lifted his hand in a wave and Lucas offered a nod.

"So, the trouble's finally poisoned the well," Navi announced, her voice echoing through the empty tavern. Her hands remained on her hips as she swaggered on in. "If we don't put a stop to Mackey and fast, we're looking at a spreading revolution."

"We got word of the riots in Virginia," Finn added. He strode past them, heading behind the bar with the familiarity of someone who'd grown up here.

"Well, golly gee," Drew continued, lifting his pint. "This day keeps getting better and better."

The door creaked, and in stepped Sierra, Dax and Jer. The door hadn't shut before it swung open again and Akio walked in after, followed by Ally.

"Did you all arrive in a clown car?" Finn called from behind the bar, tugging out the bottle of Jack Daniel's and pulling off the cap.

"Get your ass out from back there, Kelly," Sierra called from the opposite end of the room, her droll tone one she rarely indulged in. "We're already hemorrhaging cash from the break-in. Last thing we need is for you to be demolishing our top-shelf stuff."

Finn lifted the bottle of JD. "If this is top shelf, you've got bigger problems than that."

Drew could feel Ally's presence as she strode closer, a livewire connection he'd never been able to dismiss. He expected her to walk on by and head for Dax, or one of the Tribe, but instead she strolled right next to him. Their eyes met, and he couldn't help the shiver down his spine at the memory of the hot way they'd collided last night. For the brief moments when she'd stepped past her wall of snappy barbs, hope had brushed across him like liquid sunshine.

Ally reached past and grabbed his pint, lifting it to her lips. She tipped it back, chugging down the charcoal liquid.

When she set the half-emptied glass onto the counter, a grin quirked her strawberry lips. "Thanks for that."

Drew shook his head, warmth spreading in his chest. When they'd been together, Ally had never ordered beer, claiming she only wanted a sip—which fast turned into half his pint. Drew had started ordering two on reflex, knowing she'd drink more than planned. She'd stolen his drink on purpose. They hadn't been able to talk this morning at the ceremony, and he'd been wondering what would come of last night. If the collision would change anything between them at all.

But the gesture from their old relationship, how she'd come to him first—he could read between the lines.

"That's fine. I only wanted half a porter anyway." He shot her an arch look, causing her grin to deepen. Lucas glanced between the two of them, a curious look in his eyes. No doubt, his Tribe friend would be scurrying off to tell Lana the moment he got the chance.

"So, what can we do to stop this from spreading?" Dax asked the group, his question causing the casual chatter to fall quiet.

Jess sank onto one of the bar stools, her elbows hitting the chestnut bar as she stared at the glossy surface. "I'd normally say we should head to the other shifter packs in the region and rally them to fight."

"Except with the way news has been spreading, who knows how many would turn and run at our arrival," Akio spat, slamming a fist to the table.

"If only that useful trick worked on the Landsliders," Drew responded, tapping the side of his glass.

"What if I go?" Sierra asked, pacing back and forth. "We've got connections with the other packs in the regions, and we might stand a chance of convincing them."

Dax rested his hand on her shoulder. "Over my dead body, babe. You're staying and keeping the packs together. They need at least one of their leaders here, because I'll be heading out."

Sierra's scowl threatened to turn into a full-fledged argument when Finn strolled over with his bottle of JD sloshing around in his hand.

"Come on, Kanoska. Don't tell me I show and you're already ditching. You've got to catch me up on everything that's happened since I've been gone." The former Red Rock beta glanced to Dax who passed him a grateful look.

"You might as well ax off the next few weeks if you want to be filled in, brother," Jer said, cuffing Finn in the shoulder. A grin rose to both of their faces, the familiarity there driving daggers into Drew's chest. He had that once, with Dax, with Greg, with Ally and Lana. Spirits above, he missed the camaraderie of those childhood friends every damn day.

"You shouldn't go alone, though," Ally started to argue, whipping toward Dax.

"Which is why I'll be going," Drew interjected. If he had to sit behind waiting with the packs he'd once helped splinter, he'd go insane.

"Bullshit." Ally's glance sparked with irritation. "You've earned too much notoriety through the region. It's like bringing an assault rifle to a peace talk."

"Actually, Drew's right," Lucas stepped in. Gratitude flushed through him in a fierce sweep. The man hadn't just become one of his closest friends but someone who fought for him at every turn. "He might have gained a bad rep in the Red Rock and Silver Springs packs, but he's been working with us for close to a year now, visiting the other packs and helping break up issues. Besides, if anyone can convince folks how much of a danger Mackey Kendricks is, he can."

His stomach twisted at this praise he didn't deserve. He tightened his grip around his pint glass, and he stared at the glossy wood grain of the bar, more than aware of the stares descending on him.

When he looked up, Ally's gaze softened. "Maybe you two should go."

Drew's forehead creased. He'd expected far more fight from his firebrand.

"Wait, you're agreeing with Drew?" Dax called from the other side of the room. "Are you having a stroke? Do you need medical attention?"

Ally rolled her eyes, ignoring him as she crossed her arms. "While I still think I'd be a better asset in a fight," she emphasized, eliciting a grin from Drew. "Many of these packs fought against the two of you in the trials for Silver Springs alpha. Seeing the Williams brothers united on this front might be what it takes to convince them."

"Glad that's figured, because we've got to divide and conquer here. Every second is important," Navi said, leaning back in her chair. "Ava will be arriving in an hour or so, and we're going to need to brainstorm with her to figure out some sort of resistance against the device. Either the humans and Coalition who banded with the Landsliders set off the device, or Mackey and the other shifters have figured out a way to combat the effects."

"We should outreach to the humans anyway," Lucas interjected, spreading his palms flat against the surface of the bar. "We don't have any compulsion over them, so they won't have the same fear of us."

"We've got connections with the cops we should tap into," Jess agreed.

Ally nudged her hip against his, the touch drawing his attention. Their situation had been changing ever since they'd headed out on assignment together, and last night had brought the tissue-paper walls they'd erected tumbling down. The touches between them were open and the affection not hidden even as they swapped caustic jabs, their form of foreplay. She offered a half-smile before she headed over to talk to Dax.

Drew lifted his pint and chugged the rest of the contents, drowning out the chatter of the others who had devolved into separate conversations. The Tribe members exchanged connections and plotted their next move while Jer and Finn had begun to talk pack issues with Sierra. Ally and Dax spoke in low murmurs in the corner. His brother's eyebrows drew tight together when he cast another glance over to Sierra.

Drew's heart squeezed tight. If they managed to take down Mackey Kendricks and the Landsliders, drinking by his lonesome was the future he hurtled toward. While he had worked alongside the Tribe, he wasn't one of them. He didn't belong amongst the Red Rock pack either, and he'd lost his place in the Silver Springs.

If he managed to survive killing Mackey Kendricks, and that was a *big* if, Drew was a kite without a string and the strong breezes would carry him away from this place. The thought devastated him. As much as pain splattered across every surface of these lands, connections existed here forged through sorrow, bravery forged through pain and hope forged through a community who refused to back down, no matter what life threw at them.

He wanted to be a part of it.

However, he'd fucked his chance up the day he followed his father into the Landsliders.

Dax sauntered over to Sierra, interrupting her conversation to press a kiss to her lips. She wrapped a hand around the nape of his neck, crushing her mouth to his. He knew a kiss goodbye when he saw one. Ally headed in his direction, and when she tilted her head toward the entrance, Drew pushed his pint aside to follow.

Once he exited through the front door, the reek of bleach dissipated, softening to the sweet spring breezes that swept through. The gentle citrine hues of the afternoon sun gleamed on his skin and the crispness in the air tasted like hope, even in the wake of their mounting problems.

He hadn't taken two steps out when Ally grabbed him by the front of his shirt and closed the space between them. Her mouth crushed to his with a desperation he could feel pulsing through his veins. Drew drank in the taste of her, a hint of porter and a sweetness he'd craved from the day they first kissed. Drew slipped his fingers through her sunlit waves, gripping the strands tight when he claimed her mouth.

He slid his other hand to her waist and took one step forward, then another until she bumped against the wall. She rested her arms on his shoulders, tightening her grip like he might disappear. Even as he sank into the raging heat and fury of their kiss, relief coursed through him so strong he almost sagged against her.

Spirits above, he'd missed her so much. He missed the casual touches, the glances across the room and the silent communication that always existed between them. He missed someone giving a damn if he came back or not.

Her lips were soft and yielding to his, her mouth scorching and the scent of gardenia lingered in her hair. Her golden skin looked bitable in the tank top and jeans she wore, ones he wanted to peel off her with his teeth. His mountain lion rammed against him with base demands he was half-tempted to give in to. She let out a sharp inhalation before she lunged back in for more.

Ally had always been everything he dreamed of, from the fierce way she fought to hide her vulnerability to the way she bled loyalty, the sort of fighter who wouldn't fall back even in the face of unsurmountable odds.

The door creaked beside them and, a moment later, a cough sounded.

Reluctantly, Drew separated from Ally, letting her golden strands loose from his grip. Her shoulders heaved up and down, her berry lips glistening, and he couldn't tear his gaze away from the warmth shining in those ocean eyes.

Dax stood feet away from them with his arms crossed and slight disbelief creasing his features. Drew sucked in a deep breath, ready to drop some excuse.

"Way to be a cockblock, D," Ally said, casting Dax a glance. "You don't see me peeping in on your and Sierra's long-ass makeout sessions." She paused, looking Drew's way. Her eyes flashed with the bronze of her mountain lion. "Drew and I are back together."

Drew shook his head, unable to help the grin rising to his lips. Of course, his brimstone girl would drop the news to both her alpha and him like that.

Dax tugged at the brim of his baseball cap. "I'd say I was surprised, but most of the pack had a betting pool going the moment Drew reappeared."

Ally shot Dax a glare, followed by a punch to the arm. "We were broken up for real."

Dax lifted his finger in air quotes. "For real," he said, the sarcasm heavy.

"Don't blame Ally," Drew joined in. "I can't help the fact I'm irresistible."

Ally's glare in return was pure acid. She lifted her middle fingers at them. "Both of you can fuck off, kindly. Sierra and I will be hard at work with Ava while you're gone. Go get us some allies. Keep your sparkling personalities at home."

Drew slipped to her and snuck a quick kiss. He leaned in to whisper, "Stay safe, Car Crash."

Her irritation faded as fast as it descended, and the side of her mouth quirked. "You too, Train Wreck."

Ally stepped back first, offering a salute to the two of them before she headed inside Beaver Tavern. The door echoed with a click.

Drew faced his little brother, someone he'd once been closer to than anyone else. Time, the Landsliders and

Williams Sr. had ruined the bond for good. Dax might've grown taller, broader and more muscled, but he still possessed the gentle brown eyes of their mother, and even though he'd become hardened and mature as the Silver Springs alpha, Drew would only ever see the little brother who chased after him, trying to be part of the fun. Now, the gaze held a caution bred from everything that had broken between them.

They'd beat each other bloody in the fight for alpha of Silver Springs, a position he'd never wanted, but no amount of physical pain wounded him like the grief in his brother's eyes. He had hated hurting him.

"Let's get on the road," Dax said, slipping his hands into his pockets. This awkwardness had never existed between them in the past, but no matter how hard he hoped, some wounds couldn't be healed.

"I'll drive," Drew said, dangling his keys as he took the first strides toward his Caddy. He tried to ignore the prickle of loathing along the nape of his neck, the familiar hatred mirrored in the eyes of most of his former pack. If the Williams brothers working together again didn't convince the surrounding packs of what a major threat this was, he didn't know what would.

Chapter Seventeen

The next morning, Ally waited in her car outside Beaver Tavern for Sierra to show and unlock the joint. She'd already swung by the salon to take on a few early clients, but her work was flexible with her schedule in times of crisis. Ally buzzed with nerves and kept slipping glances to her phone. She flipped to the text Drew had sent her last night. He and Dax had stopped by to talk to a couple of the local packs already and had gotten a few nos and a few noncommittals. Then he'd snuck into the bathroom of the motel and snapped a filthy pic she couldn't stop staring at.

Spirits, that body was criminal. His shoulders were broad and arms muscular, the ones that had lifted her around in the past like she'd weighed nothing. And his six-pack was cut perfection, all the tan skin making her want to lick him from head to toe.

Ally had snapped a pic of her own, stripped to her black lacy bra and panties.

His response had been *Dirty girl*, which caused her to bite her lip and moan. She'd needed to retreat to the shower for a while after to masturbate. In this bubble, their relationship turned into all sex all the time — she'd been there before. But sooner rather than later, Ally would have to tell Drew the reason why she'd broken up with him, even if the mere thought made her palms sweat.

The crunch of car tires over gravel snagged her attention. She slipped her phone into her pocket, preparing to hop out and greet Sierra. A car she didn't recognize rolled into the parking lot, screeching to a halt in front of Beaver Tavern's entrance.

Ally rested a hand on the latch, ready to take action if needed. After Mackey and his crew had done their drive-by massacre, she wouldn't get taken unawares. The driver's side swung open, and the younger guy from the fragmented pack they'd taken in stepped out — Sam. He opened the back door of the car and Eli hopped out with a pensive frown. Together, they strolled to the front of Beaver Tavern. Sam sank to Eli's level, placing a hand on his shoulders. They seemed to be discussing something serious, but then Sam stood again, clapped the kid on the shoulder and headed for his car. Sam's eyes flashed with a familiar look, one she knew far too well.

Self-loathing.

Ally watched as Sam drove away, leaving Eli standing by himself in front of the tavern.

Eli sat down, placing his backpack beside him, and drew his knees to his chest.

A steady thrum rose in Ally's mind, one that grew when the pieces began to click together. Maybe Sam had been running an errand and couldn't bring Eli along. Maybe another member of their former pack was coming to pick him up. Except Ally couldn't shake the bottoming out inside. She stepped out of her car and approached the kid.

"Hey there, Eli," Ally called out, waving to get his attention.

He looked up, those big brown eyes wary, but he didn't say a word.

Ally sank to crouch beside him. "Where did your friend Sam go?"

Eli shrugged, his little legs like matchsticks he clutched tighter to him. "He said he needed to head back to our town to get something."

Ally swallowed hard. Even as Eli said the words, she could see in his dull expression he didn't believe them either. Anger welled deep inside her, the pulse growing to a steady throb. After everything this kid had been through, how could one of his packmates abandon him? The self-loathing in Sam's eyes doled out the sentence—he wasn't coming back.

Sierra's junker pulled into the gravel lot, and within seconds the alpha heaved herself out of the car, her stomach round and swollen. Ava slunk around from the passenger's side, the short Indian woman in her normal attire, thick glasses, and one of her T-shirts, this one with the Ctrl button and 'freak' beneath it.

Ally reached out to offer a hand to Eli. "Want to come help us? We're going to be meeting with a shaman today." He looked at her, the hesitation clear in his eyes. Not like she blamed him. Ally leaned in closer and offered a conspiratorial grin. "I can get you some apple juice."

That sealed the deal. Eli slipped his hand in hers and together they rose from the ground. Her gut clenched at the slight tremble in his hand. He might not be in tears and he might be fighting hard to hold back his fear, but Eli was scared.

Sierra's brow furrowed when she approached and glanced over the two of them.

"We'll talk about it later," Ally mouthed, and Sierra had the sense to remain silent. The Red Rock alpha stepped past them to unlock the door to Beaver Tavern.

"What's with the kid?" Ava asked, not having any same sense.

"He's graciously agreed to be our helper today," Ally said, glancing to him. She gave his hand a light squeeze. "We've got important work to do, so we could use all the help we can get."

"Hope you like reading, kid," Ava said with a shrug. She strode past them and entered Beaver Tavern.

With the lights on, Ally couldn't help the shiver coursing through her. Every time she entered this place, she half-expected to see Kyle's smiling face behind the bar. Every time she didn't, all she could remember were the twisted bodies that had been strewn across the floor. Ally focused on following Sierra to the table they'd be setting up shop at. As Sierra headed for the back to grab drinks, Ally caught her gaze.

"I promised this guy apple juice if you have it," Ally called out to her. If they didn't, she might just drive out to the grocery store to pick some up. Eli's hand hadn't stopped shaking like a leaf in a windstorm, and she'd take any help she could get right now.

Sierra nodded. "Want to help me grab a cup?"

Ally chewed on her lip before she let go of Eli's hand. The loss of connection speared through her. She needed to help him, somehow. "Be right back," she said, knowing the phrase didn't matter, since he'd already gotten the same lip service from another adult in his pack.

Ally followed Sierra to the back of the house where the alpha rummaged through the chrome double door fridge. By the time Ally reached her, Sierra passed over a plastic container of apple juice.

"What's going on?" she asked, casting the glance to the front.

"He was part of the pack Drew and I sent this way. His parents died in the bombing, and when I pulled up today, the guy who had been watching out for him, Sam, dropped him off and drove away."

Sierra slammed the bottle of beer she'd been holding onto the counter so hard Ally thought the glass might break. "Piece of scum. Who abandons a kid like that?"

"I'll take him in for now," Ally said, the words coming out before she could even process them. For all they knew, he didn't have any immediate family coming to claim him and searching for blood relatives would take time. In the meanwhile, she couldn't leave this kid out in the elements.

"You sure you want to take on that responsibility right now?" Sierra asked, handing over the bottle of beer to Ally as she pulled out a cranberry juice for herself. "There are families in the pack who could watch after him while we figure out his situation. We'll need you on the front line when we bring the fight to Mackey."

The Red Rock alpha wasn't wrong. She lived in her best friend's house, had just gotten back together with her ex-boyfriend and they were gearing up for a fight their packs might not survive. She looked at the cup of apple juice in her hand and thought of those wide chocolate eyes looking up at her. Her chest tugged tight, the feeling that beset her every time she saw other people's kids and yearned for her own.

She and Drew were the only people he even recognized here. Eli had been abandoned yet again. She couldn't drop him off with more strangers now, even if the extra responsibility got tough. Ally's grip tightened around the cup of apple juice. "You'll still have me for the fight, boss. No need to bother the other families in the pack. I've got this."

Sierra nodded, rubbing a hand over her stomach, the way she did often these days. "You're a good one, Coleman. I'm glad Dax has you as his second in command."

The alpha's eyes softened when she glanced at her stomach—the baby would be arriving in a month. Ally's chest twisted at the sight, the familiar ache pulsing through her. Yet the warmth in Sierra's eyes when she looked up coursed right through her, banishing away those shitty feelings.

"You're just glad he's got someone else to argue with," Ally teased, trying to shove away the yearning.

"Definitely that," Sierra agreed, flashing a fierce grin. She lifted her drinks and took the lead out to the front of house. "I'm not shouldering the burden myself."

Ally shook her head, a smile lifting her lips as she followed Sierra out. Time to dive into the books to get to the bottom of this device.

* * * *

After they'd spent most of the day at Beaver Tavern sorting through old books and dealing with the updates Jer and the Tribe members brought them, Ally was beyond exhausted. It hadn't helped that she'd agreed to be Ava's guinea pig. The shaman had the idea a tolerance might be built up against the effects of the device, and Ally had volunteered. She'd seen the glint in Sierra's eye and how her mouth had opened to offer herself. No fucking way, not while she was carrying a little one.

Sierra had already left, needing to show Ava over to her house where she would be crashing since the pack cabins were currently a charred wreck. They'd be calling in the shamans across the region, trying to summon any help they could get for the fist-to-a-brick-wall fight they were preparing to bring to Mackey.

Eli had hung in there the entire time, even though now his eyes drooped with exhaustion. He'd been flipping through books but had glazed over, not understanding the advanced language inside them, and had remained a lot quieter than the last time she'd seen him. Throughout the day, she'd stepped outside with him for walks so they could stretch their legs and kick around some gravel, but even then, he brimmed with a silence that spread outward.

Except now that everyone had left, she needed to confront the elephant in the room — where he was going next.

Ally plunked in the seat across from him, holding the key to lock up Beaver Tavern. "Hey, kiddo," she said, trying to keep her voice low, soothing. He looked to her. "Do you want to come home with me tonight?"

He swallowed hard when he stared at her, his eyes so, so lost. Eli shook his head 'no.'

"I've got to stay here," he insisted, gripping tight to the seat of the chair.

Ally's forehead creased. *Fuck.* How the hell could she tell this kid Sam wasn't coming back? If she ever saw the man again, she'd show him the full strength of her fangs and claws.

"Hmm," she said, doing a slow scan around the room. "I think the ground would be pretty uncomfortable to sleep on, though, right? Why don't you come stay with me for the time being?"

His lip quivered, and his eyes glossed over with tears. He shook his head again. "I don't want to. I want to go home." A shaky breath came from his lips, and tears coursed down his cheeks. "I want my mom and dad."

Ally's heart split in two for him, sitting there with his hands balled into fists, trying with all his might to hold back the tears even as sniffles escaped. She reached forward to place her hand over one of his small fists. At the touch, his breath hitched and he looked up at her. Eli scrubbed at his cheeks with his free hand, even now trying to stay strong. Forget showing Sam retribution — she'd kill the fucker.

Ally kept her gaze on his and her tone gentle. "What if we leave a note? So, if anyone comes looking, they know where to find you?"

He glanced at the door, as if he waited for someone to walk in through it. Except, no one was coming. The thought twisted her chest something fierce.

Finally, Eli nodded. "Okay, we can leave a note."

Ally snagged a pen and paper from the stacks of books that were staying right here. With the pack cabins out of use for the time being and after the massacre here, Beaver Tavern would stay closed to the public for the next week. They needed a congregation point for when the shamans arrived in town and when the Tribe wanted to meet up and talk. This was the one spot the packs still had.

Ally scribbled a note onto the paper, and Eli watched her, soaking in the words. Spirits, she wanted to scoop the kid in her arms and fill him with lies about how it was all going to be okay. But at his young age, he'd experienced devastating loss and he'd witnessed the ugliest sides of humanity. She understood what that did.

"All right, let's go." She led the way to the front of Beaver Tavern and locked up behind them. Night had already fallen, turning the gravel parking lot inky, yet the sweet fragrances of blooming azaleas trailed her way with the spring breeze. Her phone buzzed with another text from Drew—they'd been in constant communication all day, something she had sorely missed.

Ally patted the top of her hatchback, gesturing to the backseat. "This one's mine."

Eli slipped into the back as she looped around to the front and settled into the driver's side. The keys jangled in her hand when she put one in the ignition. Another flashed into view, the old copper one she hadn't used in a long time. Maybe tonight it was time to. As much as her current place belonged to her per the lease she'd signed with Lana, right now her bestie and her mate were living there too, and they hadn't asked for a kid in the mix.

"Remember Drew?" Ally asked, her gaze flicking to the rearview mirror to check he'd clicked his seatbelt on. Eli nodded. "We're going to head to his house. He's out helping the other packs in the area like we helped yours, but I know he'd love to see you when he gets back."

Eli's eyes lit at the mention of Drew, the first bit of excitement he'd shown all day. Ever since Drew had plucked him out of the burning house and calmed him down, the kid had developed a hero complex. As much as she'd never admit the words out loud, Drew deserved the attention. He'd weathered his father's abuse, violation from Mackey Kendricks, the hatred of his former family and home and being mated to a fuck-up like her. If anyone deserved a bright future, he did.

Ally swallowed hard. Step one was to tell him the truth when he returned, to offer up the last piece she'd been holding back. She switched the engine on, the rumble beneath her feet feeling a lot like resolve.

Soon, they'd be heading into a fight they might not all come back from. Life was too short to waste any more time running.

Chapter Eighteen

"Well, I think we left an impression there," Drew said, wiping the spit from his cheek as he headed for his Cadillac. He'd fared better than Dax, who had gotten socked in the eye. After the way Dominic Enrico had been permanently maimed in the fight against Dax during the trials, they hadn't been expecting an ice cream social from the Yellowrock pack. At least they'd scored a win this morning with the Underwood pack who remembered them from the trials in a far fonder light.

"Yeah, endearing in a get-off-my-lawn way," Dax muttered, touching the puffy skin around his eye. "Enrico's wife has a mean right hook."

Out of the seven packs they'd visited between yesterday and today, they'd batted a single yes, three maybes and three fuck-right-offs.

He leaned against the side of his car, catching Dax's gaze. "So, the only one left on the list is Cairncross pack, right?" The weight of their failure settled over him like the flu. When they'd launched into this, he'd been sure at least his brother's smooth talking would rally some of these packs. However, the alliance that existed between Red Rock and Silver Springs was rare. Most shifter packs kept to their own kind, interacting only when they needed to, hence why the Tribes had become a necessity in the first place.

"Let's hope that goes better than this last one," Dax said, slipping into the passenger's side.

Drew settled into the driver's seat and turned the ignition on, the engine rumbling through the entire car. He clung to the comfort of the leather scent of the interior, one piece of familiarity in a landscape tumbling out of his control. His music rolled out through the speakers, a saving grace amidst the tension between him and Dax, thick enough that he couldn't even cut a knife through it — the steel would snap.

He set off down the road, pumping the gas to get far away from the Yellowrock pack where they'd exhausted the zero amount of goodwill the crew had for them. Dax stared out of the window, the brim of his cap casting a shadow across his features.

"Hey, Drew," Dax said. "Ally told me to ask you about Dad's training."

The inhalation he took turned icy, prickling through his lungs. Drew white-knuckled the steering wheel, not saying a word. He wanted to kick Ally as much as he wanted to kiss her for doing that. She'd known the one thing he'd never broached with his brother, something that had changed the cracks in their relationship over the years into a chasm he could never cross.

"She wasn't the only one who mentioned there's a lot we haven't discussed," Dax continued. Even though his voice remained light, Drew could barely breathe in the heavy air that descended.

"Let me guess," Drew drawled, clinging to casual like his life depended on it. "Lana?"

"Bullseye, brother," Dax said. "We've got a half an hour before we get to Cairncross, so if you want to dig into the steaming shitpile of our past, I'm here for it."

White noise reared in the back of Drew's mind, louder and louder by the second. He could do this. Dax wasn't asking for details. He didn't ask him to go back there. Sweat pricked on his forehead. Even though Dax wasn't asking, Drew could feel the blows strike his arms, his stomach, his thighs like fifteen years ago was yesterday. The phantom bruises lingered, as did the throb of broken bones.

"Look, I know you always wanted Pop's attention," Drew said, not bothering to hide the bitterness in his voice. "Let's just say if I could've been in your shoes, ignored by our father, I would've chosen that every time."

The silence in the car held enough weight to smother them both.

"Don't tell me he..." Dax trailed off, horror in his tone.

"Nothing sexual." Drew stared out at the asphalt ahead of him, trying to ignore the roar in his brain. "Just your garden variety abuse." The droll tone that rolled out of him was devoid of any emotion. It was the sole thing he latched onto now, even as his body and soul rioted, threatening to come apart at the seams.

He couldn't go there now.

To the nights he'd spent shaking in his room, knowing what would come in the morning.

To the way he'd staggered to one of Dad's yes-men to get fixed up after a bad bout, and the discomfort in their eyes. They'd known what their big bad alpha was doing was fucked up, but they'd never spoken up.

To the patchwork of bruises across his skin, ones that reappeared so often he forgot what life was like without them.

"How come I never knew?" Dax asked, his voice hushed.

Drew couldn't look over at his brother or he'd break. He didn't want to see the disgust or repulsion. He didn't want to see the disappointment in his little brother's eyes that his big brother was such a weakling.

Drew tried to shrug, but his shoulders refused to move. "You were just a kid, Dax. No way in hell would I have let him expose you to the nightmare."

Dax's hands balled into fists. "So were you." Dax's voice grew raw, ragged in a way that scored Drew's skin like sandpaper. "You were just a kid too, Drew. All those years, I thought you both hated me. I could never figure out why until I realized about a year ago Mom did some sleeping around."

"Welcome to the Williams family," Drew muttered. "Leave your sanity at the door."

Dax slammed his fist against the side of the car, so hard the frame shook. "Fuck him. Fuck the stupid old bastard for everything he did. The man didn't deserve to be called a father." Dax swallowed, the sound audible. "I'm so fucking sorry, Drew. I'm so sorry I didn't know. I'm so sorry I wasn't a better brother."

Drew's throat tightened, and he tried to ignore the heat stinging his eyes. He tried for cavalier again, but his voice shook. "What he did wasn't your fault. I'm your big brother. Big brothers are supposed to protect, which I royally fucked up on when the old man signed us up for the Landsliders."

He stared at the open road ahead, all the memories threatening to suffocate him. His life had become a patchwork of pain and missed opportunities, and yet he was stupid enough to keep hoping. Ally had been his bright spot. No matter how many times they'd fought, she'd been there for him through the lowest lows.

Dax tugged the brim of his cap, staring downward. "You know, I was always so jealous?" he said, his voice scratching. "You were so damn strong and had Dad's approval, which I'd been chasing my entire life. Back when we fought for alpha, it fucking killed me to face you there. No matter how much Dad neglected me, you were there for me every birthday, every holiday. We once had a bond I thought would be unbreakable."

"Don't worry, I fucked that one up too," Drew responded, hating the way his eyes stung. "It's a specialty of mine."

Dax shook his head. "That's not fair. Every time you got the chance, you've proved yourself. You've tried to make up for the things Kendricks forced you to do when he placed you under his control. The actions that belonged to you, the ones Drew Williams made, not our father and not Mackey Kendricks, those have been *good*. Those have been brave."

Fuck. His skin crawled like he wanted to shed it, like he could drop the loathing that had become as much a part of him as his mountain lion. His brother hadn't been the only one seeking approval. As much as the shame coursed through him, Drew had sought their father's praise at every turn and treasured every crumb the old bastard offered. He'd needed — *needed* — to believe that all the pain was for a reason, that he wasn't just a sack of garbage to be beaten and tossed around.

Drew rolled down his window to air out some of the tension broiling around the car. He should say something to Dax. Yet the press of his brother's stare, sympathy flashing there like he didn't hate him—Drew couldn't stand it. The kindness in his tone, the forgiveness dripping from him was the same that Ally and Lana had offered. Compassion should've washed him clean, but he felt filthier, like he'd never be able to scrub his sins away.

Ahead, the looming oaks and surrounding forests began to dissipate, and the nearest town came into view. They were almost at the Cairncross pack, fringes of residences poking into view first, followed by the obligatory town post office and the rinky-dink general store.

His nose twitched, the breeze carrying the scents of butter-yellow tulips planted along the side of the road, fresh-cut grass and smoke. Drew didn't halt his drive as he searched the skyline for the telltale signs.

Dax sat forward in his seat. "Do you see the trail of smoke?"

Drew followed his gaze. Ahead, oily tufts drifted up to the blue. The déjà vu smacked him in the face—mere days ago, he'd chased down the same thing with Ally. Mackey Kendricks wasn't wasting time in his total annihilation of pack stability. And the more he made his presence known, the more the shifters would be alienated from the Tribe. After all, one of their own had committed these atrocities.

Screams filtered into his hearing next, from the right, farther down a residential road. Chances were, they'd started bombing homes.

"Let's go hunt some Landsliders," Drew growled, slamming on the gas.

Chapter Nineteen

The last thing Ally had expected to be doing today was racing through Ricketts Glen.

However, Ava and her friend Melody had set to work deep in the state park's forest, tapping into nature's own magic to fuel theirs. She and Jer had agreed to be the test subjects for the shaman's attempts to combat the device, a choice she already regretted. Her paws churned dirt, her mountain lion running free through these woods. She hadn't considered Ricketts Glen a home growing up, but once their packs allied, the forest had fast become one.

The sparrows trilled in the trees above and snowdrops sprouted across the muddy surfaces as spring infiltrated. Water churned in the distance, the steady splash from the falls. Jer shot ahead of her, the russet wolf showing off for kicks. Not like she could let that stand. Ally sprang forward, her coiled muscles even more powerful in this form. She kicked past the rocks, the soft mud and the moss until she ran neck and neck with the Red Rock beta.

Sierra had agreed to watch Eli today, for which Ally was grateful. The kid had been staring out of the window this morning, clutching the window pane. His big eyes shone with so much hope it hurt, because Sam wasn't coming back. Nor were his parents.

Ally slammed her paws to the ground harder, rocketing ahead. She scaled the slick stones of the slope, one of the many waterfalls throughout this place roaring beside them. The fresh water tickled her nose and several drops of water imprinted on her coat.

Jer lunged forward, his neck stretched out. She loped faster, trying to gain the edge. Ally's pulse sped, the thrill of the chase rising within her. These were the sorts of games she loved, a competitive edge she never lost. Every stride she took was measured, every vault placing her inches past him. They raced in tandem toward the top of the slope where it plateaued next to the churning falls.

Ally surged ahead by an inch, sailing through the air. Her paws landed on the base with a hard thump she could feel in her bones. She panted as she resumed a slow prowl to where Ava and her friend waited, a whole mess of chalk symbols marking the stone surface. Jer rammed her in the side and she nudged back. Amusement welled in her chest, the sense of play something she needed right now. As if she could forget why they'd showed up here.

"If you two could stop romping around, we've got some spells to perform," Ava called, her voice ringing out.

She'd dressed in hiking boots and a hoodie today, for once nothing sarcastic written on the front or back. Already, the shaman appeared out of her element, usually surrounded by dusty tomes or her glasses glinting in front of the blue light of a computer screen. Her friend, on the other hand, had the shaman routine on speed dial, all sweeping bohemian skirts, beads through her tawny strands and painted henna marks up and down her arms.

Ally sauntered up to them. Ava had told her and Jer to arrive in their animal form. Since the device made their animal side tweak out, they'd be testing the effects in that form. If they were already shifted, the device would either be worse, or maybe they'd be able to exert more control. They couldn't tell until they tried.

"Hey, guys, I'm Melody," the other shaman introduced herself, offering a wave and a friendly smile. She was the polar opposite of Ava in every way. "I'm sorry, but this spell might hurt."

Ava shrugged. "They signed up to suffer. They knew this wouldn't be a picnic in the park."

Jer dipped his head, a wet whump noise coming from him that sounded a lot like laughter. Ava had saved their pack multiple times over since she'd replaced Joe Ganzorig as their local shaman and everyone had fast adapted to the woman's lack of tact. Ally preferred it.

"Come stand here," Ava directed, pointing them to the center of the chalk circle she'd constructed. Several piles of herbs had been sprinkled around the line, from lavender to wormwood. Ally stepped into the circle. Even though they hadn't begun the incantation yet, the magic of their movements and their intent reeked in the thickened air.

Jer settled into place beside her, and the russet wolf cast her an amused glance. Ally tilted her head in a nod. Without warning, Ava began to chant, and Melody hustled to catch up. Together, the shamans sank into the spell, an emulation of the device based on Ava's previous study of the object and the effects they'd described to her. They were all throwing darts blindfolded, but Ally would take any help offered.

As their chants filled the air, Ally stared at the dirt by her paws in a paltry attempt to focus. Concentration became impossible with the thoughts clanging around in her head — her new situation with Drew, what might happen with Eli and if she'd even be around to worry after the confrontation against Mackey and the Landsliders. A buzz started, slow and steady, churning her problems into a frenzy.

The buzz continued, rising in volume — the spell.

Ally clenched her jaw. In this form, the sound grew so loud even now, but her body didn't riot to shift at least. Jer let out a low whine as he pawed at the ground. The buzzing started to get more painful, radiating through her bones and weighing them down like platinum. The sound crawled beneath her skin, making her want to shrug it off, to leap forward and dive off the waterfall.

Ally's claws flexed, and she dug them deep into the ground, as if she could anchor herself there. Jer's whole body began trembling, and his muscles grew taut.

So. Damn. Loud.

The noise engulfed her until the pain jolted through, like someone had Tased her.

Ally's whole body was stricken, frozen completely.

The world around her flashed black once, twice, then stayed that way.

* * * *

Ally's body ached like someone had gone to town on her with a sack of baseballs. She rolled to the side, still in her mountain lion form. The experiment had been a failure. She didn't know how they were supposed to combat this brand of shamanic magic that knocked them out on the spot. Since the device had worked on Lucas at the cabin, the Tribe wasn't immune either.

"About time you got up." Ava's voice rang through the air. "I figured the two of you were going to sleep the rest of the day away."

The waterfall roared beside them, which meant they hadn't moved locations in her time out. Ally blinked, trying to clear her sight, her mind — anything to dispel the fog.

Jer sat beside her, already shifted back into his regular form, all charming smiles with dimples. He'd dressed in baggy gray sweats they hadn't brought with, so the shamans must've come prepared.

"Leave it to the cat to nap longer," he commented, a playful grin on his lips.

Ally pushed herself up to look around. The chalk markings remained beneath them, but the herbs had been replaced, used in the spell. Her insides turned at the idea of enduring the blast over and over. Her bones trembled with the reverberations, the way they had when Mackey had originally used the device. She still felt like an idiot for thinking it was anything as simple as a bomb.

Of course, Mackey wouldn't go for a one-use item. He strategized for maximum impact. Why devastate an area with a blast when he could paralyze and wipe out entire communities with no end in sight? The power he wielded poisoned her from trunk to root.

"What are you waiting for?" Ava asked while she wrapped twine around a bundle of sage. "An invitation to shift?"

Melody strode over to her and placed a pile of the same shapeless sweats Jer wore. "You can wear these. Since the effects seemed to hit as strong if not stronger in your animal forms, we're going to try a different route."

Ally sank into her shift, the claws retracting to form nails and her limbs elongated as she changed form. The fur dissipated to reveal smooth arms and legs, and her hair grew in length until it brushed against her back again. She dipped to grab the pile of clothing, even though she'd be just as comfortable buck-naked. With the way Ava and Melody averted their eyes, they wouldn't have the same levels of ease.

She tugged on the five-sizes-too-large sweatpants, pulling at the string to tighten them, and slipped on the tank top.

"So, what's the deal, shaman-in-charge?" Ally asked, striding over to where Ava fiddled with more herbs. "Are we going to try getting device-Tased in this form until we build a resistance? I bet I can hold out longer than Taylor."

Jer snorted. "You wish, Coleman. You might've run a little faster, but the cards are stacked in my favor when it comes to endurance."

"I'm sure Raven is thrilled." Ally rolled her eyes.

"She's got no complaints," he responded, his voice dripping with the insinuation. Not like Ally had any doubts. Ever since the two of them had mated, they'd been slipping off to fuck every spare chance they got. The muttered excuses, rumpled hair and mussed clothing were always telltale.

"While I'm sure the two of you would love the masochistic thrill of getting zapped over and over again, I like to work smarter, not harder," Ava interjected. She handed them each a round pebble with markings painted over the surface. "In the hours you two were knocked out, Melody and I got to work on a different solution."

"Ava did a lot of study into the spell Ganzorig used to separate your human and animal forms," Melody explained. "We're going to try dampening the animal form. Since the device doesn't seem to work on humans, we're going to see if you respond differently while you're masked as human."

Ally clutched the pebble tight in her hand. Her mountain lion rammed into her chest, not satisfied with this option, but she'd try anything, take any advantage they could get. The idea of ever being that helpless again crawled under her skin.

"This might not work," Melody warned. "It might zap you again."

"Don't tease," Jer responded, his eyes glinting.

Ally lifted her chin, meeting Ava's gaze. "Bring it."

Chapter Twenty

Drew had dropped Dax off at Sierra's house, the lights glowing on the porch. His brother's mate had waited up for him to come home, and Drew couldn't help the pang of envy. He kept the windows rolled down even though the tension in the air and the hint of ozone in the rising breeze signaled a storm on the horizon.

A tempest was the closest thing to his mind right now. The Cairncross pack had been shattered by the Landsliders, halved from the way he'd torched their homes. Due to the device, they'd been defenseless to stop him. The film of smoke clung to his skin from the fires he and Dax had dived into, hoping to retrieve anyone from the wreckage.

The pack alpha had promised retribution, which made them the second pack in the region to join their alliance against the Landsliders. Two wouldn't be nearly enough, but they couldn't back down. Not after what they'd experienced at the hands of the

Landsliders. Mackey Kendricks needed to be stopped, even if they all died trying.

Drew tapped his fingers along the steering wheel. He zoomed along the highway, the familiar trees leaning in, knobby oaks with thick foliage. He was going to turn the shower to scorching and drink for the rest of the night. Not like hot water would help scour the memories clean. If the hour hadn't been so late, he'd have swung by Lana's. He needed to see Ally beat at the same steady pulse as his heart did.

His driveway peeked into view from along the roadside, the familiar sentinel oaks on either side, withered and aged yet still standing proud.

He pulled down the driveway, the crunch of his tires over twigs, the bumps along the way he knew by heart. Drew almost pumped on the brakes once he reached his rancher.

Ally's car sat in the driveway, and his porchlights were on.

A harsh breath slipped from his lips at the wash of relief that swept through him. The sight punched him in the chest, the culmination of night after night longing for this, for her to come back to him. They still hadn't discussed where they stood, even after she'd declared them dating again in front of his brother. He hadn't dared to ask, the idea of her slipping from his grasp too much to bear right now.

By the time he pulled into Park, his door creaked open and Ally snuck out.

Her honey strands fell in gentle waves that brushed along her shoulders as she strode to his stoop. She wore jean shorts he couldn't wait to tear off her long-as-sin legs and the lavender tee placed the curve of her tits on perfect display. She was mouthwatering, but when her gaze met his, the look reached in and grabbed him by the chest. He was home.

Drew shut his car door with a click that echoed through the clearing. With the tension flickering between them when their eyes met, he might as well have cocked a loaded gun.

"Couldn't stay away, Car Crash?" he said, a genuine grin slipping to his lips, even as he fought it.

Ally cast him the side-eye. "Please, I just came for the extra space. Your place is a lot roomier than mine with Lana and Lucas getting busy every three-point-five seconds."

Heat coursed through him when he soaked in the sight of her sitting on his stoop. Except then she tugged her knees toward her chest, a hesitation surrounding her that stopped him short.

"Drew, we need to talk," she said, the words snuffing out the flickering glow in his chest. This wasn't a reunion like he'd hoped. This was a goodbye.

His mouth dried and, for once, the words evacuated him. He slumped onto the stoop beside her, his legs numb.

Ally stared at her bare feet, refusing to look up at him. He had just gotten her back. He had cracked open the battered chest he'd let rust over for far too long, and now she was slamming the lid shut. The air brimmed between them, a bomb waiting to explode. Drew's hand curled into a fist, his nails digging deeper and deeper into his skin. Maybe if he bled, this wouldn't hurt as bad.

"The last time we broke up, I didn't tell you the truth," she murmured, the words so faint he almost lost them.

"You had every right to break up with me," Drew responded, not wanting to hear the period at the end of the sentence, not wanting to let this fragile, tenuous thread he grasped slide out of reach. "I didn't tell you I joined the Landsliders, and I was getting more and more distant by the day."

Ally stared at him, the desolation in her eyes stealing the words from his lips. "Let me get through this. I'm not going to be able to do it a second time."

Fuck. He couldn't back away from this precipice even if the result would break him beyond repair. He'd been an idiot to hope. Fucking stupid to think a piece of shit like him could retain the slightest bit of happiness.

"When we lost..." She trailed off, her eyes growing glossy with unshed tears. Drew didn't have to ask. He remembered the miscarriage like it had been yesterday. He remembered running her to the hospital and the way she'd sobbed in his arms after they'd lost their light. He remembered how her fingers had curled into his shirt and how a piece of him had forever fractured.

Drew didn't dare reach out and touch her—when Ally brimmed like this, she'd snap back or retreat further inside. Instead, Drew slipped his hand to the space between them. Ally glanced to the offering he made. She rested her own hand over his, the touch between them the one thing he held onto right now.

"I had to go back to the doctor's a week later," she said, her voice dull, lifeless. "Lana took me."

His brow creased. He didn't remember this trip at all.

"They gave me the diagnosis, and I came home and broke up with you," Ally said, her words so tremulous they might shatter. She squeezed his hand so tight his bones protested, but he didn't dare move away. Ally looked him in the eyes at last, unshed tears glittering in her beautiful blues.

"I'm broken, Train Wreck." The words came out in a gasp, and her shoulders trembled. "You're never going to be able to have the family you want—not with me." The first tears slipped down her cheeks, ones the proud woman rarely allowed herself. He could see the way her shoulders rounded, how she braced herself like she prepared for the worst blows—the ones he'd been steeling himself for.

Her words sank in past the numbness, past the worry that they'd reached the end of the road.

Ally couldn't have kids.

Part of him died then and there, the part that had dreamed of sitting around a kitchen table with her and their little one. The part that watched the tender way she interacted with kids and how her walls melted away. He felt the pit open in his chest as visceral as the day they'd lost theirs, a hollowness he'd never believed would fill again.

Drew squeezed her hand. She was waiting—waiting on a response from him.

He'd believed she hated him, that his time in the Landsliders and all the terrible things he'd done had damaged him beyond salvation. Yet even back then, when he'd been shitty and distanced, she hadn't pulled away. Ally had always given him shit for the way he dove in to protect everyone at the expense of himself, yet she'd been doing the same all along.

A sob rose in his chest at how alone she must've felt, at the shattered glass in her voice, and how the self-loathing must have choked her daily, the same way it did him.

Drew reached forward, wrapping his arms around his gorgeous, stubborn as hell, resilient mate. Ally stiffened at first against his chest, but the moment he gripped her tighter, she sank against him. Her shoulders shook and the wet heat of her tears printed on his shirt, just like back then. He clung onto her with all his might like he had years ago, after his dad had beaten him black and blue. They'd always been clutching to each other like a safety raft in the storm, the one thing keeping them from being drowned by the tempests life delivered.

"I love you, Ally Coleman," Drew murmured, his voice ragged with the emotion coiled tight in his chest. "I have always loved you. I will always love you."

Spirits above, she must've felt so alone. She must've felt so isolated with the weight of the reality forced upon her. And even now, she'd summoned the bravery to tell him. The fear in her eyes hadn't been regret. She'd been terrified he'd view her the damaged-goods way she viewed herself. That he would be the one to leave her.

Ally shook, her whole body trembling with the force of the sobs ripping from her throat, ones that welled in his own. His fingers traveled through her golden strands, and he stroked her hair, her back. Drew held her tighter to him, wishing he could take the pain away, wishing he could cross time and be in the doctor's office with her to tell her the diagnosis would've never scared him away.

Except that time had passed. All they had was now.

"Babe, you're all the family I need," he murmured into her hair. His voice grew rough, low, and his eyes stung with heat he forced back. "You don't need to try to protect or preserve my dreams. They came true the day I mated to you."

Ally let out a shaky breath, looking at him. Her eyes glittered with tears, the same soft glow as the moon. She tried on a quavering half-smile. "Sucker," she responded, fighting to blink away the remaining tears. "I trapped you early."

Drew traced the slender line of her chin with his thumb, brushing across her plush lips. That smart mouth of hers, the bitter snark she relied on when she was at her worst—they'd been kindred spirits from an early age. If sacrificing those dreams for a kid of his own meant returning to the soft glow of the porch light left on, to this beautiful woman in his arms who smelled like gardenia, fresh berries and hope, he'd give them up in an instant.

Drew had been hurtling a hundred miles an hour toward his own annihilation, but Ally Coleman was the one person who could bring him back every time.

"Come on now," he murmured, inches between them. "You're the one who got saddled with my hot mess."

"Emphasis on hot," Ally responded, her eyes gleaming with amusement. "You're lucky you're gorgeous." The teasing in her eyes returned, and after the whiplash of their conversation, Drew welcomed the blaze. The look in her eyes was pure seduction, and her tongue trailed along her lips in deliberate perfection.

Drew closed the space between them. He pressed his lips against hers, tentative for a split second before the hunger reared up. He gripped the back of her neck and devoured her mouth with slow, scorching kisses, his tongue tracing along hers. She twined her arms around his neck, sinking into the kiss with a desperate need that raced through them both. Ally's moan vibrated against his mouth, the sound traveling straight to his cock.

The winds whipped around faster and the first raindrop splashed onto his skin.

Drew pulled away from her, their breaths mingling together as he stared into her eyes. "Let's take this inside."

Ally glanced to the side. "Uh, slight problem with that."

Drew lifted an eyebrow, and he pulled back. She leaned on her elbows against the wooden planks of his stoop, and he rested his palms on either side of her. Part of him didn't give a damn if he walked in to find she had hulled out the inside — he wanted to pound into her until they both forgot they'd ever been apart.

Ally cast another glance to his door. "You've got another guest in the house."

Drew pulled away, even though his body let out a protest. "This wasn't something you could've just texted me about?"

Ally shrugged. "Figured you'd understand. Plus, it's easier to explain in person. I put him to bed in the guest room a while ago." She let out a sigh. "Sam dropped Eli off at Beaver Tavern the other day and drove off."

Drew's claws pricked out before he could help himself. Anger roared at an accelerated thump in his chest. "I'll kill the fucker."

After everything the kid had been through with losing his parents, the last thing he needed was to get abandoned again by one of the only people he knew. Drew should've pieced the puzzle together earlier. He'd seen the reluctance in Sam's eyes back at the ceremony, how he'd shied away from dealing with Eli.

Ally placed a hand on his chest. "You'll have to fight me for the chance. The kid's so lost, and he didn't have anyone."

The realization settled over him. Warmth soaked through his chest at the sight of the woman he adored more than words could ever convey. *Of course. Of course she would've.*

"You took him in," he affirmed. She nodded, biting her lip as if she waited for the criticism and condemnation Rylie Coleman had pounded into her daughter day in and day out. She'd never get that from him.

"Spirits above, I fucking love you," Drew said, the words slipping out before he could help them. He didn't care. He wanted to stand at the road and shout it out to the sky in the hopes that those words reached the stars. He would've done the same thing—the kid deserved so much better than the shit hand life had delivered.

"Thought you might be okay with the judgment call," Ally murmured. "I wasn't going to bring him home to Lucas and Lana. They both have enough on their plates, and besides, he doesn't know them. The last thing the kid needs is more strangers. You should've seen the way he lit up when I mentioned I was taking him to your house."

Drew's insides twisted with sharp longing, the kind he always got being around little ones. Even though he'd have to give up the idea of a kid of his own, he and Ally would share that burden together. Eli was in for a tough next couple of years and a lot of nightmarish adjustments he wouldn't wish on any kid, let alone one as sweet as him. Drew wanted with everything in him to shield the little guy from the pain he'd face.

"Hey, where are you at?" Ally's voice softened and regret shadowed her gaze. None of that. Drew brushed his thumb across her cheek, drawing her focus front and forward to him.

"I'm thinking if we can't make a lot of noise in there, I'm going to take you out here," he murmured, his voice coming out rough and low. "Because I'm going to fuck you senseless."

Ally wrinkled her nose, glancing to the sky. "What about the storm?"

The drops increased in frequency, several slipping past the brief alcove overhead to print on his shirt. "Just means you can scream as loud as you want, babe," Drew said, prowling overtop her. Ally leaned back, her elbows digging into the wooden planks.

Drew hunched on top of her, pressing his lips along the slip of her tan skin that peeked out between the hem of her shirt and her waistband, the firm, velvet skin of her toned arms. He bit down on the thick muscle of her traps, and Ally moaned out loud, her legs spreading open in response. His cock hardened at the feel of the woman beneath him, the one whose body he knew like these back roads.

Ally's hot breath puffed against his skin, and he bit harder, sucking at the tender skin. The raindrops splashed down a bit heavier, but even the bursts of cold didn't threaten the building inferno between them.

"I need you inside me, now," she moaned. He wanted to toy with her, to make her cries echo out into the moonlit air, but they had all night. She fumbled with his belt, and within seconds, the snick echoed through the air when she pried it open. His button popped, the zipper dragged down and Ally tugged it further. His erection was stark in the space between them and her legs spread like a plea to be filled.

Drew slipped his hands past the waistband of her shorts, the elastic of her panties, and his fingers swiped against her slit. The oncoming storm couldn't compete with how soaked Ally was. The slick feel of her against his fingers dosed him with desire, and he pumped his fingers inside her faster and faster until he drowned out her soft cries with his mouth. He drank in the taste of her lips, sweetness and tea.

Ally reached out to run her hand along his length and he almost came on the spot. Spirits, he needed to be inside her. Drew pulled his fingers out and dragged her shorts off, almost tearing her panties in the motion. Ally kicked them to the ground past the stoop. She leaned against the steps, her pussy soaked and the look in her eyes drenched with desire.

Drew shunted his pants to the side and knelt on the steps in front of her. His cock brushed against her slick entrance and her entire body shivered at the contact. He ignored the pelt of the rain soaking into his shirt as he nudged his head into her. Ally wrapped her arm around his shoulders, and he began to rock inside. The moment he slid all the way in, she wrapped her thighs even tighter around his hips, and a shuddering sigh escaped him. The relief was the same as rolling up to this familiar driveway after a long time away.

He was home.

Ally leaned against the steps, one elbow steadying her while she gripped him hard with the other. He drove into her, his knees biting into the grain of the boards beneath him. Drew savored the burn against his knees and the creak and groan of the steps as he slid into her again and again. Because this was real. He was here with his mate and this time neither of them would run away.

Drew braced one arm at her side, leaning against the slope as he rammed into her faster and faster. Drops from the rain slid through his hair, mingling with the drip of sweat down his forehead. Already, the tension formed a fist inside begging to shake out. Ally tilted her head back, her cries louder than the breezes whipping around the place, sending leaves skittering across his uneven drive.

Drew reached between them with his other hand to brush his thumb across her clit. He circled around and around, enjoying the way she thrust against him. Pleasure made her this wanton, needy thing. The pounding in his cock intensified. He was going to blow, any second now.

Ally's core throbbed tight around him and she let out a gasp, her lashes flickering. She closed her eyes in bliss. Drew let loose, careening over the edge with her. He emptied inside her, almost sagging against Ally on the steps. His mind blanked, all the tension escaping his body in one blinding sweep.

Drew leaned down to press his lips against her throat, a tender kiss, a promise.

"Don't worry, babe," he murmured in her ear. "We're just getting started."

Chapter Twenty-One

Ally curled her fingers into Drew's shirt as he crushed her against the steps. Her entire body thrummed in the wake of the orgasm he'd wrung from her. She could barely dare to believe her truth lay out in the open. He'd seen into the rotting grove she tried to hide from everyone, every last bit of ugliness, and he'd accepted it. Drew still wanted to be with her.

Ally sought out his lips, tasting the smoke on them, the scent surrounding him — he must've been diving into fires again. Thunder crashed and the rain listened, coming down hard enough to pelt against her bare legs.

After all the secrets that had splintered them apart before, everything lay out in the open now to be swept away by these aching, bracing winds. The contact between them wasn't enough — she wanted full skin on skin. Ally reached for the hem of his shirt and tugged at the fabric.

Drew grinned against her mouth and pulled out of her. He took a step back and with a fluid motion tugged the shirt up and over. It hit the ground with a wet thump. The thunder crashed again, the rain coursing down his body. Ally licked her lips before she could help herself. He towered over her, all his luscious tan skin a perfect canvas for her teeth. His erection hung heavy between his muscular legs.

Drew lifted two fingers and beckoned her forward.

A tentative grin rose to her lips. Ally tossed her damp tank top to the ground, unsnapped her bra and that followed suit. Her calves tensed. She leapt forward, sailing through the air toward him.

Ally slammed into Drew's chest, but his arms already looped around to brace her. She didn't even question if he would catch her—she knew her mate would, every time. They'd both spent so much time running from the truth, breaking apart when the blows life dealt got too tough, but she had known ever since they were kids she was meant to be with Drew Williams. Ally didn't believe in a lot, but she believed in him.

Her legs twined around his waist and his strong hands gripped her thighs, which kept her hoisted around him. Ally crashed against his mouth, the fury of the storm riding through their kiss. Overhead, the sky trembled, it quaked and the foreign light flashed as the first strike hit the sphere. However, they'd weathered the worst storms and had both grown stronger for them.

Ally sank her teeth into his lower lip, tasting copper. His hands gripped her thighs so tightly that they might bruise, and she'd relish each and every one. The rain slapped against her bare skin and coursed down her back, her legs, dripping off her toes. The slithering cold didn't come close to dousing the heat in her core or the insatiable hunger that drove her to him again and again.

Drew growled, the sound a deep thrum in his chest. Her nipples brushed against his bare skin, the tips tightening when drops of rain splashed onto them. The torrent pounded harder, turning the ground to mud around them. Droplets burst on her lips, mingling with their kisses and slithering down her scalp. Her sodden strands of hair plastered on her cheeks, her neck.

She dug her heels into his muscled ass, and she drank in the taste of him like she might never get it again. They clashed together with the frenzy of two addicts returning for a hit, their love something they'd never been able to quit. Drew gave her legs a squeeze and he lowered her to the ground. He moved her around like she weighed nothing, the sheer power he'd gained throughout the years turning her on even more.

She circled her legs around his waist, but her back thumped against the muddy surface beneath her. Not like her ass had a chance to follow, because Drew hoisted her legs up and over his shoulders. Her elbows dug into the dirt beneath her, the mud streaking them. Grit tangled into her hair, but before Ally could move, Drew's tongue slid across her clit, and she forgot everything else.

He lapped at her with a precision that got her panting within seconds. The rain smacked against her skin, sliding down her face, but Ally closed her eyes and went along for the ride. Drew thrummed against her clit, a tightening bud begging to unfurl. Her core throbbed and even though he'd just filled her to completion, she needed him again. Spirits above, she needed him tonight.

Ally's back arched, the rain splashing around her. The winds swept it across in choking torrents. Water dripped from her hair, slid down her cheeks and slithered down her legs, but none of the chill came close to extinguishing the heat of Drew's mouth against her clit. Her breath came out in ragged pants and her nails changed into claws as they sank into the mud on either side of her. Ally thrust her hips toward him as the tension mounted. She sank into the bliss of his touch, the melody of his mouth an old song she'd forgotten how much she loved.

Drew sucked at her clit, the pressure pushing her over the edge. The bliss rocked through her with all the force of this descending storm as she surrendered. Ally cried out his name, her claws digging into the ground and her back arching with the force of the orgasm. She rode out the waves of pleasure, the sensations short-circuiting her brain. As they receded, she slumped on the ground, her legs still twined around Drew's shoulders.

Ally unhooked her legs and rolled to a crouch, bringing her eye level with Drew. She shoved out and her palms smacked against his slick chest. He moved with the motion, his ass slamming to the ground. Ally prowled above him, giving him another push to send him onto his back. His eyes shone with a mix of tenderness and molten heat, a look that coursed right through her.

She slipped her legs on either side of him to pin him down, and his erection slid against her ass. The firm length caused her core to clench. He lay there before her, his longer tawny hair plastered against his cheeks, some of the strands stained by the mud beneath him. Rain soaked her through, pounding so hard she could barely hear anything else.

Ally memorized the man before her, the elegant arch of his nose, the firm slope of his chin and the wicked curve of lips most often in a smirk. His skin was a patchwork of scars, from the old ones that had thinned with time to the newer ones slashed across his legs and arms. She'd gained her own in their time apart too, the mottled one along her thigh and dozens more from the countless battles they'd been in. Ally inhaled the ozone from the rain, the smoke all washed away. They carried their past with them, but the rain brought the hope of a new future, one where they could shed their sins and move forward. *Together.*

"You're fucking perfect, Drew Williams," she breathed, even though her words got drowned out by the storm. Based on the gleam in his eyes, he could still tell. Ally's heart twisted tight.

Drew wrapped his hands around her cheeks. She dipped with his movement when he guided her mouth to his. Their lips connected, as electric as the flash of lightning scorching the indigo skies above. Even though her skin had numbed from the cold slap of the rain, his mouth burned against hers and she slid her hips down. Ally lifted until the head of his cock brushed against her core. She sank onto him, taking his full length inside her.

Drew's thumbs pressed into the hollow of her hips, and he clutched each side tightly before he thrust into her. Ally rocked up and down, pressing her palms into the mud. Their lips were inches apart. Each time she dropped down and their hips smacked together, the tips of her nipples brushed against his chest, the sensation sending her into overload.

She began to pick up speed, and Drew rocked along with her. He slipped his hands around her waist. He thrust into her harder and harder, her breasts slapping against her with the force of the movement. Ally's breath hitched in her throat. The rain pounded around them, almost as deafening as the roar inside her chest. They clashed together, fueled by desperation and the hope for salvation they'd both been chasing since the day she met him.

Drew thrust harder into her, every glide down bringing her closer. They smacked together with enough strength that the delicious sting coursed to her toes. Her core twisted tighter and tighter, bringing her right to the edge of shattering apart.

The incessant pound of the rain numbed her fingers and toes, yet she and Drew moved with a dogged determination, as if they fought the sky itself. Their gasps came out harsh and ragged, smothered by the quaking thunder which reverberated through the air. Their back and forth was as natural as always, an endless push and pull.

Drew slid his hands around her breasts, and he squeezed tight as she rode him harder. He grazed his thumbs across her nipples, the sensation traveling straight to her core. He pinched them hard and a gasp flew from her throat. The dose of pleasure rolled through her, honey-sweet. The splattered mud across her skin, the grit against her knees and the wet strands of her hair plastered along her neck, down her back — all of it faded away.

Her focus tunneled in on the man beneath her, the one who moved with the strength of a storm. The rain splashed all around them, drops pounding against her back. She tightened to the point of pain, to the point where she needed release more than her next breath.

Drew thrust into her hard, hitting deeper than before. She blinked white and pleasure slammed into her like a two by four. Ally's whole body responded, her toes curling, her nails digging into the dirt, and her back arching as the orgasm tore through her. Drew continued pumping, until, several thrusts later, his cock pulsed. He tightened his grip around her waist. Heat flooded inside her, and she coasted out the aftershocks.

Any energy she'd been clinging onto vanished. Ally crumpled against him, leaning down to steal a kiss. Drew's lips curled in a smile.

"Babe, you're filthy," he murmured in her ear, the words dripping with intent.

"You're one to talk," she muttered, trying and failing to summon the energy to lift off him. "We've got enough mud between us to plant a garden."

"We're both due for a bath," he responded, pulling out of her. "Hope you're ready to get steamy."

"You're insane," she responded. "If we try to go for another round, I'll probably die."

"Drama queen," he shot back.

"Slut."

His lips curved in response. Drew kept his hands around her waist as he pushed up from the ground, bringing her with him. Ally's legs quivered, spent after the multiple orgasms and numbed from the rain that continued pounding down. By some miracle, Drew was upright and still had energy. He scooped her into his arms and she went with the motion, leaning against his chest. His strength radiated through the easy way he lifted her, how he clutched her tight then strode toward his house.

Ally glanced at him. Her heart glowed at the satisfaction on his lips, the way his eyes looked less lost, less haunted. She would take every second they could steal together. One thing she knew for sure — she was never walking away again.

He fiddled with the knob, pushing the door open.

Ally tapped a finger against his chest to get his attention. His eyes locked on hers before he stepped inside.

The certainty descended in her chest, the same she'd felt the day she'd accepted their mating bond. "Welcome home."

* * * *

Ally woke up in Drew's bed, and for a moment, she thought she'd transported back in time. Sunlight streamed through the blinds, the golden rays splayed across his navy comforter. The scent of him spread everywhere here, making her mountain lion purr with appreciation. She stretched, her muscles sore in the best way. After the marathon sex they'd had last night, continuing even in the bath, she was surprised she could even move.

The low murmur of voices came from outside the room, drawing her attention. Ally slipped out of the bed and shrugged on one of his T-shirts, dragging on a pair of baggy sweats she tightened at the drawstrings. She finger-combed her waves, wishing she had a brush and some conditioning spray stowed away. Ally opened the door with a creak.

The scent of pancakes and syrup wafted her way, causing her stomach to rumble. As she crept ahead, the voices grew clearer, Drew's rich, deep tenor, and Eli's higher tone. She peered in past the doorway and warmth snuck into her chest. Drew stood at his stovetop, flipping pancakes in his cast-iron skillet. Eli sat at the two-seater table in the kitchen with him, his head tilted and curiosity gleaming in his eyes.

Drew snagged a plate and placed several small pancakes onto it, the steam rising into the air. His gaze snared on hers as he crossed the space over to Eli and a genuine smile lit his face. Fuck, she was so smitten with this man.

"You need anything else on your pancakes besides syrup?" he asked. Drew passed Eli a secretive grin. "Ketchup? Jelly? Mustard?"

Eli wrinkled his nose. "That's super gross. No one eats pancakes that way."

Drew arched an eyebrow. "Hear that, Ally?" he called out to her. "You're super gross."

Ally snorted when she entered the room, her bare feet skating across the hardwood floor. "Yes, yes, I'm the weirdo who likes jelly on my pancakes. Don't knock it till you've tried it."

Eli's eyes widened. "I didn't mean..." he started, glancing between the two of them. As comfortable as he seemed, the kid had been plunked into a brand-new setting and they were one step away from strangers to him.

Drew shook his head, his eyes alight with the way he loved to irritate. "You stick to your guns, kiddo. It *is* super gross."

Ally didn't have to fake her smile. Listening to Drew encourage him, to be the opposite of everything she grew up with, made her heart soar. She reached inside the fridge and pulled out the strawberry jelly. Ally grabbed a plate and flipped the pancake cooking on the skillet, checking the other side before she snagged it. Drew strode behind her with his calm, measured tread.

His hands slid around her hips and he squeezed, a brief touch before he returned to skillet duty.

Ally leaned up to press a kiss to his cheek. The smirk in return was all sorts of worth it. Spirits above, this was everything she'd dreamed of, everything she'd told herself she didn't need when she'd lain awake at night by her lonesome, hands clutched to her hollow stomach. She never believed she could feel this complete, this elated.

She spread the jelly on her pancake, clutching the knife a little tighter. Ally needed to steal these moments while she could. Their assault on World's End loomed, and survival wasn't a guarantee. She rolled the pancake and took a bite from the end. Here and now — that was what was important.

"Come on," she said, strolling over to Eli. She plopped into the other seat and offered the other end of her rolled pancake. "At least give this a try."

Eli cast her one wary look, but he reached out to take the tiniest bite. His nose wrinkled when he swallowed. She didn't need to look over to the stovetop — she could feel the amused grin on Drew's lips. Eli didn't say a word as he averted his glare.

"Stop trying to win allies to your side," Drew called over.

"You can be honest," she said, ignoring him as she focused on Eli. He shook his head, his nose wrinkling again. A laugh escaped her lips. "Don't worry, we'll figure out your weird food quirk sooner or later. We all have them." Ally leaned in to give a stage-whisper. "Drew eats the ends off his burritos first. Like a monster."

A hesitant grin reached Eli's lips, one she'd fight for.

Drew snorted and pulled up an extra chair to the table with them, a plate of pancakes piled high and drenched with syrup. He slammed his fork in and began to chow down. "I'm just getting rid of the baggage before diving into the good stuff. Perfectly reasonable."

"Chew a little louder," Ally shot back. "They can't hear you in France."

A giggle escaped Eli, one he tried to cover up with his arm, as if he were about to cough. Ally's chest tightened when her gaze met Drew's. His blue eyes glowed with a warmth she hadn't seen from him in a long time, a serenity radiating off the man who she'd worried would be haunted for the rest of his days. The love was evident in his gaze, in the tender touches and in the way he teased her, because he knew her better than anyone else.

If she had to take one memory with her to the upcoming battle ahead, it would be this one.

Chapter Twenty-Two

The last time Drew had seen the parking lot of Beaver Tavern this crowded was when he and the Landsliders were attacking it. Cars covered every square inch of the gravel lot, even more than the normal pack influx. Representatives would be joining them from other packs, the human law enforcement and the shamans.

Ally brimmed in the seat beside him. They'd dropped Eli off with Marcy and Rick, one of the families tasked with guarding the littles while the rest of their packmates went to war. Trying to say goodbye to that kid as they'd dropped him into yet another unfamiliar situation had been torture. Eli had stared up at him with those big brown eyes, a pleading there that reached inside his chest and tugged. *Not like we had another choice. Can't bring a kid to the battlefield we'll be entering.*

Before they'd left, Marcy and Rick's oldest, Daria, had approached, offering a friendly smile and an outstretched hand. Drew took solace in that.

His heart lurched when he pulled in to park beside Lucas' Explorer. A couple of weeks ago, he would've been hurtling toward oblivion at a hundred miles an hour. However, for the first time in a long while, Drew wanted a future.

"Perfect timing, right?" Ally's voice cut through their silence. "We get back together right before a fight we might not return from."

Drew forced a smile, even as he curled his hand over hers. "Well, you've always had a flair for the dramatic."

"You're one to talk." Ally shot him the side-eye, even as she squeezed his hand tight.

For a moment, they sat in the stillness together, the dread sweeping over with a hurricane force. It leeched the will from his bones, suffused his world with gray and the horizon line that once stretched out unending narrowed to one, defined point.

Yet as the warmth of her hand soaked into his and the thread of their bond tightened rather than going slack, the wave passed. Resolve settled in his bones, the oath he'd sworn from the day he escaped the Landsliders. Drew caught Ally's gaze and she flashed a smile neither of them believed. In the wake of the overwhelming odds against them, bravery wasn't about conviction but in taking steps forward even when they shook.

He stepped out of his car, staring at the homey lights that beamed from Beaver Tavern's windows in the early evening. No matter how many times their enemies had destroyed this place and no matter how much blood stained these floors, it remained a beacon for the packs, a symbol of their resilience.

Headlights flashed and Finn's Challenger pulled in beside them. Akio and Jess hopped out from the backseat while Navi and Finn exited the front.

"Don't tell me you've repurposed your baby as a Tribe clown car," Drew drawled, hooking his thumbs through his belt loops. Finn Kelly took care of his Challenger with a holy man's devotion.

Finn shook his head with a grin. "Don't tell me this is what you're passing for humor nowadays?"

"Please, this is on the better end of the shit that comes from his mouth," Ally responded, slinging an arm around his shoulder. Drew tugged around her waist to drag her closer, unable to help the grin that snuck to his face.

Jess' gaze flicked to his, an inquisitive look in her eyes. "Thought you didn't have time for romance, Williams?" He caught the note of envy in her tone — she'd been interested when he'd first come around to the Tribe, and he had turned her down. He'd been too fucked up and broken to get into the nitty gritty that his own mate didn't want to be with him.

Ally tightened her grip on his, a possessiveness he adored, part of the passion and fire that dripped from her pores. "Trust me, he still doesn't have time for romance," she responded. "The sucker had the misfortune of being mated to me." Even as she said the words casually, he could feel the intensity in her gaze when she looked at him. Fucking hell, he loved her so damn much.

Navi's eyebrows lifted, same as Jess' when the realization settled home. Finn let out a low whistle, while Akio rolled his eyes and headed for the front door.

"Let's be real—you're the sucker here," he responded, taking the first steps toward the entrance. The rest of their group followed behind as he approached the door. Ally snorted and squeezed his shoulder before pulling away. She strode in first and, one by one, they all entered Beaver Tavern.

The wall of noise from the dozens of groups crammed inside slammed against him. At least thirty people if not more crowded the roundtables, lined the bar stools and leaned against the walls of Beaver Tavern. Raven stood behind the bar, handing out pints of ale, water, whatever their visitors wanted. With the way the bartenders of this place kept dying, Raven's willingness to stick with her job showed the woman's mettle.

Dax and Sierra lingered by the front of the bar, deep in conversation with Lucas and Lana. Drew didn't hesitate in his stride toward them. In the past, the tug of regret might've followed, shame dragging at his heels. However, in the wake of his conversation with Dax, the first gasp of clarity in years descended. They'd both wasted so much time chasing after affection from the father who'd never give it.

Dax glanced his way and waved forward, a grin breaking out on his brother's face, one that reached his eyes at last. The breath Drew had been holding released. That look in his brother's eyes took him back years to when they were dumb kids running through the woods together. Ally strode ahead of him, ducking past the familiar faces at the tables where members of the Silver Springs and Red Rock packs sat.

Unfamiliar folks clustered at a roundtable, at least six of them. Based on the amount of carnelian, amethyst and other stones around their necks or dangling from earrings, the shamans had arrived. Besides, the stench of their magic gave them away. He passed by another table filled with cops, most of them still in uniform. The human scent was devoid of the animal undertones he caught from shifters.

The beta of the Cairncross pack hunched against the wall, catching his eye and throwing his hand up in a wave. A throng of shifters surrounded him, all ones Drew recognized from the grand tour he and Dax had done the other day. The clash of different scents and sounds warred throughout Beaver Tavern, combining with the gunpowder tension that descended among everyone who joined them.

They all arrived here for one reason.

Ally slipped her hand through his when they approached. Lana cast them a knowing glance, a not-so-subtle grin playing on her lips. Drew didn't doubt for a moment her best friend had an instrumental role in Ally telling him the whole truth the other night. For the way Lana pushed both of them to be honest and for her forgiveness, he would always be grateful.

"Who are we still waiting on?" Ally asked.

"The gang's all here," Sierra said, scanning over the crowd. She clutched a hand to her stomach which strained the fabric of her maternity shirt. Sierra squinted, trying to single out members amidst the sheer volume of people crammed into this place. "And if they're not, we're done waiting for them."

"You're the pinnacle of patience, darling," Dax commented, earning an elbow jab from Sierra. Drew didn't hide his grin like so many times in the past. His brother had found himself an equal in the Red Rock alpha, a perfect balance to him in so many ways. For a long while, every time he saw the happy couples together, the sight had dosed him with poison, a reminder of what he'd lost.

However, he stood here today at Ally's side, her hand pressed against his. He stood here today amidst a group of people who mere months ago would've snarled and growled him from the room, yet for the first time since he'd joined the Landsliders and careened down that brambles-and-thorns path, he felt like he'd taken the initial step home.

"I'll leave it to you to wrangle the pups," Lucas commented, casting Sierra an amused glance. "Consider it practice." Lana tried to hide her snicker at the comment but didn't manage.

Sierra passed them a murderous stare before she balled her hands into fists and stepped to the bar. Jer leaned up from behind the bar where he helped his mate and slammed a bottle of Jameson onto the counter, loud enough to echo. A couple of stares flickered in their direction, but with the chatter of so many different groups, they failed to snag their full attention. The Tribe began to weave their way to the front — on a normal day, they'd be the ones taking the lead, but in the wake of the distrust Mackey had sown, Dax and Sierra were who the shifters would look to for guidance.

Ally placed her hand to her mouth. "Shut the fuck up and pay attention," she called, her voice echoing to the rafters. At once, the conversations severed, and Sierra passed her a grateful glance.

"Pack," she called out, sweeping her gaze across the room. "Brethren. Allies." Her voice resounded in the hushed, iron tone of command Sierra wielded as naturally as she breathed. "We've gathered here today because the threat against our region, the threat against our nation, needs to be stopped. Mackey Kendricks and the Landsliders have torn apart our packs, bombed our homes and murdered so, so many of our kind. Tomorrow, this stops."

"What about the device he used?" one of the leaders of Cairncross called out. "How are we going to combat that?"

Lucas gestured to the table of cops and other humans. "The Landsliders aren't just shifters. Humans have joined in with them too and they can withstand the device. If Mackey uses this against us in battle, we'll have our own force to defend."

"And a human is supposed to take down Kendricks?" one of the Red Rocks called out, the skepticism clear in his voice. A couple of the cops shot from their seats, their hands balling into fists. They might as well have been snarling with the way their brows furrowed and their expressions stormed.

"This is our fight," Lucas announced, his voice rolling through the crowd like thunder. Drew had gotten used to seeing the soft side of the big guy, but with his chin lifted and his eyes flashing like lightning, those Tribe tattoos marked clear up his arms, he remembered why people thought he was one scary motherfucker.

"Mackey Kendricks was East Coast Tribe who defected, and the Tribe is responsible for taking him down. Ava has figured out a way to thwart the device—she's only had the time to make a handful of pendants to suppress our shifter sides. We'll be going into this fight without claw or fang."

A hush settled over the room at the realization. Their best fighters would be robbed of their greatest assets when they rushed into this suicide mission.

Drew frowned. "And how are we going to guarantee Mackey will be at World's End when we march?" Back in the fight against Ganzorig, they'd been able to draw him out using the device as leverage, but once Kendricks had stolen that, he had everything he wanted.

Sierra let out a sharp exhalation when she scanned around the room. Based on the troubled expression in her eyes when her stare rested on him, she and Dax hadn't teased out a solution to that massive problem yet. However, part of leadership was acting like they held the answers, even when they were clawing ahead in the dark. "Have any suggestions?"

Drew's mind raced. Kendricks had gotten the device to paralyze shifters, he had a horde of loyal Landsliders at his beck and call and he'd crossed off all the names on his hit list.

"What about his parents?" Ally asked, glancing his way.

"You mean the two skeletons he keeps stabbed to the wall as trophies?" Drew lifted an eyebrow. "I don't think they're going to be doing too much reprimanding in that form." He glanced over to the table of shamans. "Unless you lot can raise the dead. If you want the surefire way to draw Mackey Kendricks in the area, his parents were the core of his entire agenda to bring the Tribe and packs tumbling down."

"See this lot?" Ava spoke up from the wall she leaned against. "I'm pretty sure they think we're a miracle delivery system. Press the button, shamanic wonder delivered."

One of the Elders at the table pursed his lips in amusement, but he stood to address the room. "We're not able to resurrect the dead—that sort of spell is taboo for good reason."

Drew's chest sank. Apart from Mackey's parents, nothing else would keep the man in the region if he got even a whiff that forces headed his way. He avoided direct fights, so the full-frontal assault the Tribe planned wouldn't matter in the end. The man would leave everyone to die and start over somewhere new, in true cockroach fashion. Loyalty wasn't in the monster's makeup, no matter how many Landsliders fought and died for him.

One of the other shamans rapped a hand on the table, a slender woman with her beaded hair pulled back into a loose bun of braids that jangled with the movement. "What about summoning their spirits?"

"A good, ol'-fashioned haunting?" Ava's forehead wrinkled. "We could pull it off, but would that be enough to keep him in the area?" The entire table of shamans focused in on Drew. He swallowed under the intense attention, each individual wielding a pack's worth of power.

"Yeah, it would," Drew said, slipping his hands into his pockets. "You have no idea the grip his parents have on him even now. All it took was a pair of monsters to create the biggest threat we've ever seen."

"Right," Dax stepped in, taking the reins again. "So if the shamans can summon some mojo to keep him in the area, then tomorrow, Mackey Kendricks will meet the full power of our packs and allies."

Ava rolled her eyes and several of the shamans murmured in wry tones together. The lot of them were so reclusive he'd never seen this many collected in one space before. Chances were, he might not again.

Sierra lifted her chin as she strode a step past her mate. Even eight months pregnant, the woman radiated a wild ferocity.

"Tomorrow, we face Mackey Kendricks and the Landsliders." Her voice rang out like the tolling of a bell. "Tomorrow, we stop their reign of terror on this region. For too long, he's been working in the shadows, spreading tainted drugs and turning our kind into berserkers. He's roused the Coalition to a fury, their hate affecting both shifters and humans. He's bombed our homes, murdered our packmates and our cubs to tear us apart."

The silence spread in the wake of her words. Drew's skin prickled at the memories of what he'd helped bring to power and part of him wanted to bolt from this room in shame. However, he stayed.

"He's used the gifts passed down to the Tribe to violate our kind in the worst sorts of ways." Her gaze traveled to Raven then to him. Drew swallowed, his throat too dry. Sierra continued, raising a hand as she gestured around the room. "He's tried again and again to ruin us, to reduce our people to chaos. However, tonight, we aren't just pack. We aren't just humans. We aren't just shamans. We're a community, one that tragedy won't break. One that won't falter in the wake of bloodshed.

"Every single one of you, in standing here tonight and standing with us tomorrow morning, is the reason why that monster will not win.

"Tomorrow, we will show him the power of the people he's tried to reduce to nothing. Tomorrow, we fight." Her voice reached a roar, one that reverberated around the room.

For a single moment, silence reigned.

Then the howls began, the roars, the cheers, the hoarse yells filled with all the grief, all the rage and all the injustice they harbored.

Ally's hand slipped into his and she squeezed. She tilted back her head and let out a pure animal roar, the sound of her mountain lion. Drew opened his mouth, needing to be a part of this, needing to be part of something again. Dax's hand rested on his shoulder, and his brother gave him a brisk nod.

The roar ripped from his throat, joining the many voices shaking the planks of this quaint tavern on the side of the highway.

Tomorrow, they went to war.

Chapter Twenty-Three

"Come on, babe," Drew's voice sounded as he rocked her back and forth.

Ally let out a groan. Mornings were already stupid and they'd started extra early today. She tilted to the side and wrapped her arms around his waist. The skin-to-skin contact thrummed through her, stoking her coals to a blaze. Ally reached down to brush her fingers along his cock, stiff with morning wood. Well, if she hadn't been awake before, she was now.

"Down, girl," he responded, placing his hands over hers. He pinned her arms above her head, pressing her against the bed. He tightened his grip around her wrists, and she bucked her hips against his. Drew sank overtop her, the delicious weight of him keeping her from floating right off.

"Tease," she murmured.

Drew brushed his lips along her neck, the featherlight touches coursing through her like whiskey. She ground her hips against him, gliding his stiff length against her core. A moan slipped from her—she couldn't help herself when the mere scent of leather and vanilla turned her on.

Drew released her wrists and slid off her, a wicked grin on his lips. "Now, *that's* being a tease. Come on, up and at 'em, Car Crash. We've got a date with a whole passel of Landslider critters at World's End."

Ally heaved a sigh and rolled to the side, her heart thudding even harder in her chest. She didn't want to go. After all the ups and downs from the past few years, she'd cracked the code, gotten that first taste of bliss, and she didn't want it to end. Whatever happened today at World's End would change the future. She knew that deep in her bones.

Drew reached around to drag her close to him, squeezing her tight. "I don't want to go either," he murmured, brushing his lips against her hair. "I've been fucking terrified of this confrontation from the second I escaped the Landsliders. Mackey doesn't tolerate defectors, and this fight against him — well, back then I didn't have a future to hope for."

Ally's throat tightened. She couldn't lose him. Her grip tensed on his arms, and she surrendered to the solace of his embrace. The heat permeated from the inside out, strength she'd fallen back on so many times.

"You're going to survive this," she said, the words coming out low, hoarse. "No matter what. Even if Mackey gets away, I need you to come back to me."

"Same to you," he murmured, running his fingers through her hair. Ally shuddered against him, the panic clawing fresh wounds into her chest. "My future doesn't exist without you by my side."

Ally turned around to face him, their noses brushing against one another. She placed a kiss on his lips, and he responded in turn. She drank in the taste of him, the mint from his toothpaste, the desperation of departure. His heat wrapped around her like a blanket and she sank into every stolen moment. With each caress of their lips, the gravity descended between them, the knowledge heavy in the air — this might be their last.

Ally broke away first to stare into those beautiful ocean blues, the sort she'd lost herself in once, and the ones she'd forever fall for. "I love you, Drew Williams." The words came out butterfly-wing fragile, a whisper of vulnerability she exposed around few. He was the one person she would descend to the depths with.

"I love you, my mate," he whispered, and her heart splintered.

It wasn't fucking fair. They'd just embarked on their future together only for it to be stolen away. This fight loomed on the horizon, and her scar throbbed with the reminder of just what the Landsliders were capable of.

Drew pulled away first, even though he kept his fingers on her shoulders when he stood. Ally pushed up on the bed, sliding to the edge. The air thickened to the point where she could barely breathe, to the point where the memories between them and the hazy fears for the future rose to such heights that the plummet would destroy her. Ally stood, regardless.

She was the beta of the Silver Springs pack. She was Drew Williams' mate. And she was a part of this beautiful community she'd defend with her life.

"Let's get ready to go."

* * * *

Ally leaned in the backseat of Lucas' Explorer, the heft of the knives weighting her down and the pistol she carried along unfamiliar. The pendant hung heavy around her neck, the cool, smooth malachite resting against her overheated skin. Like she needed a reminder that the connection she'd had since birth had been temporarily severed. While she wore this, she couldn't shift. Her mountain lion wasn't just quiet but snuffed out, like a part of her had vanished.

"All we need is Sierra crammed back here with us and I'm getting some major déjà vu," Ally said, breaking through the quiet.

"I don't know," Lucas said from the driver's seat. "The lack of constant bickering is making me worry."

"Never fear," Lana responded. She turned back to wink at Ally. "Whether they're on or off, they're always fighting."

"I can't help if everything he says incites me to violence," Ally responded, elbowing Drew in the side. He pulled away from his broody staring out of the window to offer her a grin.

"Says the woman with the shortest temper on the planet," he responded, a teasing spark returning to his eyes. "You even butt heads with Lana, who's a freaking Disney Princess in shifter clothing."

"Damn, did I mate to royalty?" Lucas shot back, his tone light even with the loaded pistol tension that descended through the car.

"I call bullshit," Lana responded, lifting a hand in defense. "If I were a Disney Princess, I'd have a whole bushel of critters to help with housework. Either my starter package got lost in the mail, or it's no dice. Speaking of." She halted to pivot around and look at them. "Are you taking permanent residence at Chateau Williams?"

A flush spread across Ally's cheeks as both Drew's and Lana's stares drilled into her. If she were being honest, she'd almost forgotten she didn't live there. The place was such a slice of their past, where she'd left a piece of her heart when they'd split up.

"Didn't realize I was driving with the Spanish Inquisition," Ally muttered, avoiding their stares.

"Is that a dig, *mi amiga*?" Lucas joined in from the driver's end.

She let out an audible groan. "Not you too. These two are already unbearable."

"So unbearable you mated me," Drew reminded, a wicked grin on his lips. Spirits above, her fingers itched to punch him, even as her heart twisted tight. Lana snickered from the front seat, her best friend well aware of the pot she stirred.

"Let's focus on the fight ahead," Ally responded. "I'm not going to go making plans for a future I'm not sure I'll even get to enjoy."

Her words came out blunter than intended, dropping into the car like a bomb. She clutched the ledge, staring out of the window at the looming oaks and pines growing denser the closer they got to World's End State Park. She waited for her nails to shift to claws on instinct, but they remained intact, the familiar tug from her mountain lion missing.

Drew rested a hand on her thigh, the warmth from his palm slicing through the shell of cold surrounding her. His lips turned up with an earnest smile, even though the same fear flickered through those ocean blues.

"Don't worry, babe. Even Mackey Kendricks isn't going to save you from a future of waking up next to my irritating ass every morning," Drew responded, his touch her salvation.

Lana leaned back again. "That pretty much answers my question. Thanks, Drew. My best friend here's allergic to emotions."

"My condolences," Lucas called from the driver's seat. "I've woken up next to that irritating ass in the morning. Tribe funds don't cover separate rooms."

"You guys are idiots," Ally responded, a grin rising to her lips. Even though the fear brushed across her skin like oil, they cracked jokes in the face of the upcoming danger same as always. Lana and Drew had been a part of her life from the beginning, when they were cubs racing through the fields together and muddying their paws. She wouldn't want to head into the final fight with anyone else.

The terrain changed, the road growing narrower as the familiar trees and crags of World's End surrounded them. No matter what the future held, she'd made her mark on this area. She had lived, and cried, and fought throughout this region with these individuals. The side road they'd taken before cropped into view.

"Turn there." Drew gave the directions to Lucas.

Her entire body brimmed with energy, and she kept tugging the pendant around her neck, the same as the ones Drew and Lucas wore. They were part of the final attack force who'd be carving their way into the depths of the lair.

The Explorer bumped up and down along the uneven path bringing them closer and closer to the alternate parking lot. When they'd arrived before, a handful of cars had spread across the space, but today, even with everyone at max carpool capacity, the sheer volume of sedans and SUVs had them parking each other in. Dozens and dozens of cars, from Finn's Challenger to Jer's Jeep, took up space. Packmates milled between the cars and strolled along the fringes of the parking lot, more of their kind than she'd ever seen crammed into one spot before.

Drew peered out of the window and let out a low whistle. "Well, damn," he murmured. "Looks like the other packs showed."

"The ones who agreed to come fight with us?" Ally asked, running a thumb across the handle of the knife strapped to her waist.

Drew shook his head. "Only Cairncross and Underwood agreed to help. Everyone else was either noncommittal or turned us out. But there are at least five alphas out there I never expected to show." He gave her a wink. "Doubtless, they were swayed by my charming personality."

Ally snorted. "More like word spread about the last-minute rescue you and Dax did for the Cairncross pack. Talk is easy, but the two of you showed your commitment back there."

Lucas slid behind two cars and crammed into what might be considered a spot. "Looks like once we're parked, we're here for good. No one's going to be pulling any daring car chases."

"Well, there goes my grand plan of driving through World's End to slam grill-first into Mackey Kendricks," Drew drawled. He'd been assembling his armor piece by piece ever since they'd left his bedroom. Ally had done the same.

"Poor baby," she responded. "You'll have to make do with shooting him right in his stupid face."

Lana let out a laugh, pure sunbeams, and cracked her door open. Once the sound echoed through the car, heaviness settled into Ally's bones. Approaching the lair the first time had been terrifying, but this attack—

her mind couldn't even broach the consequences or she'd falter.

The moment she stepped out of the car, voices filtered her way, some familiar, some foreign, but all of them the sounds of their army. She scanned across the crowded lot. What seemed like chaos before fast grew organized. Raven followed Sierra's lead as the two loped around barking orders — though, mostly Sierra — and directing individuals into different units. Every member of this force would be part of a squad to disperse the attack, and every squad of shifters needed humans mixed in, on the high chance that the Landsliders utilized the device.

Lana and Lucas stepped off to the side of his Explorer. Based on the quiet murmurs and the glossy shine in Lana's eyes, they were saying their goodbyes. Lucas would be joining them on the Mackey Kendricks Death Squad while Lana was on team healer.

"Let's head closer to the woods," Drew murmured, tension simmering through the air. His features darkened when he focused on the narrow pines that loomed before them, and she didn't miss how his fingers skimmed across the thigh with his Landslider mark. Unlike the other Landsliders, with the help of Ava, Drew had broken free of the compulsion — for good.

Dax stood on the opposite side of the clearing next to Jer, so she nudged Drew in their direction.

"I'm going out of my mind with this thing," Jer called to them, lifting the pendant around his neck. "Three seconds away from ripping it off and taking the risk."

Dax gave him the side-eye and tipped the brim of his baseball cap. "Streaky, I'm not going to carry your ass if you go fainting in the middle of the battle. Keep the pendant on."

Ally lifted her hand over her eyes to scan between Dax and Drew. "Do my eyes deceive me? Is that both of the Williams brothers going to battle together? If someone told me this a year ago, I'd say they'd popped five too many Prozac."

"What can I say? Nothing brings people together like war," Drew responded.

Dax cracked a grin and Ally's chest uncoiled, a tightness she didn't realize she'd been holding on to. The day she'd reclaimed her relationship with Drew, she had prepared to fight fang and claw for it, but watching the rift between the brothers begin to heal soothed her more than a cold seltzer after a long shift. She would fight for her mate, but she respected Dax. The fact that they'd talked out their past, that they'd begun to heal gave her hope.

All they needed to do was survive today.

Lucas approached, a grim look in his eyes, while Akio and Jess followed close behind. Finn and Navi raced in after them, skidding to a sudden halt as they reached their circle.

"I won that race fair," Finn said, his shoulders heaving up and down. A boyish grin spread on his face and his eyes crinkled.

Navi crooked an eyebrow, her breaths coming in even. "You keep telling yourself that." Even though the woman emanated cool and composed, her mouth quirked in amusement.

"This is everyone, right?" Lucas asked. Each member of their group wore the green and silver pendants around their necks and more weapons than sense. This was the first fight Ally had gotten in since she was a cub where she'd be operating without the use of her fangs or claws. The last time she'd watched one had been Drew and Dax's final face-off in the ring.

Raven slipped behind Jer, a searching look in her eyes. He slipped his hand into hers, and he tugged her off to the side. Before they'd taken two paces, his lips descended upon hers with the hungry ferocity of departure.

Sierra strode up to stand beside Dax. "The squads are ready to mobilize. Once your crew gets a head start, I'll send them off after. They'll draw the attention from you guys." She met Dax's gaze and Ally's chest twisted tight. She couldn't imagine being separated from her mate in a fight like this.

"Come back to me," Sierra said, the command in her tone unshakable. She slipped her hands around his neck and pressed in for a kiss goodbye. Dax's grip on Sierra was possessive and his kiss the sort to burn down a forest. The two alphas shared the sort of steadfast love that had only grown stronger with time, one that had managed to unite two packs. One that that managed to summon an army.

Drew's fingers threaded through hers. Ally gripped tight to his hand as she glanced to him. His somber eyes reflected the task they faced. After everything they'd been through, everything the packs had faced through the past year, they'd reached this precipice.

"Stay safe," Sierra called out to their crew, her eyes flashing. "And kill the bastard for me." With that, the Red Rock alpha strode away, Raven following close behind.

Lucas stepped to the forefront of the group. "Time to march."

Chapter Twenty-Four

Last time, Drew had sneaked through these woods. Today, he ran.

They vaulted through the trail he and Ally had uncovered on their search for an entrance to the lair. He followed the path his memory had carved. All eight members of their hit squad barreled through, launching at a full charge. Guaranteed, they'd run into Landsliders in these woods. However, the rest of the troops would handle Mackey's expendables. Their packs would be causing enough noise and clamor to draw attention away from them.

His heart thundered, and he waited for the normal tug from his mountain lion, like a dog yanking at a leash, yet it never came. Without the constant presence, he felt hollow, even if the effects only lasted as long as they wore these pendants.

The thud of their steps echoed through the woods, which had grown eerily quiet. The normal rustle of squirrels, the trill of bluebirds and the *thunk-thunk-thunk* of the woodpeckers all silenced. The animals must've sensed the sheer mass of shifters arriving to this state park and fled. Not like he blamed them.

Ally raced neck and neck beside him, her streaming golden hair soaked in sunbeams. Ferocity sparked in her eyes. Even if they didn't flash bronze, the thrill of the hunt remained. No matter how this spell severed them from their mountain lion sides, they were raised and honed by their beasts, an integral part that bled into their human forms. As much as he hadn't wanted her in this sort of danger, he couldn't imagine fighting alongside anyone else in the final confrontation against Mackey Kendricks.

His senses dulled compared to when he tapped into his mountain lion, noticing every snapped branch or rustle in the bushes. Drew's fingers brushed against the handle of one of the many knives he'd slipped into the band around his waist. The shift in the cool winds prickled against his skin, the only reason he caught a scent.

"Shifters ahead," he called out.

Fur flashed up, the russet and black visible under the steady beams of the sun.

Three coyotes raced for them at top speed, kicking up dirt and leaves behind them. Their eyes flashed with territorial aggression—Landsliders. Drew flexed his hands, but when the claws didn't emerge on reflex, he reached for the knives at his belt. The snicks of blades being drawn sounded all around him, as well as the click of safeties turned off when Lucas and Dax drew their pistols.

The coyotes soared through the area with finesse bred from familiarity, dodging past trees and sailing over roots. Drew's whole body mutinied to reach out for the connection to his mountain lion.

Lucas lifted his pistol and aimed. He squeezed the trigger and the bark resounded through the clearing. The bullet zipped toward one of the coyotes who attempted to swerve. Too late. The shot tunneled into the beast's leg and he stumbled.

"Charge in," Jess commanded, rushing forward with a dagger in each hand. From behind, footsteps rumbled louder and louder as Sierra mobilized their forces. Soon, their army of shifters, cops and shamans would be catching up.

Drew burst ahead, his calves squeezing tight. He raced for the coyote shifters who hadn't faltered. The beasts moved in a blur, with a speed he envied. He tightened his grip on the blade, the hilt heavy in his hand — if he couldn't have his claws, this would have to suffice. Ally surged ahead of him, faster, like she'd always been, her ponytail streaming behind her. She bolted for the coyote on the far right and Drew followed.

Those fangs gleamed as the coyote sailed for them, the claws flexed for maximum impact. Ally hunched, her blade out.

Drew pivoted around to the other side.

The coyote sailed above her, and she lifted her blade. Ally cut a vicious slash with the knife, the blade glinting like silver under the sunlight.

Crimson followed.

The coyote rebounded to circle around with animal quickness, faster than she ever could in this form. But before the beast's fangs snapped forward to clamp onto her arm, Drew attacked.

His blade descended, the tip snagging along the haunches with a wet slice. The coyote didn't whip around at the attack in defense, smarter than most of his brethren. However, Drew bought her a second. Ally dodged away right as gray fangs snapped for her throat this time. The coyote landed on all four paws, even as drops of blood speckled the grass beneath them.

A wet whump sounded from beside them, followed by a human grunt. Drew couldn't afford a second to search for the source. He trusted the competence of their crew.

Behind them, the clamor of shoes crunching over twigs and the soft thump of paws echoed through the air. Another shot rang through the clearing. Whether it was Dax or Lucas, he had the feeling they hadn't missed. Other Landsliders bounded past them, not bothering to engage in the fight as bears, wolves and humans barreled in the direction of the army they'd assembled.

Drew caught Ally's gaze as the coyote stalked toward her again, on a mission to take his mate down. Her muscles tensed in her fighting stance, and she twitched at her knife hand. *Perfect bait.*

The coyote loped for her other side to avoid the pendulum swing of her knife. Too bad the guy didn't pay attention to Drew.

Inches remained.

Drew vaulted forward, springing off the soles of his feet to sail through the air. The coyote lunged for Ally right as Drew landed behind him. The tip of his knife sank into the back, plunging past fur and gristle. Drew dragged down. A sharp howl ripped from the coyote and Dax whipped the muzzle in his direction.

Ally dragged the blade across the shifter's throat.

Blood spattered across the earth, droplets flecking across her tan arms. Drew tensed, his blade at the ready for retaliation. However, the beast dropped to the ground and the blood from the open wounds fast formed a pool.

Dax strode forward, pistol in hand and a hurricane expression on his face, followed close behind by Jer, whose knife dripped with blood. Navi and Finn prowled after them. Ally nodded to Drew before she skipped ahead, while he stepped in line with Lucas.

"The more time we waste scrapping with the low-tier Landsliders, the more time we give Mackey to escape," Drew said, shaking the drops of blood off the edge of his blade.

Lucas nodded, a grim look carved into his features. He cast a glance behind. Landsliders had vaulted past them while they'd engaged and those forces would head to greet their main crew. Already, he caught the flash of fur in the distance as squads of Landsliders bolted through the trees in the direction of the clamor. The sounds of their approaching army of shifters, humans and shamans gave enough of an indicator that their forces weren't far behind.

"We'll need you and Ally to lead us there," Lucas said, meeting his eyes. He understood the risk — they'd be the easy bullseyes of any attacks. However, Drew had known the danger from the moment he'd accepted his place on their strike team. Even after he'd begun to heal the rift with his brother and even after he and Ally had finally clicked into place the way he'd always hoped, he couldn't let Mackey Kendricks roam free any longer.

Drew jogged ahead, tapping Ally on the elbow as he passed her by. Her eyes crinkled. She took the cue, loping up beside him.

Katherine McIntyre

"From here out, this is a flat run," Drew said to Dax. "Ally and I will lead the charge. No stopping for any disruptions."

His brother tipped the brim of his baseball cap in acknowledgment. "Got it, man—though I'm not opposed to snagging any clear shots."

Ally bounced on her soles, her lithe muscles flexing as she prepared for the run. Drew stepped beside her.

"Ready for this?" he asked. Her eyes gleamed with the same churn of excitement and terror threatening to drag him under.

Ally flashed a blinder of a grin, all bravado. "First one to the lair wins."

At that, she took off.

A smile tore across his face when he leapt forward. For a single moment, the fear slicing ragged lines across his insides melted away. For a single moment, the years vanished and he and Ally were six years old again, racing through the forest at top speed, spurred by the cool shadows, the warm bursts of sunbeams and the feel of packed dirt beneath their feet.

Drew's calves pumped as he tried to match pace with her. No matter how many folks tried to claim the title, Ally was the fastest among their combined packs. His girl had always been a runner. Drew lagged a few paces behind, but together they vaulted past the cragged trees, past the moss-covered stones and past the patches of grass and clover that had just begun to grow. The sharp spring air whistled in his ears, plastering across his cheeks. He sucked in the sweetness, sinking into the ferocity of the hunt. Even cut off from his mountain lion, some instincts had bred into his bones.

A group of five humans bolted toward them, carrying a familiar silver box in their hands. The device.

250

Fuck. He needed to stop them, tear into them, anything to keep them from reaching their destination. The device would knock out over half of their army with a single press of a button.

But the Landsliders raced away from the lair with it because once activated, the buzzing would knock out their forces too. Which meant the shifters were protecting their stronghold. Drew caught motion by the trees — wolves threaded through, focusing on the human squad, which meant Mackey was keeping the bearers protected.

Drew began to veer away from the crew, as did Lucas. They needed to stay focused.

Finn, Navi and Jer continued running forward, as if they planned on hurling themselves in front of the humans.

They hadn't made it five paces when Navi let out a bone-shaking howl.

She dropped to the ground.

The group of humans swerved away from their group and the throng of six or so wolves sprang out from the trees, running close behind them. No matter how much he wanted the device out of their hands, stopping now would give Mackey the chance to escape. Drew joined the others who crowded around Navi.

The incriminating bear trap shone with the gloss of silver. He would've guessed as much even if he didn't see the way it caused her flesh to sizzle or how her palms came up scorched after she shunted it from her ankle.

"Are you okay, babe?" Finn asked, kneeling in front of her. Concern gleamed in his eyes.

Navi grunted. "Just dandy. We shouldn't have tried to stonewall the humans. We already planned for this eventuality." Finn looped an arm around her shoulder, which she accepted while she ignored the pain creasing her forehead. She looked up at Drew and Lucas. "Lead the way."

Drew nodded and launched into a flat run. He couldn't stop now.

They continued racing through the woods, past the dips in the earth and the slope of the valleys that led to trickling streams. The sun slipped through the trees overhead, the beams glinting across his skin. His gaze flicked to the markings carved into the bases of the trees, the trail they'd followed last time to lead them to the lair.

They'd only been racing through the woods for a couple of minutes before buzzing hummed through the entire woods. Startled birds flew from the trees en masse, clustering across the sky in swarms. Even the ground beneath them reverberated with the force of the device.

His packmates would be knocked out and their throats slit before they had a chance to defend themselves. Every ounce of him longed to run back and protect them. Lana would be fighting there, and Sierra with his niece or nephew. The sound quaked through the trees, trembled the leaves, and the oily residue of magic followed. Spirits, he needed to know they were okay.

Before, the sound increased in volume until his mind rioted, his body raged and his mountain lion fought him tooth and claw to burst free. His pendant glowed with the effects of keeping his beast restrained, the stone warm as it thudded against his chest. This time, the sound faded away, and not even a buzz lingered in his mind.

They kept running.

His worries reached a deafening roar, but he clenched his jaw and raced forward. Ally glanced back, as if she might catch some glimpse of the armies they'd left behind. Some sign that they were okay.

He caught a moving blur from the far left between the pines. Drew guided their group to the right. More Landsliders surged through this forest in the direction of the explosion. Now that Mackey had leveled the playing field, he'd sent out the rest of his shifter troops. The bastard was smart. Drew only hoped and prayed that the humans and shamans could hold them off until the shifters woke back up.

He'd seen the alternative.

The trees around here grew more familiar, and once he spotted the first rocky crags of those stone stacks, an unsettling foreboding swept over him. This was it. After all the time he'd spent running from Mackey Kendricks, after the way he'd kept his distance because the memories dropped like bombs, the sight of the entrance to his lair struck Drew dumb. Last time, the sound of the man's voice in the hallway had frozen him on the spot.

Today, at last, they'd take their fight to him.

Ally slowed her steps, minding each footfall to not blindly crunch over twigs or rattle around stones. Drew followed suit, focusing on a quiet tread, same as the rest of their squad. They carved past the massive oaks dominating this forest and headed for the tall stacks of stones. Even though they'd found the side entrance to the lair, these woods crawled with Landsliders who wouldn't hesitate to tear them apart.

The device had scared off the rest of the wildlife, leaving the woods hushed with a resonant quiet that crawled across his skin. He approached the massive crag they'd found the lever on before and Ally sidled up to him.

"The man must've spent an exorbitant amount on contractors," Lucas murmured upon approach. He leaned against the stone, spreading his palm across the surface.

Drew snorted. "No wonder he resorted to selling drugs."

"The terror of the East Coast is just a misunderstood shifter with a redecorating habit he can't quit," Dax added in with a smirk, tugging at the end of his baseball cap.

"Right, and I'm a wolf," Ally muttered.

Drew's fingers latched onto the seam he'd found before to the side entrance of Mackey Kendricks' lair.

A pair of growls lit the air.

Of course, Mackey Kendricks wouldn't have left this area unguarded. Without the connection to his mountain lion, he missed the changes of the scents in the breeze, the slight crunch telltale. He turned to face the pair of guards.

Mackey had sent his heavy hitters.

The pair who approached from around the side of the massive rock face couldn't be classified as wolves anymore. One of them had the same mottled patchwork of stone as the other mutants he'd seen, while the other looked like the one they'd fought back in the caves, with a tangle of thick, choking roots moving around like they had a life of their own.

Drew's fingers slipped to the latch they'd found before, the door to open the lair. They didn't have the time to fight, not if they wanted to get to Mackey

Kendricks. But these beasts wouldn't just let them enter.

"Finn and I will handle them," Navi called out, her voice echoing through the clearing. The shortest woman in their crew emanated enough fierceness to bring them all down. "My leg's useless to keep running, but I've got plenty of magic to burn." Her gaze met his, then switched to Lucas. "Go."

Finn took the first step toward them, an excited gleam in his eyes. "Leave the fun job to us."

Jer clapped a hand on his shoulder, his gaze serious. "Stay safe." Finn nodded in response as the growls grew louder, the wolves approaching step by careful step. Those deadened eyes glowed.

Finn let out a whoop, tossed his pendant to the ground and vaulted toward them.

Drew found the latch and pressed down. The door to the lair slid open.

"Hurry," he barked out to the others. Ally ducked in first and he slid behind her. The others slipped in one by one before the door ground shut, leaving Finn and Navi behind.

Chapter Twenty-Five

The last time they'd entered the Landsliders' lair was permanent nightmare fuel. One escaped breath and they would've been sentenced. Yet, back then Ally and Drew had been scouting. This time, they were here to hunt. To kill.

The darkness and the stench of this stale place suffused through Ally. Cut off from her mountain lion, she didn't catch half of the normal animal scents or the clear trail of the Landsliders. Drew stepped past, his fingers brushing against hers in the process. She followed him toward the sallow beams spilling through the entrance of the corridor ahead.

Already, their crew had been reduced to seven. Akio, Jess, Jer, Dax and Lucas strode close behind them, maintaining a static silence. The steady pound of her heart echoed in her ears and her skin vibrated from the tension. They needed to get to Mackey Kendricks, no matter the cost.

Ally sucked in a sharp breath when they reached the corridor they'd crept through on their first arrival. Today, they marched.

The doors lining the hallway lay open, devoid of the shifters who roamed these halls. The shuffles and the steps they could hear came from the sections deeper inside the lair they hadn't explored while they'd been searching for a way out.

Ally's gaze lingered on Mackey's shrine when they passed by, the bones of his dead parents still suspended by spears through the skulls. Her heart thundered. After they'd uncovered the room, filth had clung to her like a coat of oil. She hated sharing anything in common with the monster, even loathing for the parent who'd raised her, the one who'd inflicted wounds she struggled every day to erase.

Except, everyone had wounds. Each member of their pack bore the weight of tragedy. Yet, they took those strands of their pain and their past and began to weave. Together, they created a magnificent tapestry stronger and more vibrant than alone. She might still struggle with her past and hit some gravel roads, same as Drew, but they'd managed to carve space for their own healing after all these years of running. Their flesh and blood might have hurt them, but they'd found a family and a home to belong to in their packs. This community, this was what they fought for.

Footsteps pounded louder from the opposite end of the hallway, but their squad marched onward, unfaltering.

Lucas caught up with them and turned to Drew. "Can you sense Mackey in here?"

Drew nodded, pressing the spot on his thigh where the Landsliders' mark had been carved into him. He might've severed the compulsion with the help of Ava, but the blood connection still existed. "He's deeper inside."

"Then we'll slash and burn our way to him," Dax announced from behind.

They were past hiding. Past running. The sconces lit the way in increasing intervals like an airplane runway, and the march of footsteps reverberated through the hall. Mackey and his Landsliders could've scented them out the moment they entered, but Ally would bet her lucky pair of cutting shears the bastard hadn't shown up for an in-person meet and greet.

No, Mackey Kendricks would try to run.

They followed the curve of the hallway to where it emptied out to a massive atrium. Bumpy stone walls had been painted the creamy white of milk, same with the ceiling of this underground lair. Fluorescent bulbs lit the circular space, casting off-hue beams. Where the side rooms along the way displayed a cozier, more personal feel, this emanated the cool lines and chrome fixtures of a place of business. Glass rooms separated out the space, one filled with an array of chairs around a table. The other was coated from top to bottom in painted gray markings, featuring an altar inside strewn with herbs and stones. On the far end of the room, glass double doors led deeper inside.

The moment their squad stepped into the entryway, at least a dozen sets of eyes flashed on them. Landsliders had been waiting here, and they fast assembled. Four shifters were in human form while an array of bears, wolves, coyotes and mountain lions prowled through the room.

Two wolves, a coyote and a bear loped toward those double doors led by a tall man with raven-black hair and Tribe markings down his arms. He didn't need to turn around for Ally to know. The mere sight of him was enough to coat Ally's skin in acid, to remember the icy grip he'd claimed on her mind back in the fight against Ganzorig.

Mackey Kendricks was heading further inside. The doors clicked shut behind them. The rest of the Landsliders were left to kill or be killed, because their illustrious leader wasn't concerned about their survival.

"He's going to get away," Drew murmured low, his hands balling into fists.

They couldn't let that happen.

Dax clapped a hand on his brother's shoulder. He glanced to Ally and Drew. "I've been hankering for a fight. Go on ahead." Ally's chest tugged, but she didn't speak up. Even though she wanted to leave with her mate, her place in battle was by her alpha's side.

The bear let out a roar and began to charge in their direction. Dax surged forward to meet it midway.

"I'll keep an eye on this bastard," Jer said, slapping her on the back and offering a meaningful glance. The thread of hesitation snapped and Ally pressed her lips tight together before nodding. Jer ripped off the pendant and flung it to the ground with a clink. He hadn't taken two steps forward before the shift overtook him, his bones mutating and the fur sprouting across his skin. His war cry fast-changed into a howl.

Drew had already started to race across the atrium, his gaze focused and his moves steady as stone. Ally bolted after him. Lucas loped alongside her, determination in his knit eyebrows and golden stare. Behind them, Akio followed Jer's example, and in place of the short Japanese man, a tawny lion emerged with a thick mane, massive paws, and enough height to hulk over the competition.

One of the shifters in human form lifted a pistol, his finger slipping to the trigger. The bastard aimed for Drew. *No, no, no.* She needed to be faster. Faster. Her calves burned. She needed to reach him.

The bark of a pistol reverberated through the air. Ally's heart lurched.

The Landslider took a step forward, the gun still raised. Red bloomed across his chest. Lucas lowered his pistol, his gaze dark and steady. The Landslider collapsed to the ground.

She raced past the glass rooms, closer and closer to the double doors on the opposite side. Behind her, Dax shifted into his mountain lion form to join Jer's russet wolf against one of the bears. Their remaining squad were outnumbered seven to three in here yet Jess loped close behind her.

The four of them charged for the doors. Mackey Kendricks would die today.

Each one of them knew what fate they risked when they'd agreed to be on this squad. At the end of the day, she, Dax and Jer couldn't even face Mackey in a direct fight. They couldn't battle his compulsion, and he could order them to slit their throats or kill their own packmates.

Drew was the one with the pulse on Mackey's location. He was the one who'd be facing the monster with or without her. The thought dragged her to crevasse depths even as her sneakers echoed against the cold stone floor.

The double glass doors swung back and forth from the force of the shifters who'd passed through them. A lion's roar reverberated through the air, Akio's rage permeating every pore of this place in a wall of sound. Drew burst through the double doors in hot pursuit of the shifters who'd vanished through mere moments ago. Ally sped ahead, the breaths snagging in her throat as she caught up with him.

Ally slammed through the doors and stopped dead in her tracks.

The hallway stretched out before them, lighter and brighter than the one they'd entered through. A door lay open at the end, leading to what looked like another large room. Chances were, it contained one of the many exits built into this stronghold. The four shifters paced along the hallway, on guard, and the frosted sconces along the way enhanced the sharpness of their claws and the glint of their fangs.

However, they weren't who froze her blood. Here he stood, after all the time they'd spent chasing after him, in the flesh and bone.

Mackey Kendricks.

The man's thick, dark eyebrows rivaled Lucas', and his eyes burned with a confidence that rallied humans and shifters alike to his side. His sort of conviction had led to the fires raging through this region, to the countless bodies dropping to the floor and to her family, her friends, her packmates taking their final breaths. His features bled with a nobility the bastard didn't deserve, one the murderer, the traitor to their kind hadn't earned.

Being in the same room as this man sucked all the air out. Ally's nails bit into her palms, and the need to be connected to her mountain lion pounded louder and louder. She wrapped a hand around her pendant, ready to tear it off.

"Long time no see, kids," Mackey drawled, his gaze landing first on Drew, then on her.

The Landslider they'd seen in the mini-mart appeared through the doorway closest to Mackey.

"Boss, the route's clear."

"Oh, hell no." The words ripped from Drew's throat. His growl vibrated in the air between them.

Mackey turned to them and tipped two fingers in their direction. "Then, I'm off. Landsliders," he addressed his crew, the tone of command shifting with the gravity of compulsion she'd become well-versed in. "Stop them from following—at any cost."

He threw a bag, which sailed toward the four Landsliders. The moment it smacked against the ground, the drawstring opened and the powdery contents poured out. Ally didn't have to guess hard at the white snow that spilled onto the floor. The Landsliders lapped the substance up, taking the edge their leader forced upon them even if the shamanic-laced meth cost them their lives and sanity. The control he exerted with those simple words left a graveyard mark. This. This was why they fought him today.

The bear, two wolves and the coyote whipped toward them, unable to resist the compulsion of their leader. They charged.

Mackey was going to escape. All their careful plans, each member of this squad who'd stayed behind to give them a chance, and the packmates who'd fought and bled scattered all across World's End like fallen leaves—it would all be for nothing.

Drew leaned forward and pressed his lips to hers. The kiss only lasted a second, but the full weight of each fight, each touch and each scar they'd left descended upon her. Yet beyond the pain and anguish resided an ocean-deep love. In the split second, the future sprawled out before them, all blinding sunbeams, hesitant spring breezes and endless fields of wildflowers.

Then the connection severed.

Their goodbye had arrived.

Ally couldn't voice the words, but neither could Drew. The single look he cast sufficed, heartbreak, fear and a faint, flickering hope.

Drew bolted forward, his calves flexing and his soles slamming against the ground. Those meth-addled shifters would tear him apart, forced to annihilate anyone who tried to pass. Ally's job was making sure her mate made it through. Jess plunged forward paces behind Drew, veering toward the big bear to divert attention. The Tribe member flung her pendant to the floor and began to shift into her jaguar form.

Ally couldn't follow him on this chase, but one person stood a chance. If Drew took on Mackey Kendricks alone, he would die. That was a guarantee.

Her gaze snared on Lucas. "Help him," she pleaded, not bothering to hide her desperation.

Lucas nodded and took off after Drew.

Ally ripped the pendant from her neck and flung it to the side wall. All the numbness, the haze that had settled over her while she wore it vanished. At once, her mountain lion flexed her claws inside and she could feel her girl snarl in her chest.

Ally tossed caution to the wind and let her mountain lion take the lead. Already, the effects of the tainted meth had begun to contort the remaining Landsliders. Their eyes grew redder and the way they pawed the ground and paced became more erratic.

Two wolves leapt after Drew. A coyote tried to snap at Lucas who bare-hand slapped him aside, the *thunk* echoing through the room.

Ally shifted from two feet to four paws and the moment she hit the ground, she loped in the direction of the wolves. In this form, her senses exploded to life. The stench of the Landsliders grew a thousand times stronger as well as the tinny tone of the magic laced through the meth that lay scattered on the floor. The metal and cave dust made her nose twitch. She raced so fast her fur ruffled from the breezes she created. The scrape of claws to stone grew louder, as did the shuffle of footsteps from the other room while Mackey attempted his escape.

Drew ran fast, but the Landsliders in their animal forms were faster.

The first wolf leapt for his back.

Ally burst forward. They might be quick, but she was quicker. She wouldn't let her mate down.

Before the wolf landed, Ally flexed her claws, snagging into the beast's back leg. The wolf's front paws crashed down harder, throwing her off-balance. The moment's hesitation gave Drew the inch to escape. When the other one lunged for him, Ally rammed into the beast headfirst. The solid blow sent him flying.

Drew reached the door. His gaze flashed her way for a single moment, those blue eyes holding the wishes they'd murmured in secret, the ones she held close. Drew ducked through the frame.

Before the wolf could follow, Ally threw herself in the way. Fangs snapped at her, too close to dodge. The tips sank in past fur, and Ally winced when she tried to step back. She tugged out of the grip even as blood welled to the surface.

Lucas barreled toward her at top speed, the coyote hot on his tracks. She couldn't let these shifters pass.

The two wolves tried to lunge for Lucas, but Jess launched into the air. She came crashing down onto the wolves, claws first. He vaulted past them and through the open doorway to follow Drew.

The coyote raced toward her, determined to leap past. No fucking way. Ally would hold the line.

Chapter Twenty-Six

The moment Drew stepped inside the room, his heart roared louder than the falls of Ricketts Glen. His bones buzzed and his veins rioted. Every remaining scrap of sanity told him to run.

Harry stood by a cage on the far side of the room, fiddling with the latch. One of the mutants paced behind the bars, a half-coyote glowing with encrusted coals close to combustion. Copper piping stretched overhead in this room, leading to a boiler in the opposite corner. On the far wall lay a massive iron door deadbolted shut. Guaranteed, that was the way outside. Mackey Kendricks strode across the room with his back to them. The casualness to his gait suggested he never found them to be a threat in the first place.

Drew had spent his entire life feeling weak.

First, at the hands of his father. Whatever blows Williams, Sr. dealt, Drew had never been big enough, skilled enough. He had never been strong enough to fight against the abuse, too small, too weak.

And he'd never even got a chance to step out from his father's shadow. The day dear old Dad had enlisted him in the Landsliders, Mackey Kendricks had violated Drew's mind again and again. Every time he'd tried to resist, Mackey had doled out harsher commands. Every time, he'd been forced into committing some atrocity that had haunted him along with the others, another failure to stitch onto his quilt.

Never. Strong. Enough.

Yet as he stared at the monster who walked away from him, at the man who'd held callous court over his nightmares for months, for the first time Drew stood tall. Even though his legs quaked and even though his instincts screamed, he clenched his jaw and took those steps forward.

The oath he'd sworn the day the Tribe had extricated him from the Landsliders echoed in his mind now, the mantra he'd repeated until it became his sole mode of surviving each excruciating day.

Kill Mackey Kendricks or die trying.

Except the oath wasn't what pushed his legs now. He'd stopped drinking from a poisoned well and the first sip of clear, pure water had tasted a lot like hope. Drew marched for the Red Rock and Silver Springs packs who'd fought for them throughout these forests today. Drew marched for the kids like Eli, left facing the harsh realities of life too soon. Drew marched for Ally Coleman, his mate.

Another pair of steps thundered in behind him and Drew spun around.

Lucas raced into the room, determination burning in his gaze. "Don't think you're doing this alone, brother."

Drew shook out his fist and warmth rushed through him. Despite everything that had shattered and broken,

Drew managed to forge new connections. Even though his past had robbed him of the family he'd known, the new terrain hadn't mutated into the wasteland he'd once feared.

At the sound of Lucas' voice, Mackey Kendricks turned around.

"I should've figured the two of you wouldn't stop." Those dark eyes gleamed as Kendricks stared at them. He lifted an eyebrow. "Come on now, Williams, what did you expect would happen here? We've seen this story play out again and again, and I'll be honest, the struggle is getting dull." He stared at Drew, his eyes gaining that hypnotizing quality, focused, the way they always got when he used compulsion. The air tensed. "Kill him."

Drew's throat dried, his entire body braced for the tug of the command. His muscles clenched tight. He waited for the eventuality that Ava's spell had failed and the man would break him once more.

Nothing happened.

The overriding force, the smothering, violating sensation that had once choked out reason as his body acted on someone else's accord—none of it rose up now. Heat pricked his eyes and relief washed through him like a summer storm. A giddy thrill surged in his chest.

Drew took another step forward, his chin lifted and his gaze focused solely on Mackey Kendricks.

"Try again, asshole."

In the entirety of Drew's time in the Landsliders, he had seen Mackey Kendricks cocky, assured and confident. The surprise flashing across his eyes when his thick eyebrows drew together was a first.

"Kill him." Mackey repeated the words even louder this time, echoing through the room. Not like they did a damn thing. Ava had succeeded. Mackey Kendricks couldn't control him anymore. A snick sounded from the cage's padlock which hit the ground with a thump and Harry backed away from the cage.

Drew pulled off his pendant and he strode toward the monster responsible for so much suffering and so much pain. He clutched that stone and flung it back behind him. The connection that had been stifled returned in full force, like an epinephrine shot vibrating all the way through his body to his fingers, to his toes. His mountain lion leapt to the fore, his nails turning into claws on reflex.

Lucas raced past him with that straight-arrow gaze on the door. If Mackey Kendricks wanted to leave, he'd have to get through the two of them.

Drew's fangs slipped out before he could help himself, his mountain lion battering in his chest and begging to be free.

"Do you really think you'll be able to stop us?" Kendricks asked, returning to the languid tone Drew loathed. His eyes gleamed in amusement and bile corroded Drew's throat. "Once I get out of here, I'll just rebuild. I can always find more Landsliders, but out on those fields today, your packs are getting slaughtered."

Drew's jaw flexed and his claws scraped against his palms. Even now, the bastard didn't make a move to bolt, pace or indulge in any nervous behaviors. Mackey Kendricks never got ruffled, not when he always, always held a royal flush. Drew caught the twitch of Kendricks' shoulders and his glance to Lucas, as if the man evaluated how fast he could get past him.

"Too bad you're not leaving this building alive," Lucas responded, his voice low, like granite scraping shale. His eyes sparked with a chasm-level ferocity he'd seen before in the man, one he felt take light inside him.

"Harry, kill them," Mackey intoned, the pressure in his words.

At once, the Landslider began to sink into the shift. The cage door creaked open and the coyote vaulted out. Between him and Lucas, he happened to be the closest target for both the bastards. Lucky him.

The coyote was faster, fueled by hysteria and whatever shamanic mojo scrambled the beast's brains in the first place. Drew sank into his shift like a free-fall off a plane, knowing his mountain lion was eager to take the reins. The coals along the coyote's skin glowed, sparks hitting the ground to flicker out as the creature loped forward. Drew's clothes tore, and the knives clattered to the ground. Not like he needed them anymore—he'd face this final confrontation with his claws and fangs.

He lowered onto all four paws, his senses adapting to the shift. The shadows grew sharper, lines precise enough to slice, and the stench of Mackey Kendricks became even stronger. The smoky, rich scent of cloves burned into his memories from his time bonded to the bastard, and the permanent mark carved into his skin throbbed.

The coyote sped up, closing the distance between them. Drew crouched, his back legs tensing as he prepared to spring. The coals would scorch his fur in an instant. Harry had already shifted, and the black bear loped in his direction under Mackey's order.

Inches away.

Brimstone emanated from the coyote, and corpse breath blasted in his face. Drew didn't budge. When outnumbered, cleverness was the only way to win the day. The coyote's teeth snapped for his flank.

Drew didn't move until the tips of those fangs scraped against his fur. He vaulted forward, the beast's teeth leaving a slight graze along his side. He soared toward Harry, claws at the ready.

The bear kept his head down when he charged, and the burly guy had a slower response time. Drew took ruthless advantage.

He landed on top of Harry with a thud that trembled through him, his claws sinking deep into the flesh with a squelch. Before the bear could snap that ugly mug up to take a gander, Drew lunged in, fangs-first. He gripped tight to the ear and yanked. The flesh tore and the ear flew off to hit the ground with a wet slap. Harry's howl echoed to the ceiling, reverberating around the piping. Drew launched to the side right as the coyote barreled toward him too fast to stop.

Drew tumbled to the ground and the beast's hot coals brushed against his flank. His fur singed and the sizzle of his flesh hit a moment later, the pain enough to numb his teeth. Harry rebounded, and the bear was pissed. He lumbered Drew's way, those big paws slapping the ground with heavy footfalls. Drew continued to roll until he swerved right out of the bastard's lane. He sprang up on four paws and whipped around to face both opponents.

From behind him, a familiar tiger's roar split the air. Lucas had shifted. To Drew's shock, so had Mackey Kendricks.

The man rarely shifted, preferring to sever the animal side of him as often as possible. Besides, he couldn't bark commands in that form, losing the precious, precious tool of his compulsion. However, Mackey Kendricks must be feeling more desperate than he was letting on if he'd shifted to face off against his old Tribemate. The man morphed into a hulking great wolf with fur the color of midnight in winter, far bigger than any he'd seen in the Red Rock pack. Those yellow eyes glowed like fluorescent lights.

The coyote landed in front of Drew with a whump, dragging him back to the present. Those jaws snapped and fangs sank deep into his front leg. Drew fought the reflex to yank away, despite the way his nerves screamed. Instead, he slammed headfirst into the beast. His skull met the mutant's with a resounding thud, and his skin sizzled when he caught one of the coals. The coyote let go. Drew yanked his front leg back, even though the pain throbbed.

He needed to take one of them out, fast, and Harry made for an easier target.

Drew swerved to dodge the snap of the coyote's jaws, the fetid breath blasting in his face. The coals glowed along the mottled coat like cancerous sores. He launched off from his back paws to vault forward. Every time his front paws slammed to the ground, his right one pulsed.

Harry lumbered at top speed towards him, which was still slower than Drew. No matter how heavy the big guy could hit, he was fueled by forced compulsion to continue attacking, which would always make him sloppier. Drew knew firsthand.

Drew sprang forward, sailing through the air. The landing caused him to tense as the bite on his leg radiated pain, but he didn't hesitate. The moment he hit the floor, Drew lunged in for Harry. The bear lifted his paw to swipe, the big claws looming overhead. The fool left his neck open.

Drew's fangs sank in deep, and he whipped his head from side to side. The force tore skin, and blood began to gush. A low gurgle came from Harry's throat, and his claws raked against Drew's back. He gritted his teeth harder, not releasing his grip even as the thick, metallic liquid oozed into his mouth. The tips of the claws stung, but Drew thrashed back and forth, tearing deeper and deeper.

The light blinked out of Harry's eyes and the arms stopped battering at his back. Drew's chest thumped with regret. With Kendricks' Landsliders, he could never tell who was there out of genuine devotion or coercion. While Harry had been loyal, who knew how long he'd been stuck following Mackey's whims, or how warped he might've become?

Whump.

Drew didn't even have the chance to turn around when the coyote rammed full force into him from behind. His grip on Harry loosened, and the bear crashed to the ground. Drew stumbled forward. His entire back stung from the scorch of the coals protruding from the mutant's body.

Crimson dripped from his fangs when he whipped around to face the coyote.

That was when he caught sight of Kendricks.

The massive wolf leapt on top of the tiger, and his teeth latched tight onto the back leg to pin Lucas down. One of the pipes creaked above them, the jostling growing louder and louder as the metal squealed. The length broke free.

Each member of the Tribe had an element they were connected to, and Mackey Kendricks bent metal to his whim. The twisted copper length hurtled through the air, Mackey's dark eyes glowing yellow as he focused his Tribe magic.

Lucas twisted to the side. Not fast enough.

The copper pipe descended with the speed of an arrow, spearing right through his other leg. The crunch reverberated through the room.

Lucas let out a furious howl. The raw, strangled pain of that sound dosed Drew with Novocain fear.

Lana had already suffered so much. She couldn't take another loss like Greg, and Drew had promised to bring Lucas home alive. Hell, he couldn't lose Lucas. The man had become more than a friend, a brother. If anyone should be fighting Mackey Kendricks, it was Drew.

Even as the coyote charged behind him, Drew already loped toward the enormous black wolf whose claws outstretched to maul one of the people who mattered most to him. He might be a little reckless and maybe a little stupid in thinking a pack-less nobody could go toe-to-toe with one of the Tribe, but Drew had found his reason to fight. This monster wouldn't hurt anyone else.

Drew soared across the cold stone floor, ignoring the throbbing cuts along his back and the charred skin that pulsed. He might not have Tribe magic to summon and Mackey Kendrick was about three times bigger than him, but he didn't care. He sailed forward on fury alone, the flames combusting in his chest until they scorched past any remaining doubts and fears.

Drew dipped his head so the flat of his forehead was front and forward as he surged closer. Mackey's citrine gaze flickered to him. The bastard stepped away from Lucas, who crumpled to the ground. Lucas' front paw groped forward for his speared leg, his features contorted in pain. Mackey Kendricks faced him, each of his movements deliberate.

Drew hurtled too fast to stop.

He crashed headfirst into Mackey Kendricks, getting a whiff of those noxious cloves melded with wet dog. He wanted to gag. The hulking bastard barely budged from the strike. He lashed out, his paw sailing for him at top speed, but Drew hadn't paused to get caught. He pivoted out of the way and dropped to the ground. This wolf might be far larger than the ones he'd wrestled with, but Drew had spent time training with the East Coast Tribe and they hadn't taken it easy on him.

The moment Kendricks' blow sailed overhead, Drew hopped back up. Mackey Kendricks loomed on his right, and the coyote mutant closed the distance, fast.

Lucas had managed to knock out the pipe and pushed himself up even though his back paw slumped to the ground. A deep look of concentration overtook him, the tiger's gold eyes glowing. The ground, the ceiling quaked. Rocks loosened, bits of gravel and stone that descended only to circle faster and faster in the air while the Tribe member whipped them into a cyclone.

He'd battled by Lucas' side so many times in the past he didn't need to guess the strategy.

Drew closed the feet between him and Mackey Kendricks.

The man had rarely fought—after all, why lift a finger when lackeys could sacrifice their lives? However, he knew the reputation of the Tribe and he could see the mottled tapestry of raised white scars along his dark-as-a-void fur. Any simple feints wouldn't work. Speed wouldn't work. Strength wouldn't work. This close, the man smelled like copper, cloves and death.

Closer.

Inches away, and the calculating bastard still hadn't budged, leaving Drew to cast his line too early. Drew darted forward to nip at his side, an exploratory bite. Kendricks moved like a striking cobra, lashing back with his paw. Drew crouched, the claws sailing so close above him his fur vibrated.

A crash echoed through the room, dozens of blunt objects plummeting to the ground, and a muffled howl followed. Lucas' movement might be hindered, but that didn't stop him from whipping those stones around at bludgeoning speed.

Drew ducked beneath Mackey, the wolf's legs long enough to fit under. He might be smaller, but he was fast and he'd use the size difference. Drew swiped up and his front claws latched onto his underbelly. Mackey let out a low growl and jerked to the side, thrashing back and forth. Drew hung on for dear life, the back of his head slamming against the ground.

That was when Mackey dropped his full weight.

Drew had barely slid to the side by the time the force descended, knocking the breath from him. Half of his body was pinned down by the fucker. *Shit, that was a terrible plan.* He struggled to tug himself from underneath the weight, trying to rock back and forth out of the hold. Mackey's teeth gnashed in his face, the hot breath slamming into him. His weight pressed onto his chest and Drew's mind blanked, the tightness so, so familiar.

Torch the place on the way out.
Kill every member of the pack you can find.
Don't leave survivors.

Order after order from the monster had squeezed his chest the same way. The commands had pinned his mind down and forced his body forward even as his mind had screamed.

Mackey Kendricks couldn't control him any longer.

The muzzle slammed him in the face with enough force to knock his head to the side. The room swirled. Claws dug into his flank, the pain piercing through the memories he drowned in, until he surfaced.

Drew rammed his head forward again and again, bashing into the claws until wetness trickled past his eyes. He smashed into the solid form of the monster pinning him to the ground, keeping him immobile. Drew sucked in a shallow breath and forced his body still, going lax.

The fangs glinted in the sallow light, and Mackey lunged to bite him in the throat.

Closer. His entire body screamed with the need to move, the need to run and his vision turned white around the edges as his mind threatened total shutdown.

Mackey's body tilted the slightest, and he dove for the bite.

Drew shunted his entire weight to the opposite side. Those legs faltered for a moment, and Drew rammed in again, even harder this time. He rocked out of the grasp, the muzzle snapping by his ears.

Drew sank his teeth into the bastard's flank on his way around, biting down hard. Kendricks growled, the sound reverberating through his big body. Drops of blood splattered across the ground, most of it probably his.

Mackey whipped around, claws raking across his side. The pain scorched and liquid dripped past his eyes, but he clung on tight. Mackey shook his entire body until he separated from Drew's hold. Drew staggered away, the piece of flesh between his teeth. He spat it to the ground and charged.

Except, he recognized the concentration in those amber eyes.

The creak was the one indicator he got as the bars from the silver cage zipped toward him.

Chapter Twenty-Seven

Ally couldn't compete with the sheer desperation of Landsliders under compulsion.

However, she had a Tribe member on her side.

Ally leapt between the two wolves, barely landing before she launched off to lead them on a merry chase. The wolves snapped after her, foam dripping at their muzzles, and their eyes glowing cherry red.

Wind began to whip around the corridor, bigger than a draft from a window or open door. This was a growing force, and she happened to be fighting alongside the woman wielding it.

Bits of gravel swirled around from the strength of the winds, and right before Jess reached the big bear who raced her way, she slammed her paws to the ground. Ally darted past them, the snicker-snack of the jaws behind her echoing through the air.

Jess' winds descended, one slash, another, and another, so razor sharp they sliced into the side of the bear like massive claws. The coyote took a running leap and launched for Jess.

Ally whipped around, letting the wolves close the space between them. Her back legs tensed. They neared, and Ally led to the right. She pivoted at the last second, switching to the other wolf. Her fangs descended into the side of his neck, and the beast let out a garbled growl. He stepped away as claws razed across her back, and Ally restrained her wince. From feet away, a thump reverberated across the floor, followed by a low whine from the coyote.

The wolf behind her leapt on top, flecks of foam splattering across the floor. They began to change into the mindless beasts, and fast. Ally crouched low, gaining leverage before she bucked back. The wolf tumbled off right as the other one vaulted her way. Fangs sank in past the skin above her front leg and the stubborn asshole wouldn't let go. His breaths grew more frantic as madness rode his bones.

Even though her instinct was panic when the teeth dug in deeper, Ally remained patient, the way she'd been taught to since she was a cub. She just needed the slightest opening.

The other wolf charged in.

Gray teeth flashed and Ally whipped her head to the side to protect her neck.

A whistling sound pierced the air and a blast of wind burst between them, traveling so fast and hard it formed a barrier.

Jess dropped in a second later, barely making a whump as she landed.

Ally seized the distraction. She rammed her skull into the wolf whose fangs buried into her leg. The thud jolted them both enough for the grip to relax. Ally pivoted around, leaping away even as her right shoulder ached. The bear barreled in their direction, the beast's back leg dragging. Ally didn't wait around. She hurtled toward the wolf at top speed. They needed to end this, fast. She couldn't hear anything from the room Drew had disappeared into, but she'd felt a tug in her gut, like he'd reached in and yanked their mating bond.

One of those massive lion's roars quaked the doors at the opposite end of the hall. Akio.

Ally leapt on top of the wolf and she sank her claws deep into both sides of the beast. She latched on, snapping around the back of his neck. This time, she found a solid grip. Ally yanked away, flesh and fur tearing with the motion. Blood spurted from the open wound, the coppery liquid filling her mouth. She spat it out as she pushed off the wolf to soar through the air.

Jess smacked into the wolf, knocking the beast off-kilter before she launched after the bear again. The winds whipped around, faster and faster, like the woman summoned miniature cyclones as she ran. Jess slammed to a halt mid-run and she slid her paws back and forth. The winds obeyed the movement, the wild breezes splitting. One launched into the bear, slicing across the beast's skin again, droplets of blood spattering on the floor. The other descended onto the wolf, tripping it up mid-stride.

Ally loped after the wolf while Jess chased down the bear.

She closed the distance to her quarry, mere feet away, when the double glass doors smacked open.

Two bloodstained beasts raced her way. *Fuck, fuck, fuck.*

Until the mountain lion and russet wolf came a pace closer—Dax and Jer. The door opened and she caught the whiff of smoke, the scent still burned into her memory from the bombs. They barreled through the corridor at top speed, rushing in her direction. Their eyes were wild, frantic. A single glimpse past the glass doors rewarded her with the familiar gold-red glimmer of flame. Terror swept through her, fast turning to action.

Ally charged for the wolf. The slam of footsteps reverberated behind her, but she didn't need to look back to feel the presence of her alpha there. Ally headed for a direct charge, snaring the wolf's attention. It raced toward her and at the last second, she swung to the left.

His attention moved to her right. Dax charged from behind.

When Jer leapt in from the side, the wolf didn't stand a chance. All three of them tore into the beast with mechanical motions, fueled by necessity. Blood flecked onto their fur, spittle flew and the wolf crashed to the ground, flesh rent from their fangs and claws.

The bear swayed, and Jess lunged for the throat. The jaguar sank in her teeth and tugged, causing the massive beast to buckle. It offered a weak snap back, but Jess wouldn't give up. She slashed at the face with her claws, and she sank her tips in. Moments later, the bear slammed to the floor.

Jess cast a glance to the double doors, her ears down. She met Dax's gaze, but he shook his head in an unmistakable 'no.'

Akio wasn't following.

Ally's heart lurched — at the loss of the Tribe member, at the dangerous flicker of the flames, and at the idea of her mate facing off against the biggest monster on the East Coast.

She needed to get to Drew.

A raw, painful howl reverberated through the hallway, coming from the room they'd disappeared into, one she'd heard before during the fight against Ganzorig. Lucas was in trouble. Ally didn't bother looking to Dax or Jess for confirmation. Her legs started moving before her mind could catch up, and Ally didn't just race—she soared.

Her vision narrowed to the end of the hallway. To the open door that could spell her worst nightmares come to life.

Ally ran faster.

The wounds she'd collected ached, her muscles burned and blood tickled as it trickled down her legs. She didn't care. She needed to help her mate.

Ally burst past the door, sailing through the entrance to land hard on all fours.

Rubble coated one half of the room and, based on the pockmarks, bits of gravel and stone had been pulled from the ceiling and the walls. Something lay buried beneath the pile of shale and earth, a bit of matted fur poking out amidst the wreckage. Lucas limped away from the heap, and his leg dragged. Blood coursed from that wound, enough to give concern.

However, the sight of a massive black wolf on the far side of the room stole her attention. Ally had never seen him shifted, but she didn't question for an instant who he was. The gleam in Mackey Kendricks' dark eyes was a memory she'd tried to bury. The thought of how easily he'd forced her still and crushed his vile lips to hers corroded her insides like every jab her mother had made, every stab of regret when she and Drew had split up and every clench of her too-hollow stomach.

Drew faced off against Kendricks, the tan, brawny mountain lion as fearless and brave as she always knew he could be. In this form, Mackey Kendricks' eyes glowed yellow with concentration. Silver glinted under the sallow light of the room as the metal bars zipped in the direction of her mate.

Ally raced across the room at top speed, a roar ripping from her.

She moved fast, but the bars whizzed faster.

Ally's heart lodged in her throat and she forgot to breathe, forgot to think—all she could do was run.

Paws slammed to the ground behind her. The twisted silver bars zoomed down, in direct line for Drew's throat.

The wind that rifled her fur blew past, heading for the projectiles. Drew leapt to the side but Mackey Kendricks' gaze never left him. He simply made the adjustment. The man directed the metal toward his target with undeterred focus. Ally's chest squeezed so tight she couldn't breathe.

No. No. No.

The silver bars drove down with a sickening crunch.

The twisted metal pierced his paw instead of his throat, still burying deep. Jess' breeze had moved the bars a couple of inches, barely in time.

A howl escaped Drew's throat filled with the fresh scrape of pain and the ragged edge of desperation. His agony reverberated through her, pulsing in a phantom ache as if her own hand had been gored through. Ally couldn't stop now. She slammed her paws against the concrete even though the gashes along her flank ached and bled.

Mackey Kendricks had tried to destroy her home, her pack and her mate too many times. She would pay him back in blood.

Ally soared at this point, her paws barely hitting the ground, because Mackey Kendricks wouldn't be offering Drew a grace period, or any chance to recover.

The monster vaulted on top of her mate with a sickening determination in his eyes and his claws extended.

Other footsteps echoed from behind. The sounds rose, multiplying like their entire army of shifters, humans and shamans stood behind her and not the handful of their attack squad who remained.

Mere feet lay between them. Ally tensed her back legs and she sprang forward to sail through the rest of the distance. Mackey dipped his muzzle, his fangs flashing. This close, the weight of his presence slammed into her like a battering ram. The great wolf would rip Drew's face off. Not on her fucking watch.

Ally didn't try to stop the impetus. She tilted her head down and threw her whole weight forward. She crashed into him with a thud that clapped through the room like thunder, hard enough that her bones creaked and her mind spun. The massive great wolf tipped to the side a step, and Ally couldn't help but fall with him.

Mackey Kendricks smelled like blood, brimstone and betrayal, the stench filling her senses and making her want to vomit. His fur brushed against hers as he loomed over her in his wolf form. He snapped for her throat and drops of crimson splashed onto her. Ally swung her head to the side just in time for those fangs to flash in front of her.

Drew rammed Kendricks in the side even though he limped, his paw a mottled wreck of scorched flesh and broken skin. Determination flashed in her mate's gorgeous blue eyes. How she'd ever stopped believing him was a mystery in the wake of the sheer adoration that swept through her.

Ally bucked forward, trying to roll out from beneath Mackey Kendricks. Every time she attempted to move, his jaws snapped for her throat again. The man moved with a swiftness that rivaled hers and a grace that she'd only seen from the Tribe.

Dax landed on top of the bastard's back, his claws descending to rake across the surface. Mackey whipped around to try to shake him off. Ally seized her escape and slipped out from beneath him.

The others approached, closing in on the man who had tormented them for so long. Jer raced behind in a streak of russet, and he looped around to Drew's side. Jess prowled closer, the jaguar moving with graceful, steady steps. Lucas followed behind her, his gold eyes glowing with the retribution they all sought.

The winds swirled.

The stones shook.

Ally launched back into an attack. Mackey Kendricks whipped around to try to bite her alpha. She landed in front of the monster and sank her teeth into his front leg. Dax whipped his claws down in an arc again, raking across his fur from behind. Jer lunged forward, nipping at the man's hind legs with a dogged focus.

Ally recognized the look that flashed in Mackey Kendricks' eyes. She'd felt the same at his hands too many times, when he'd bombed her friends in their homes, when he'd torched their pack cabins and when he'd used that insidious compulsion on her, forcing her body to lock up. The man experienced true panic, at last.

Kendricks had survived through Tribe powers he didn't deserve, and he'd kept himself surrounded by a horde of shifters he'd forced into submission.

For the first time, he was alone.

The East Coast Tribe members, Silver Springs and Red Rocks had all fought together for years. Some of them had been scrapping with each other since they were cubs, and they continued to stand side by side to fight and bleed together. No matter how many times their packmates were murdered and their homes were torched, they understood one thing the leader of the Landsliders never would.

Pack wasn't some corralled group of individuals or even hatred repackaged as a common cause. Pack was an instinct bred deep among her kind, the knowledge that none of them could survive on their own.

Pack was home. Pack was safety. Pack was family.

Together, they would always be stronger than any threat that descended.

Jess' paws slammed to the ground, and Lucas joined her.

Gravel began to whip around, faster and faster until it churned into a full-fledged tornado that zeroed in on one individual. The air reeked of the Tribe magic as their combined efforts grew into a primal force.

Ally clenched her jaw tighter around Kendricks' front leg even when he thrashed to try to kick her off. Drew lunged in on the other side to bite down on the leg, pinning the big bastard in place. Their eyes locked. She and her mate — they were in this together until the end. She squeezed her eyes shut and spread her paws flat. The winds and gravel descended.

Her fur rifled around under the force of those breezes, which brought dirt and grit smashing into her, hundreds of tiny pinpricks. Stray stones smacked against her pelt, hard enough to bruise, but Ally didn't falter. She kept her jaw wrapped around Mackey Kendricks' leg even as he bucked forward, trying to shake them both off.

The wolf hunched under the onslaught of rocks and gravel. He tugged at his front legs and lashed back and forth, using that formidable weight to try to hurl them off him. Creaks and groans sounded from above, the whine of metal. Any moment, he'd use those powers in retaliation. Yet Ally didn't budge. She and Drew held steady. The wind settled, and dozens of thumps sounded beside them as the stones hit the floor.

Kendricks' yellow eyes gleamed with focus. Despite the dozens of cuts along his flank and despite the open wounds dripping in crimson rivulets, the bastard refused to die. The creak from overhead was telltale. He'd bring more of those copper pipes down to spear them through.

Drew let go of the leg.

With Mackey Kendricks' focus up on the metal above, her mate found a new target.

Drew lunged forward. His fangs sank deep into the neck of the man who had overridden his own mind, the one who had used him like a tool to bomb his friends and family, and the one who had forced him to fight his own brother. Her mate clamped down hard, his eyes flashing with relentless determination. Even after he'd been beaten down for so long, by first his father then this monster, that spark never died.

Drew yanked back, and the neck tore open. Blood sprayed across the floor, drops coating her fur and those eyes shuttered.

Ally unclenched her jaw from around his front leg and took a tentative step back. Her muscles remained poised to spring forward at the slightest start. Mackey Kendricks wavered, his body swaying. Drew backed away, the limp from his mutilated front paw even more pronounced. Dax tensed, his fangs baring at the ready to dive in again.

The massive black wolf swayed back and forth, blood running from dozens of scratches and gashes along the flank, matting the fur. He flexed his jaw in a feeble attempt to snap, but that only caused crimson to gush from the gaping wound across his neck. Those yellow eyes lost their focus and the man managed a single step forward.

Mackey Kendricks crashed to the ground. The great wolf lay slumped to the side and a final, shuddering breath escaped him. All six of them didn't dare move an inch, waiting for the monster to rise, or for some last trick to lash out at them. However, the blood continued to pool around him, and he didn't stir.

The menace of the East Coast, the leader of the Landsliders and the member of the Tribe who went rogue fell and he didn't get up again.

Chapter Twenty-Eight

Mackey Kendricks was dead.

The man who had haunted Drew's nightmares ever since he joined the Landsliders, the one he'd thought he'd waste his whole life running from, lay dead at his feet. Mackey Kendricks didn't move, the wolf's yellowed eyes closed for good. He'd never again witness the cocky gleam in Kendricks' eyes when the man forced him under compulsion. Blood pooled around the matted black fur and the massive body sprawled on the ground, limp.

For a moment, beyond the blinding pain, oblivion stretched before him. He had reached for it and tried to grasp on tight back in his time with the Landsliders and after. This was supposed to be his end.

Ally nudged him in the side. The gentle touch from his mate cracked his heart wide open and he nuzzled her back. After years of bleak misery, fighting to place one foot in front of the other, he stood here with his mate, alive. Their nemesis lay dead before them. Now, at long last, he could look to the future.

Dax hopped away from the body and headed for the large iron door Mackey had been trying to escape through earlier. Jer loped close behind him with energy that Drew couldn't summon right now. Jess shifted from her sleek jaguar form onto two feet, and in seconds she reached for the knob. Lucas trailed behind them, his back leg still dragging with his movements. Drew and Ally arrived last.

The door cracked open, and the golden rays of late afternoon poured out to greet them. A crackle and a groan sounded from farther in the lair and the approaching scent of smoke gave the indicator. The final refuge of the late Mackey Kendricks was going up in flames.

One by one, they headed out of the Landsliders' lair, out into World's End.

* * * *

By the time they reached the section of the woods where the battle had taken place, Drew was forced to focus on each step forward. His energy dwindled faster and faster, the bone-aching weariness seeping through his veins at a numbing rate.

They'd spotted bodies along the way, wolves, bears, humans, some Landsliders and some their own. However, most of the fighting had already stopped. Drew knew from experience why. Mackey's compulsion over the Landsliders had broken the moment he'd died. Many of them might've sworn their allegiance and even might've been dedicated at the start, but years of being used like tools to do his dirty work didn't translate to loyalty. The moment his hold broke, they'd fled.

The dregs that remained soon realized they were outnumbered and ran.

Their group reached a higher vantage point so he and Lucas could stop to conserve energy. Jer and Jess loped off in the direction of the parking lot they'd arrived in to get help. If he and Lucas lost any more blood, they might not survive.

Drew slumped onto the ground and the shift overtook him as he transitioned into his human form. Ally had switched to two feet before and she crouched beside him. Her long waves were tangled and matted with dark flecks of blood, those same streaks of crimson painted across her skin in wild slashes from the wounds she'd sustained. Worry pulsed in her sky-blue eyes.

Drew winced when he settled into place, unable to look at his right hand. The silver had sheared right through it in the worst agony of his life and the wound throbbed so loud he could barely hear anything over the roaring pain as his body refused to heal. Even still, he held the wound tight, trying to staunch the flow of blood.

Lucas leaned back against the trunk of a nearby tree, gripping his leg tight while he did the same. A hushed silence spread between them as they all stared out over the valley.

So many bodies littered the sloping hills before them. Shifter, human, shaman. Landslider, Silver Springs, Red Rock. Blood christened these hills, soaked into the ground and stained the rocks.

Blood had stained his hands, more than he could ever erase. He thought maybe, just maybe, in defeating Mackey Kendricks, the heaviness wouldn't clutch his heart anymore. That all the pain, the weight on his shoulders and the pulse of guilt that lingered even now would dissipate.

Ally leaned her head against his chest. The soft weight of her, the velvet of her skin and the tenderness in her motions was worth every ounce of this pain.

Maybe redemption wasn't a milestone to achieve, but a gift given.

Drew stared out to the horizon. The citrine sun began to descend, weaving together crimson, magenta and tangerine in a sunset so fierce it stole his breath away. The colors stretched out in a bright burst reflecting all the brilliant souls who had fought and died today. This glory in the skies, the depth of the color and the breadth of the fall represented all the people of this region who had banded together to defend their home.

None of them said a word as the colors burst like fireworks, as the sun dipped below the horizon and as the first breath of night cooled their skin. Yet every time the light died, eventually, those rays would burst through again.

Life wasn't as simple as hitting a reset button. He might carry this guilt, and he might carry these wounds for the rest of his life. However, he had a brother who still cared. He had a mate who was the hope of a new day. And even though he'd believed he'd lost it for a while, he had a home.

Drew threaded his fingers through Ally's and gripped tight. Here and now, he had a future.

Chapter Twenty - Nine

Six months later

"Buckle up," Drew called, placing the keys in the ignition.

Ally cast a glance to the rearview mirror where Eli had most definitely ignored Drew's directive. She withheld her snort and settled into the comfortable leather seats of her mate's Caddy. The kid folded his arms and stared at the roof of the car, the stubborn little shit. Her chest warmed at the open display of his feelings, even if he was being a brat right now.

When no relatives arrived to claim Eli, Ally and Drew came to the agreement that they'd adopt him — as if that hadn't been the unspoken hope they'd both held on to from the moment Eli had entered their lives. Lucas had helped them through the red tape on the Tribe end of things, negotiating with Eli's old pack. Just last month they'd celebrated his official adoption into their family, and on top of that his inclusion in the Red Rock and Silver Springs packs.

"Kiddo, seatbelt on," Ally reinforced, turning to fix him with the 'eye'. Eli wrinkled his nose and opened his mouth like he was preparing to argue. Ally still had an ace to play. "The sooner you pop the seatbelt on, the sooner you get to see Lila."

A second later, the click resounded through the car. Drew's mouth quirked with his grin as he turned the engine on, and they rolled out of the driveway. Worked every time. Ever since Eli had first met Dax and Sierra's little cub, he had become obsessed with his new cousin. As they'd gotten to know Eli better, his stubborn side had begun to emerge, but he had an innate sweetness she'd seen from the start, which blossomed every time he interacted with kids younger than him.

"Try to be a little more commanding next time, Train Wreck," Ally murmured. "He might listen for once."

Drew snorted. "Why would I bother trying to compete with your bossiness? You've got the market cornered, Car Crash."

From the backseat, Eli let out an exaggerated sigh. Already, the kid had started to give them attitude, but Ally lapped up all of his sass. He was getting comfortable with them, which was everything she could've hoped for.

They raced across the highway in a direction she'd traveled a thousand times before—the Silver Springs cabin. The East Coast Tribe had arrived in town, and just in time for the grand reopening of the Silver Springs pack cabin. Besides, Ally wouldn't pass up the opportunity to see her best friend.

Every member of the Tribe would be there, all except for Akio. They'd lost him in the battle at World's End. When more Landsliders had arrived on the scene, Akio had summoned one spectacular blaze to give them all a chance to survive. Ever since then, the Tribe members had been working overtime, but the bond they'd formed with the Silver Springs and Red Rock packs had been forged in iron and tempered by shared experience.

The winding path to the Silver Springs cabin grew clearer down the highway, peeking out amidst the tall pines that loomed along the way. Drew slowed and turned onto the sloping drive. Ally couldn't help the stutter of her heart as excitement flooded through her like an energy shot.

What Mackey Kendricks had reduced to a smoking hull had been rebuilt. Even though the new structure wasn't the weathered beams and wide frame she remembered from childhood, the Silver Springs cabin stood in the same section of the woods as always with that serene lake sparkling in the distance. Already, the trees had begun to change color into a gorgeous spread of gold and orange and withered leaves drifted down to collect by the roots.

At least a dozen cars littered the driveway, the way they always did at the larger pack gatherings. Over the years she'd witnessed this familiar sight, from a young age when it was her parents, then her mom, dragging her to yet another Silver Springs get-together. The cycle continued. Now, they were the parents dragging their kids to a reunion of pack, of long-held friends, and of family. Ally felt lighter than she ever had, like she'd grabbed onto a sunbeam and shoved it inside. Her chest strained from sheer joy as she caught the scent of vanilla and leather threaded through the car, the scent of her mate. The scent of her home.

The second Drew rolled to a park, Eli let out an excited yip and the door flew open. The kid bolted before they got a word in, his small footsteps clattering across the pavement. Ally hopped out from the passenger's side. Eli raced across the clearing to where Sierra strode forward, carrying Lila in a dark green sling around her shoulders.

"About time you showed, slackers," Dax called over to them, waving overhead to direct them over. He stood by one of the grills parked on the edge of the clearing, watching the steaks sizzle on the surface. The scent of cooked beef trailed over, causing her stomach to rumble. The others hung around the clearing, so many familiar faces.

"I know the rest of you are a snore, but I can't be the life of the party all the time," Drew called, his voice carrying. He slipped his right hand into his pocket when he strode ahead, something he'd started doing on reflex ever since it had gotten damaged in the fight. The wound had never healed quite right and he couldn't form a fist with that hand any longer.

Ally slid beside him and grabbed his hand from his pocket to give it a squeeze. "Save us, before your ever-expanding ego suffocates us all."

His eyes gleamed as he caught on to what she did — the same thing he had done for her regarding the scar on her leg. They both carried permanent wounds, some visible and some not, but they were done running from them.

Together, they strolled up to Dax, who had Raven and Jer for company. Back when they'd first entered Beaver Tavern, she could've never imagined this camaraderie from the wolves who'd tried to growl them out, but they'd forged unbreakable bonds. Jer caught her gaze and waved. She'd been hanging out with him more as of late. Out of everyone in the combined packs, he understood what it was like being beta to a stubborn alpha.

"I'm surprised you're back from Allentown already," Ally called to him as they closed the distance. After the battle at World's End, Raven and Jer had become their pack outreach to the shamans, forging a better relationship with the magic users who had come through for them in the end.

Raven snorted, sweeping back her thick black hair. "I am too, with the amount Ava keeps threatening to steal me away. The woman is a relentless flirt."

Jer's lips twisted in a smirk, the devil in his eyes. "There's an easy solution to that."

Raven shot him a look. "If you say threesome again, I'll slit your throat." Ally snorted, noticing that despite the way Raven rolled her eyes, a small grin lifted her lips.

Drew clapped Dax on the back. "Is Enrico's pack still knocking at our door?"

Dax let out a groan. "Don't remind me. Why the bastard thought attacking a Tribe-protected, combined pack was a good idea is beyond me." He flipped the steaks on the grill, the sizzle echoing through the air.

"They should've just sent Enrico's mate," Drew joked, his eyes crinkling at the edges. "She roughed you up pretty bad." Dax lifted his middle finger in response. Ally's heart squeezed tight at watching the warmth between the brothers now, how easily they touched and joked. That rift was one she had worried would never heal and yet those cracks had already begun to smooth. The relationship they had now was nothing like the one they had as kids, but here and now they had the chance to become a real family, something their father would've never allowed.

Ally tugged at Drew's hand. "Let's go check on our son before he sneaks off with Lila." Saying those words aloud still sparked her with a secret joy, one she knew Drew shared by the way his eyes still lit up.

"Mind sending Sierra over?" Dax said, tugging at the brim of his baseball cap. "The steaks will be done in a few minutes."

"Will do, boss," Ally responded, throwing a thumbs-up in the air. They strode across the clearing to where Eli had run off to. Finn and Navi approached around the same time, as the former Red Rock beta sidled up to Sierra and threw an arm around her shoulder.

"Long time no see, kids," Navi called to them in greeting.

Eli already stood on his tiptoes, trying to get a peek of his little cousin. Lila had bronze skin like her mother and doe eyes that seemed to win people over on the spot. She'd be a charmer like her father, for sure.

"She's waking up," he squealed, his eyes gleaming in excitement. The little one lifted her chubby fists and let out one massive yawn.

"Dax says the steaks will be ready soon," Ally said as she and Drew approached. "Why the lazy ass couldn't just call that over is beyond me."

Sierra snorted. "He's trying to reclaim what little power he has. This one's stolen most of it." She brushed Lila's thick black hair to the side, glancing down to her little one. The love glowed in her eyes, emanating from the fierce woman. From the moment Sierra and Dax had become mates, Ally knew the same traits that made Sierra a good alpha, that protective warmth, would make her a good mother too.

"She's way too big," Finn complained.

Sierra arched an eyebrow. "Maybe you just need to visit a little more."

"We're definitely planning on a little vacation soon," Navi said, rocking back and forth on her heels. "Chasing after the dregs of remaining Landsliders has been more of an annoyance than anything."

Finn kept his arm draped over Sierra's shoulders even as he looked to Navi. "You know, I was *promised* all these riveting adventures when I decided to follow your ass."

Navi let out a laugh. "You'd have followed my ass regardless, pup."

Finn's grin broadened.

Jess leaned back at one of the picnic benches, chatting with Marcy and Rick. The tables were covered in a mess of chicken salad, rolls, fresh slices of watermelon and grilled corn on the cob dripping with butter. Daria and her sister raced around in a game of tag, their pealing laughter echoing through the trees. At the edge of the clearing, Ally caught sight of her best friend and Lucas.

"I'm going to go say hi to Lana," Ally said, releasing Drew's hand.

Lana strode in her direction and Ally closed the distance the rest of the way to throw her arms around her best friend and squeeze tight.

"All this overtime means you've got to make it up in extra visits," Ally murmured into Lana's shoulder. Some knot undid inside her at the woman's presence, the way it always had. Spirits above, she missed her best friend.

Lana glanced over to Eli who lifted his hand carefully. He petted his little cousin's head, smooth strokes over her thick shock of black hair. The sheer joy in that kid's eyes as he showered Lila with affection had Ally smitten all over again. "Trust me, I want to get to know Eli as soon as possible. Aunt Lana can't be some weirdo stranger who shows up covered in spleen with a half-knitted cozy for a gift."

Drew snorted. "Well, when you put it like that, you're guaranteed to give him nightmares." He clapped a hand on Lana's shoulder and brought her in for a hug. "Glad to see you, Sunshine. And you, Lucas," he called to the massive Tribe member who strolled over, a grin on the tamed tiger's face.

Lucas and Lana shared a look, then Lucas nodded.

"We'll have to stop renting my house out next year," Lana murmured. "At least for some time."

Ally tilted her head to the side. The realization crystallized with the shy way Lana glanced to Lucas, the beaming she couldn't hold back. "You're pregnant."

Ally threw her arms around Lana again and squeezed tight. Tears heated her eyes, that combination of yearning and joy that still hit her even now at the mention of pregnancy and having kids. Those feelings would always be complicated, but so was she. And her beautiful, complicated family was the exact sort she needed.

"I'm sorry," Lana whispered in apology. Out of everyone she knew, her best friend was the one who came closest to understanding. Ally shook her head, burying her face in the crook of her best friend's neck if only to hide the few hot tears that slipped down.

"No apologies. You and Luc are going to be great parents. I'm so fucking happy for you." Ally squeezed her tighter, living with that sunlit joy for a moment more. She pulled back at last and offered a grin.

"Besides, I'll take any excuse to keep my best friend in the area a bit longer."

Drew clapped his hand to Lucas'. "Congratulations, man. You both deserve that sort of joy. Our little guy will be thrilled to have another baby to dote over."

"We've got to go make the rounds, but then we're catching up," Lana said, drilling her with a look. "I've got way too much to tell you."

"Deal," Ally said, and she reached out to tug on Drew's hand. "Come on, let's check out the new cabin." She cast a glance to Eli who hopped from one foot to the other to show Aunt Sierra his awesome balance. Sierra's eyes crinkled in amusement, and she caught Ally's gaze to give the 'I've got this' look they'd both mastered in a short span of time.

Drew took the first steps forward, leading her away from the rest of their packs. They approached the new entrance of the cabin. This was a place where they had been broken in, where childhood dreams had taken root and where they'd also been torn from the ground. This was the place where they had fallen in love, and this was the place where they had shattered apart. This home, these lands and these joined packs—they meant everything to her.

Drew met her gaze and squeezed her hand tight. Shadows sometimes flitted to his eyes once in a while, but they'd grown lighter. They bickered—they always would—but the jagged edges had whittled down. She'd always felt the glow of his presence, the warmth and steadiness he'd offered her from a young age. However, that strength had reached his features at last, permeating through the mask of pain, and the sight was radiant.

As they stepped up to the entrance of the pack cabin, Ally glanced back. Laughs filtered through the clearing, along with indignant shouts followed by more teasing. The scents of steaks grilling, of peach pie and crisp bottles of lager drifted her way on this perfect autumn day. The kids from both packs ducked past the adults, their small voices filled with reckless abandon and a wonder she hoped and prayed they never lost. Warmth suffused her chest, the same steady hearth as the cozy lights of Beaver Tavern at night. She wanted to capture this moment forever.

Her grip tightened on Drew's, and she stepped past him, leading the way into the cabin. They had a beautiful life waiting for them and Ally didn't want to waste a minute.

Want to see more from this author?
Here's a taster for you to enjoy!

The Whitfield Files:
Of Tinkers and Technomancers
Katherine McIntyre

Excerpt

Theo Whitfield had been dreading this visit before she entered the building. Any one of an assortment of grisly jobs sounded more appealing than the task she faced now, whether it be sucking down clouds of noxious black steam while repairing an airship vent, or tromping through the sewage and muck in the Underground. Blazes, she'd even rather devour her mother's charred attempts at supper, a feat that caused even the most ironclad stomachs to falter.

Yet, her sister Ellie had never come home last night, and Theo needed answers.

Theo swallowed hard as she stepped to the storefront and rested her knuckles on the freshly painted door. The polished bronze sign of Kylock Industries glared down at her from the overhang, and she gritted her teeth while gathering her courage. Autocarts rattled behind her while they raced along the cobblestones, part of the average hustle of Barnsbury. Each one that passed elicited a stream of curses from the street thugs who were half-rats by noon and reeked of gin.

She gripped the knob and turned it, entering the business.

The dim gas lamps in the entryway flickered their sallow light onto the tarnished floorboards. A woman sitting behind a mahogany desk stationed in the front of a sprawling parlor startled in her seat as if she'd been caught napping. Even with the posh and polished entrance of the shop, the scents of iron, steel and copper tickled her nose and made her fingers itch. For a technomancer like herself, the contraptions devised in this place were rife for exploration.

"How may I help you?" the attendant asked, smoothing her skirts before she stood from her seat.

"I'm here to see Silas," Theo said, slipping her hands into the pockets of her trousers.

She didn't miss the way the woman stared her down, lingering on her shocking attire. With her long black curls left free and wild rather than pinned back, and the lack of a corset to give her an unrealistic waist, Theo would never be mistaken for a lady. Though the populace's judgment didn't matter. As a technomancer in a city of industry, she would always, always find employment, whether she followed social norms or not.

"Mr. Kylock is occupied. Did you want to make an appointment?" the woman replied as she forced a smile.

Theo lifted an eyebrow. *The high-and-mighty bastard's too busy playing with his toys to spare a second? As if I'm surprised.*

"He'll see me now," she demanded, her fingers itching all the more. Whenever her temper sparked — which happened often — the magic tended to flow with it.

The attendant bristled at her demand. Based on the sharp glint in the woman's eyes when she opened her mouth, another denial was about to follow.

A fancy auto-stylus attached to a typewriter sat on the desk and bore Kylock's tinker imprint—a K with a surrounding cog. The fancy piece of tech could imprint different fonts and handwriting onto letters and would sell for a high price in a lot of the upscale salons. That would do just fine.

Theo lifted her hand, and the conductive ring she wore nearly vibrated from the magic at her fingertips. Wisps of it condensed in the air, like tufts of cumulus clouds, at her will. She urged the energy onward with a twist of her wrist, and the buttons on the typewriter began to type. The stylus lowered to the blank pad of paper.

"I can send this machine into a frenzy in about three seconds," Theo said. "I don't suppose your employers will appreciate their fancy equipment getting broken. Now, take me to Silas."

The stylus moved faster and faster, scribbling more furiously with every keystroke she manipulated from afar. Condensation filled the air with the outpouring of magic, like the steam that billowed out of the machinery in the city. The woman's eyes widened and she threw her hands up in defense.

"Stop, stop," she bit out, the fear illustrated by the pallor on her skin. "I'll take you back to the workroom."

Theo's kind was rare enough that when they encountered normal folks on the street, respect or fear became common currency. After all, not everyone had the ability to manipulate mechanics with magic.

The woman led her through the fancy trappings of the parlor, from the bookshelves filled with leather-bound tomes to the mahogany table and chairs next to a cabinet displaying crystal glasses and decanters of fine liquor. This wasn't the sort of place meant for ruffians like herself.

Theo's footsteps echoed down the hall, her thick-soled boots made for stomping, unlike the quiet click of the woman's heels while she guided her to a double door at the end of the main corridor. Her loose curls tickled her neck, annoying her enough to bat them out of the way before she came to a stop in front of the workroom doors. Her agitation threatened to bubble over the moment she stepped foot inside this place. The attendant bent forward, inputting a number sequence. A series of whirrs and clicks followed until the lock opened.

"Step along now," Theo said, swerving past the woman's petticoats to grab the knob. "I'm sure I can handle the rest." For extra emphasis, she waggled her fingers in the attendant's direction, which had the desired effect of sending her scurrying. If the ladies and gents were going to treat her like a freak, she might as well reap the benefits.

The door whispered as she pushed it open and stepped into the heart of rolling steam that kissed her cheeks and burning metal that tickled her nose. Absinthe-colored aether bubbled up in tubes lining the room. The power-source not only served as fuel but also cast rays of light to add to the meager flicker the dim overhangs offered. A large workbench spanned the entire back wall, and every spare inch of the monstrosity was covered in projects.

The *tick-tick-tick* of clocks echoed through the place, coming from at least six different sources, and scrolls of blueprints and designs covered entire shelves of the three bookcases that towered along the right wall. Gears, lavers, burnishers and drills lay scattered about, half on the floor, half on the table and in no particular order. Amidst the chaos of the room, one man hunched over the worktable, neck-deep in his latest project.

"Silas, I know where your missing automaton is," Theo called out, her voice echoing through the room.

The man's shoulders tensed, and he placed whatever he was tinkering with down before swiveling around on his stool to face her. His rust-red hair glowed in the wake of the sheer amount of steam pumping through the room, and he lifted his goggles with their magnifying attachments to rest them on his head. He smirked upon meeting her gaze, the sheer amount of arrogance in his dark brown eyes igniting her temper on the spot. The man was too pretty for his own good, yet Theo refused to be swayed.

"Well, well, whatever did I do for one of the Whitfield girls to pay me a visit?" He cocked a thick eyebrow, the elegant arch perfecting his defined features. "Last time I saw you, Theo dear, your employer required my consult on a situation because you refused to admit your utter lack of knowledge on the subject."

Her fingers curled into fists. They had both grown up in Islington, even getting into scuffs on the streets as teens, but as they'd aged, he'd become ever more insufferable. Once he'd become a full-fledged Tinker, and she'd found technomancer work as a handyman, their paths continued to cross, over and over and over again. Unfortunately, punching him in the face at a job site would get her pay docked, and she needed every penny for Mother's treatments.

"You want to talk utter lack of knowledge?" she ground out. "Where's the latest model of your line of clockwork maids?"

His eyes flashed with irritation. He leaned against his worktable and folded his arms over his chest. He was one of the few who didn't fear her kind. "What did your sister get mixed up in this time?"

Theo bristled. While he might be right—out of the two Whitfield girls, she'd gone the straight and narrow while her sister had taken to thieving with a naturalness that worried Mother endlessly—she didn't appreciate the derision in his tone.

"Do you want the automaton she stole back or not?" she asked, ready to exit this infernal room with the man who'd become a nightmare in her professional life as well as a personal irritant.

"You'll have it back here by tonight, or I'll give your sister's name to the constable," he responded, keeping his gaze level.

Despite the firmness in his voice, shadows crept underneath his eyes and the three-day stubble gracing his chin implied the disappearance had caused him more trouble than he'd ever admit. He fidgeted with one of his cufflinks, the constant motion betraying those nerves.

"That's the problem." Theo swallowed, a pit forming in her stomach. "She disappeared before she ever made the drop with your clockwork maid in tow."

The tapping stopped.

"So, you've come to me why?" Silas asked, his voice sharpening. The hungry way he eyed her suggested she was treading on dangerous ground. However, Theodosia Whitfield made a habit of stomping through delicate territory.

"Because I can get your automaton back, delivered without anyone the wiser. I just need your help. Specifically, I need the scrap metal you forged the clockwork maid from so I can trace it." She lifted her chin and matched his gaze. He might be taller and have developed more muscles than necessary while smithing, but she threw a mean right hook and knew his blind spots. If it came to a fight, she'd still bet on herself.

"And what do I get in return?" he asked, an infuriating grin returning to his face. "Because I have the blueprints—I can always make a new clockwork maid. However, you only have one sister."

Theo heaved a sigh, not bothering to hide her irritation. "You get the satisfaction of being a decent man for once."

Silas snorted. "That's not a barter in the slightest. Offer me something worthwhile."

Theo didn't miss the way his eyes lingered on her or the heat burning in them.

He might be a handsomer than average man with the sort of blacksmith's build to make most women fall into his bed—and many did—but he had the personality of a pickled turnip. Theo rested her hands on her hips while she eyed him, refusing to indulge the blatant implication he threw behind his words. She should punch the smug expression off his face and just steal the pieces, damn the consequences.

"A favor," she said, at last. "In my professional capacity." She emphasized the word *professional* to dispel any ideas he might be entertaining. The sooner she could acquire the scrap and get the hell out of there, the better. Her sister might be bleeding in an alley for all she knew.

Silas tapped the side of his chin as if he were musing over the proposition—as if he hadn't already made the call. "While a favor from you might be helpful, we subcontract technomancers on a regular basis. I'm not going to hand over my scrap metal and hope you bring back our automaton. I'll bargain for a favor from you if I'm along for the hunt when we track your sister."

Theo's eyebrows lowered with her glare. Spending more time around Silas Kylock was not only hazardous to her health but edged her closer and closer to the ledge of getting locked up for homicide.

Except he possessed the exact item she needed to track down Ellie. And no matter what trouble her little sister had gotten into this time, Theo would do anything for that girl.

She heaved a sigh. "Fine. Meet me in an hour at my residence with the scrap metal. You may as well clear out the rest of your busy calendar today. I don't know how long this will take." Her words dripped with derision she didn't bother masking. The Kylocks had made themselves quite a few shillings between his father's business connections and Silas' tinkering, but like her, they were gutter trash from Islington. Bottom-of-the-barrel ruffians didn't fit amongst the posh and pretentious folks, no matter how hard the Kylocks tried to pretend the opposite.

"You have yourself a deal," he responded, tugging off the thick work gloves he wore and tossing them to the ground.

He stood from the stool with a creak and crossed the distance between them until he stood mere inches away. Theo's hands didn't budge from her hips while she looked up at him with her back to the door. At six feet and a few, he towered almost a foot over her, but she had never found him intimidating.

Silas thrust his hand out between them to shake. She offered her own, and heat emanated from his callused palm as they shook on the deal. This close, she could smell the tinge of copper, earth and amber, an infusion that made her mind swirl. Theo realized their handshake had gone on seconds too long when a smirk curled Silas' upper lip. She yanked her hand back.

"I trust you can find your way out?" he asked, not budging an inch despite the proximity between them.

"Quite capable, thank you," she snapped, whirling around to face the double doors. Behind her, she heard the shuffle of footsteps and the clank of metal parts from myriad tools being moved around on the table.

Theo Whitfield kept marching forward. Even if she was required to work with the most obnoxious bootlicker on this side of town, Ellie was roaming out there and needed her help. Theo wouldn't let her down.

Home of Erotic Romance

Sign up for our newsletter and find out about all our
romance book releases, eBook sales and promotions,
sneak peeks and FREE romance books!

About the Author

Strong women. Strong words.

Katherine McIntyre is a feisty chick with a big attitude despite her short stature. She writes stories featuring snarky women, ragtag crews, and men with bad attitudes—high chance for a passionate speech thrown into the mix. As an eternal geek and tomboy who's always stepped to her own beat, she's made it her mission to write stories that represent the broad spectrum of people out there, from different cultures and races to all varieties of men and women. Easily distracted by cats and sugar.

Katherine loves to hear from readers. You can find her contact information, website details and author profile page at https://www.totallybound.com